Yakata waved us down. As we fanned out, I noticed a bright speck in the corner of my HUV. There, just rounding the corner of the building, was another Marine.

I charged, giving myself to whatever the hell they had put in my brain, those mnemosynes, those things, whatever they were, I begged for their help. I swore there was about seventy-five meters between me and that soldier. I bridged the distance in two heartbeats, but not before the bastard opened fire.

I felt weightless as I hurtled toward him, and when our skins touched, we rebounded with a force ten times greater than natural. The Marine struck the quickcrete and dug himself a vertical grave.

Dina and Beauregard crouched over Yakata, who lay on his back, just outside the door. His mouth moved, but I couldn't hear him. By the time I made it over there, he had died. He wasn't the first dead person I had ever seen, just the bloodiest.

"What did he say?" I asked Beauregard.

The colonel's son grimaced. "He told us to follow you."

BROTHERS IN ARMS

BEN WEAVER

An Imprint of HarperCollinsPublishers

This is a work of fiction. Names, characters, places, and incidents are the products of the author's imagination or are used fictitiously and are not to be construed as real. Any resemblance to actual events, locales, organizations, or persons, living or dead, is entirely coincidental.

EOS
An Imprint of HarperCollins*Publishers*
10 East 53rd Street
New York, New York 10022-5299

Copyright © 2001 by Ben Weaver
ISBN: 0-06-105972-2
www.eosbooks.com

First Eos paperback printing: January 2001

Eos Trademark Reg. U.S. Pat. Off. and in Other Countries, Marca Registrada, Hecho en U.S.A.
HarperCollins® is a trademark of HarperCollins Publishers Inc.

Printed in the U.S.A.

10 9 8 7 6 5 4 3 2 1

*For Robert, Eric, and Caitlin
and, of course,
Nancy, Lauren, and Kendall*

Acknowledgments

My editor, Caitlin Blasdell, is the real champion behind this novel. She read several versions of the original outline and spent many hours helping me hone the story and polish the prose. Her commitment to my work is as valuable as it is appreciated.

Longtime friend and agent Robert Drake also assisted with the story. We have worked on fourteen books together (including this one), and although Robert has since closed his agency and referred me to the adroit Mr. John Talbot, I will never forget his contributions to my career and family.

The TAWT drives in this novel originated during conversations I had with friend and neighbor Eric Popkin. In fact, Eric helped me write the tablet entry describing the drive's function. His extensive knowledge of physics coupled with his ability to consider unconventional ideas greatly inspired me.

Articles of the Code of Conduct of the Seventeen System Guard Corps (adopted from old United States Marine Corps articles)

ARTICLE I

I will always remember that I am an Alliance citizen, fighting in the forces that preserve my world and our way of life. I have resigned to give my life in their defense.

ARTICLE II

I will never surrender of my own volition. If in command, I will never surrender the members of my command while they still have the will and/or means to resist.

ARTICLE III

If I am captured, I will continue to resist by any and all means available. I will make every effort to escape and to aid others to escape. I will accept neither parole nor special favors from the enemy.

ARTICLE IV

If I become a prisoner of war, I will keep faith with my fellow prisoners. I will give no information nor take part in any action which might be harmful to fellow Alliance citizens. If I am senior, I will take command. If not, I will obey the lawful orders of those appointed over me and will uphold them in every way.

ARTICLE V

Should I become a prisoner of war, I am required to give name, rank, and willingly submit to retinal and DNA analysis. I will evade answering further questions to the utmost of my ability and will not submit to cerebral scans of any kind. I will make no oral, written, or electronic statements disloyal to the alliances or harmful to their cause.

ARTICLE VI

I will never forget that I am fighting for freedom, that I am responsible for my actions, and that I am dedicated to the principles that make my world free. I will trust in my god or gods and in the Terran Alliances forever.

PART 1

◀ ▶

Brothers in Arms

The rope snapped, and I plunged toward the canyon floor, some three hundred meters below.

Later on, Squad Sergeant Judiah Pope would learn that my rope had been cut, but his investigation into the incident would prove futile. Problem was, everyone in the Eighty-first Squad wanted me dead. Everyone except Dina, who felt more pity than resentment toward me, and my older brother, Jarrett, who would rather I experience pain. A whole lot of pain.

Pope had us ascending and rappelling a wall of mottled strata that South Point's first cadet corps had dubbed "Whore Face" since she offered so many good hand- and footholds. The sergeant had, in all of his oratory splendor, told us, "You fuckin' first years ain't gonna get the luxury of no combat skins yet. You're gonna climb this face with ropes, then you're gonna come down this face with ropes. No superhero bullshit. Now I wanna hear you call out. On belay? On! Ready to climb? Ready! Don't let me see you screwin' up."

My father, a soft-spoken mineralogist who worked for the Inte-Micro Corporation, had always told me that only the ignorant resorted to profanity. I had never heard more swearing than I had during the end of my first year at the academy, even though most of the second, third, and fourth years I had met seemed pretty bright, and right there in the South Point Academy Code—a code none of us would dare break at the risk of immediate dismissal—was the admonishment to be

3

at all times polite and courteous in our deportment, bearing, and speech. During my second day on Exeter, the rocky moon on which the ancient Racinians had chosen to build their facilities and on which Generals Ky-Tay and Jotanik of the Seventeen System Guard Corps had chosen to build South Point Academy, Pvt. Joey Haltiwanger had told me that the cadre was nervous over the mounting political tension between the colonies and the alliances. That's why everyone remained so intense, and that intensity grew even more fierce as we struggled to finish our first year's training and get onto the Order of Merit list for promotion.

While that may have been true for some, Pope belonged to a camp all his own. The twenty-year-old second year stood a quarter meter shorter than most of us, had skin like singed rubber, and had a gap so large between his bottom front teeth that you swore someone had knocked out a tooth. For a long time I considered him no more than a disgusting little man, a military cliché overcompensating for the curses nature had wrought upon him.

So I was falling, watching the rope drop away from me, feeling the wind rush over my face and flutter through my black training utilities as though it wanted to morph them into a parachute. And there, down below, stood Pope, a diminutive grim reaper, scowling, pointing a finger at me, and though I couldn't hear him, I knew he swore at me. I gaped at him, my eyes burning, and thought of breaking orders and activating my skin to save myself. Finally, he hit me with the CZX Forty, and I came to a slow stop about a meter off the dusty ground.

For a little while there, I hadn't been sure if Pope would save me. The day before, my poor time on the confidence course put my squad in third place during the platoon competition.

"What're you doing, St. Andrew?" Pope asked, still aiming the CZX Forty's big barrel at me. He thumbed a button on the antigrav rifle's stock panel. I dropped to the dirt, tripped, and fell to my knees. His boot suddenly connected with my jaw, and I slammed onto my back. Exeter's pale blue sky scrolled by and got me dizzy. The majority of the cadets training on Exeter had been raised above ground, but people like my brother and I who had spent most of our lives in the mines of Gatewood-Callista still had trouble adjusting to all that real, nonsimulated space overhead and had developed mild or even severe cases of agoraphobia that kept the academy's shrinks busy. Sure, Jarrett and I had been to the surface and had seen the heavens, but only on rare occasions, given the cost of renting an environment suit. My father had bought me a trip up for my eighteenth birthday, hopefully my last celebrated on that godforsaken satellite, and I had reveled in the night sky and had dreamed of coming to Exeter and becoming an officer in the Seventeen System Guard Corps so that I could, like so many other eighteen-year-old colos, shed my second-class roots.

As I rubbed my smarting jaw, I realized that all of my dreams had come terribly true.

"Get your ass up!"

Spoken like a true leader. "Sir, yes, sir!" I cried.

By the time I got to my feet, nine young men and women about my age had surrounded me and were staring at the dust-covered pariah before them.

Pvt. Rooslin Halitov, also a native of Gatewood-Callista, jabbed me with a stubby index finger, then turned up the blue flame in his eyes. "Don't know about the rest of you," he began, stealing a glance over his shoulder, "but I'm tired of carrying this gennyboy. I say he dusts out right here, right now." Halitov gritted his teeth, which made his blocky face seem all the more hatchet-shaped and drew out the veins in his tree trunk of a neck. He poked me again, then traced his finger along the two-inch, cross-shaped birthmark on my cheek. And that's when I grabbed his wrist.

And Staff Sergeant Claudia Rodriguez grabbed mine. The tall, humorless woman had the grip of a *shraxi*, and I was one to know since I had once inadvertently run into two of those nocturnal little bastards on my way back to First Year Barracks. Luckily, Jarrett had been with me and had pried them off before they had sunk their teeth into my arm.

"Squad Sergeant?" Rodriguez called.

"I'll take it from here, ma'am," Pope said.

"Very well." Rodriguez released my wrist as I freed Halitov's. She spun on her heel and headed back for the shade of the Eighty-first's Mobile Training Command Center, not much more than a small pup tent from where she monitored the squad's progress via her tactical computer. She could view us via three-dimensional simulacrum, old-style flat screen projection, or even a direct interface, were we wearing cerebros. I could always feel the heat of her electronic gaze on my neck. And sometimes I wish I had been nicer to her, but I couldn't have known then that I would watch her scream and clutch her spilling intestines before she collapsed to her death.

"The exercise is over," Pope said, holding the end of my rope. "This break is clean. Looks like someone gave Mr. St. Andrew a little help getting down. You know who you are. And so will I. Now we're going to hump back. Last mess formation at twenty-two thirty. Evening study period is cancelled."

A collective groan rose through the squad since in the morning we had major exams in astrophysics, composition, and colonial history. Never mind the fact that Exeter's twenty-eight-hour days taxed the hell out of us and we generally slept through our classes with our eyes open.

"We'll be back out here at twenty-seven hundred," Pope added. "And we'll do it again, in the dark. I don't give a shit how much you're draggin'. Police up your gear and move out."

"Can he do this?" someone muttered.

Halitov snorted. "Why don't you ask him?" Then he looked at me and just nodded, as though confirming to himself that yes, he would find a way to dust out the gennyboy. He squeezed my birthmark, twisted the skin, then wrenched himself away.

I stood there, rubbing my sore face and damning to hell my ancestors who had damned me. Back in 2144, Jeffery St. Andrew, his wife, and their five sons had been members of the original forty thousand to settle on Kennedy-Centauri, humanity's first extrasolar colony. With the sponsorship of NASA, Coca-Cola, Inte-Micro, and the old People's Republic of China, great-great-grandfather Jeffery and his family had mined iron ore, copper, and feldspar, and in doing so had contracted a new airborne disease called epineuropathy. The disease caused a rapid though ultimately treatable gene mutation that resulted in seizures not unlike those associated with grand mal epilepsy. It also affected a gene dubbed TIE-2, which codes for a receptor on cells that line the insides of blood vessels, and the malfunctioning receptor resulted in birthmarks. Similar to the old port-wine stains but created by microscopic parasites of an unknown origin, parasites that affect vein growth and strength, the marks cannot be removed without severely scarring the patient—laser surgery or no. Irony was, the marks themselves produced scars that ran much deeper than the skin because they branded you as a colonist, a second-rate citizen with bad genes. And you couldn't do much about hiding a mark on your face. Flesh-colored creams always rubbed off. I've learned to live with my mark, even embrace it, but back then I wanted nothing more than to rip it from my face. I sometimes thought that my handicap was the reason my mother left us when I was just three. My father still refuses to talk about it, and for years I blamed myself. I imagined that she couldn't handle a child with a mark, that every time she had looked at me, it had been with pity and disgust. The fact that my brother lacked any trace of defect only heightened my guilt and jealousy.

"You all right, Scott?" Jarrett asked with disgust.

I stiffened. "Just go."

It was bad enough that someone had had the bright idea of assigning both of us to Third Battalion, Kilo Company, Twenty-seventh Platoon. But couldn't the brass have found another squad for my brother? Or had they figured me for a liability who needed a keeper? I would never learn the truth. Official policy dictated that you were assigned to a unit and would remain there until either promotion, dust out, or death. Decisions of unit organization were made by the administration. Most requests for transfer were denied unless you had a seriously good reason; even then the staff would do everything they could to keep you where you were. They did not want to second-guess themselves.

Pope crossed in front of us. "You better watch your brother's ass," he told Jarrett. "If you don't, in the next couple of days I guarantee he'll IDO." Translation: Involuntary Dust Out. Pope faced me, and as usual I averted my gaze so I wouldn't have to watch him stare at my birthmark. "Mr. St. Andrew, they'll come for you in the night. I'm you, I don't sleep."

"Sir, I'm trying my best, sir." I sounded like a pathetic fool. Why was I wasting my time and the alliances' money trying to become an officer? Why couldn't I just accept who I was, genetic flaws and all?

Because I knew exactly what my life would be if I remained on Gatewood-Callista. I would marry some poor slob woman, bang out a couple of kids (who would, in turn, become middle-class workers like me because that was all you could get on a colony), and I would probably die painfully, in debt, and not by natural causes. Numox poisoning killed more people on my world than anything else. The stuff was layered through the rock, and you had to protect yourself from it as though it were plutonium. Exposure for just a few seconds would kill you within a day.

I had just wanted to escape. My father had wholeheartedly supported my decision, and I had even scored higher on the entrance exams than my brother.

"Sir, permission to speak candidly?" Jarrett asked.

Pope's god-ugly face spilt in a crooked grin. "Speak."

Jarrett raked fingers through his reddish brown crew cut, drew in a deep breath, then raised his shoulders. "Sergeant, this is bullshit. You're standing there and telling me that someone tried to kill my brother, and there isn't a thing you can do about it?"

"Trust me. Fourth years are investigating. But we should talk in private," Pope rasped. He turned a menacing stare on me. "You. Go."

I snapped off a salute, gathered my gear, and jogged away. I felt very afraid for my brother.

Some of the first years like myself often joked about how Generals Ky-Tay and Jotanik lacked originality and had blatantly ripped off the traditions of other military academies to create South Point. But once I had read up on the institution's brief, highly classified history, I discovered that the generals had had every intention of employing traditional models, which, in their estimation, simply worked. They had begun their work in 2278, just twenty-three years prior, had given the establishment a familiar name reminiscent of the old United States' West Point Military Academy, and had embraced the conventions of a cadet code, prayer, and medallion. All fifteen hundred of us had been organized into an officer's training regiment comprised of four battalions, sixteen companies, forty-eight platoons, and one hundred and forty-four squads.

But despite the generals' intentions to make the academy rest on the foundations of yore, South Point still lay seventy-eight light-years from Earth and stood on a moon orbiting 70 Virginis b, a gas giant over six times the size of Jupiter. Thankfully, Exeter's magnetic field shielded it from 70 Virginis b's tidal forces and intense radiation. Eight hundred thousand years ago, the moon had had a thin atmosphere of nitrogen and a gravity of .758 Earth standard; now it inexplicably maintained a breathable atmosphere and near-Earth gravity, much like the colonies of Aire-Wu, Epsilon Eri III, and Rexi-Calhoon. Some theories held that the Racinians breathed an atmosphere and preferred gravity similar to ours and had terraformed Exeter and the other worlds. Nothing in the aliens' technology had thus far proven those theories, and most experts agreed that they had left our galaxy about fifty million years before we discovered their existence.

I hustled toward the barracks, having fallen well behind the others. The trail wound tortuously along a cliff that afforded striking views of the academy lying below, all one hundred acres of her grounds cordoned off by towering mesas, some of which eclipsed the multihued bands of 70

Virginis b. The architecture of the academy's classroom buildings and library sacrificed artistry for function and relied heavily on sloping, transparent roofs set upon circular, quickcrete walls. But the administration building took your breath away with its carefully planned assemblage of isosceles triangles. We first years rarely visited the place. Going to admin meant you were in a world of trouble, IDO, or dead. On the fringe of the academy grounds lay the barracks, unremarkable rectangular structures divided into four main sectors: first, second, third, and fourth year. First years billeted in the cleanest and most orderly sector in all of the barracks. The second, third, and fourth years kept us busy cleaning it by way of "surprise" inspections six to ten times every day. Earth's military traditions had weathered the light-years quite well.

Inside the barracks and fully out of breath, I staggered to my gelrack, third down on the right, and dropped the rope and gear pack beside my footlocker. Barracks GY27 housed all three squads of the Twenty-seventh Platoon, though each squad had its own bunkroom and latrine. Any cadet venturing into another squad's room could do so only with the express permission of that squad's sergeant, which was why I frowned at Pvt. Carstaris from the Eightieth as she came up to me, her black utilities unzipped to the navel, her peach-sized breasts moving in an easy rhythm with her step. "I saw what happened," she whispered in my ear. "Halitov paid someone to do it." She turned and sauntered out, leaving nine dirty looks in her wake.

"What'd she say?" Halitov asked, wearing only his boxer shorts, sweat dripping from his steely pectorals. Of course his gelrack lay next to mine.

"Nothing," I snapped, eyeing the deck as I unzipped my utilities.

Had I been facing Halitov, I would have seem him coming, not that I could have fended off his choke hold, but at least I could have braced for it. I hadn't realized how much strength dwelled within those meaty poles he called arms. As he applied more pressure, I swore I felt a numbing electricity arc through my neck.

"Let him go," came a familiar voice.

Halitov snickered. "Uh, let's see. Fuck you, Forrest?"

From the corner of my eye, I spotted Pvt. Dina Anne Forrest, a tall woman with thick eyebrows, chestnut brown bangs, and a light sprinkle of freckles on her cheeks. She folded lean arms over her chest and came forward wearing a look so combustible that I would've given her a wide berth were it not for Halitov's grip. "What did you say?"

"I was asking why all the bitches come to this gennyboy's rescue."

"And I was asking why all of us bitches want to see you IDO. Couldn't be the fact that you're an ignorant, pompous ass who thinks teamwork means that he's the team leader and everyone else works? No, that's not it."

"I'm helpin' the squad here," Halitov roared. "You been checking the scores? We're in last place in everything. We won't make the Order of Merit list. Why? Here he is."

"We're a chain. And if he's the weakest link, then it's our job to strengthen him. You forget about the code?"

"For nearly a year I've put up with this. No more." Halitov's foul breath warmed my neck. "Close your eyes, little man. I'll do it quick. And you can still tell them it was an accident."

Clarion, Narendra, Obote, and Yat-sen had gathered around my bunk and appeared unfazed by Halitov's threat. Haltiwanger's eyes glassed up and his Adam's apple worked overtime; I knew my pudgy, redheaded friend wanted to help but was too scared. I'm glad that he didn't because later on it made what I had to do to him a little easier.

Dina sprang on Halitov. He shouted, reached back with one hand to block her—

And I rolled out of his grip and spun back to face him, my neck on fire, my knees buckling.

Paul Beauregard, who had been standing somewhere behind Obote and Yat-sen, crossed in front of me, his arms drawn tight to his chest, his hands balled into fists. Like Halitov, Beauregard stood a full two meters but boasted the slender frame of a swimmer to Halitov's wrestler. Even as Dina fought to place Halitov in a choke hold of her own, Beauregard struck a roundhouse to Halitov's cheek, sending him and Dina crashing to the deck.

And then a strange thing occurred, something that made me believe that Halitov was a lot smarter than he let on. He tore out of Dina's grasp and hauled himself to his feet. At that moment, I thought he would square off with Beauregard, but he simply fingered his reddening cheek, nodded to himself as was his wont, then returned to his gelrack.

Beauregard proffered a hand to Dina, which she accepted with a weary smile. His hand slid up her arm, behind her neck, and he began to loosen her tense muscles. I had to look away.

No one said a word. Dina and Beauregard returned to his rack across from mine, where they sat, and he continued his massage. He was madly in love with her. I wasn't sure she felt the same. She always seemed a bit reserved. Halitov lay back on the therapeutic gel mattress, eyes closed, hands clasped behind his head.

We had about thirty minutes to kill before last mess formation. Trying to calm down, I glanced out the window and swallowed back the lump in my throat. Twilight crept over the sky, and 70 Virginis b shied toward the horizon. I thought of Jarrett, and part of me argued that my IDO would make everyone's lives easier, maybe even mine. But that other part of me, the stubborn part that had driven me to South Point in the first place, had, well, other plans.

After sloughing off my utilities, I fetched my towel and headed for the latrine. Jane Clarion and Agi Narendra had already begun their showers in private stalls fenced off by neck-high walls. When they spotted me, they turned away, whispering. I showered in silence. They finished and left, then Mario Obote and Too Yat-sen came in, took one look at me, and did an about-face. Sighing hard in frustration, I dried off and padded to my rack. I collapsed on the mattress, and the gel seeped up around my shoulders as I stared at the ceiling, eavesdropping on Dina and Beauregard.

"But don't you have to be a second lieutenant to receive Racinian conditioning?" Dina asked.

"Yeah, but rumor has it that they might put us through after first year. They want us to have more time to assimilate. My father told me there have been some problems."

As we were all painfully aware, Beauregard's father, Colonel J. D. Beauregard, commanded the Colonial Wardens, a special forces unit within the Corps. The Wardens were the most highly respected group in our military, bar none. Upon graduation, only one or two from our entire class would be selected to train for that unit. At least Beauregard downplayed the prestige, though I sensed that his modesty was merely in deference to us.

"Squad sergeant on deck!" Narendra shouted.

I sprang out of my bed as though it were crawling with *shraxi* and lined up in front of my rack, my towel nearly slipping off.

Pope marched down the aisle between our racks, paused in the middle of the room, then placed hands squarely on his waist. "You people smell. Mr. St. Andrew? Mr. Halitov?"

As we shifted front and center, Halitov elbowed me hard in the ribs. I bit back the pain and focused on the patch on Pope's left breast: four equilateral triangles positioned at each of the cardinal points and pointing outward, with a ring of seventeen stars superimposed over them. That was the Corps's simple emblem, the stars signifying the seventeen explored worlds, the triangles representing honesty, loyalty, courage, and determination. Just words to me back then.

After a loud hem, Pope began. "Gentlemen. During orientation we told you that we maintain surveillance in every facility on these grounds. Some of you have managed to get around that and meet for a little unauthorized coitus. I don't see it and you keep it safe and controlled, it don't hurt me. But anyone stupid enough to attack another cadet inside the barracks deserves an automatic IDO. Would you agree with that assessment, Mr. Halitov?"

"I would, sir."

Though I wanted very badly to turn my head and watch Halitov squirm, I didn't dare move.

"What about you, Mr. St. Andrew?"

I flushed. "Sir, I agree with that assessment, sir."

"Did Mr. Halitov attack you?"

"Sir, not exactly, sir."

"Would do you mean, 'not exactly'?"

"Sir, I provoked him, sir. He asked me a direct question, and I refused to answer it. Sorry, sir."

"I see. All right, then. It's come to my attention that most of you have a problem with Mr. St. Andrew's performance. That's not only his responsibility, it's yours. Mr. Halitov, I'm placing you in charge of Mr. St. Andrew."

"Sir, thank you, sir." Halitov never sounded more pleased.

"If Mr. St. Andrew fails to pack the gear to serve in my Seventeen, both of you will IDO."

"But sir—"

"Sergeant Rodriguez has already approved this arrangement. Now then, gentlemen. Do we understand each other?"

We replied in unison.

"Very well." He lifted his wrist, squinted at his tac. "You've got eleven minutes till last mess formation." He shifted to go.

"Sir?" I called. "Have you seen my brother?"

A shadow passed over Pope's expression. "You want to interrogate me? That it, Mr. St. Andrew?"

"No, sir. I just—"

"I didn't think so." He stomped out.

2 ❯ **Dressed in fresh** utilities and with eight minutes to spare before last mess, I sat up on my gelrack and skimmed through electronic pages of colonial history glowing on my tablet. A lot of the material was review from my secondary education, though my instructor, a captain who looked old enough to have fought in the pre-alliance biowars (that's an exaggeration—he'd have to be over a hundred) expected us to know dates. Most of us were pretty cynical about the class. Why not slide those horseshoe-shaped cerebros onto our heads and let us spend just thirty seconds downloading a semester's worth of material directly into our long-term memories? We would later learn a closely held secret: Downloaded data interfered with the conditioning, which was why only colos could attend South Point and not the more genetically pure Terrans. Most people living on Earth received their education through cerebros and participated in learning communities to discuss all of that stuff "they never knew they knew." Education was about conversation, not memorization. We colos could never afford that extravagance, and we learned material the cheaper, old-fashioned way: lecture, group work, notes, discussion, surprise quiz, midterm, final exam, deep sigh, it's over.

Of course, the alliances had their ulterior motives in making the cerebros so expensive. Our ignorance, especially in science and engineering, kept us weak and, in my case, hungry, which was another big reason I wanted to become a conditioned officer. After the conditioning, we had the option to hook up to a cerebro and download to our heart's content. I would, in effect, enjoy the life of a fully educated Terran.

I tapped back to my favorite chapter, the only one that seemed relevant, a treatise that covered our first contact with the Racinians and the eventual development of the TAWT drive and skin technology.

On February 2, 2099, deep-core drillers working on Neptune's third moon, Nereid, uncovered the ruins of an immense, subterranean hangar housing a small fleet of spacecraft estimated to be 1.7 million years old. Designed to accommodate human-sized travelers and engineered to be remarkably similar to our own sleek shuttles, the ships were at first mistaken for classified military vehicles. It took another six months to verify that they were, in fact, of alien origin, and months after, on September 3, all of humanity learned that we were not the only intelligent race in our galaxy—or, as some war critics would later put it, we learned that the Racinians were the only intelligent race in the galaxy.

Historians still note that the discovery was suspiciously too good to be true. We had not found some mysterious monolith or some completely unintelligible device that would frustrate us for centuries. We had found ships constructed of high-strength, low-weight alloys similar to our own. The only thing we lacked were the pilots to tell us how to operate them, though it took us only thirty years to decipher their language, navigation, artificial intelligence systems, and bits and pieces of a process they endured that loosely translated as biological conditioning. Strangely enough, nowhere in their information systems could we find data on their culture, religion, politics, or even their name. We called them the alien race, the race; then the media finally dubbed them "the Racinians." Alarmists predicted the aliens were not long since gone but were carefully feeding us information for some diabolical purpose. Either way, we were hungry.

Because the discovery was so phenomenal—far more so than the microorganisms we had found living beneath Europa's ice crust, it sparked a renewed and vigorous interest in space exploration. During the entire twenty-first century, we had ventured out only as far as Neptune, but within fifty years after the Nereid find we would leave our solar system. Round-the-clock study of the Racinian craft led to the development of the Tecnocabalistic Drive System, which in turn yielded a second-generation Telic drive: the Trans Advanced Wave Theory (TAWT) drive, responsible for getting me to Exeter in the first place. The text described its operation as follows:

> *Toroidal Curvature of the containment field allows the formation of the mediators and the establishment of a stable family of PSTM (Primal Space-Time Matter) particles. The main TAWT drive computers, networked in a Quantum Communication Array (QCA) allow the so-called faster-than-light computations to be made which in turn collapse the wave function of any and all present conditions. As the ship's computer observes the conditions, it in effect can answer questions before they are posed.*
>
> *By forming a PSTM, the Racinian Tecnocabalistic Drive System (TDS) can indeed create the initial conditions of the universe at a time before the big bang of creation. In this field/particle state, all matter and space-time are located in the same place at the same time of the same particle or mass. In this field time,*

space and matter lose all singularity. Space and distance have no meaning, for all matter is located in the same place. Time has no meaning, for all matter is one. Matter has no meaning, for all is unification. In that primeval time, as the universe entered its inflationary stage (but prior to its expansion), no effect was realized at the quantum level. And for all time the quantum bond would be present, but unmeasured— until the TDS was turned on.

"Holy shit," Beauregard muttered.

I looked up from my tablet. Jarrett limped into the bunkroom, one eye swollen, both cheeks crimson, his utilities torn at the knees and coated with a thick layer of dust. He ignored the stares, winced as he leaned over and pulled a towel from his footlocker, then started for the latrine.

"Jarrett?" Beauregard called.

My brother waved off the colonel's son and kept on. I slid out of my rack and followed my brother into the showers.

"Scott," he said in a warning tone as he fumbled with the zipper on his utilities.

"I'm not leaving until you tell me."

He sloughed off his uniform, revealing a half dozen purpling bruises on his chest. I grimaced and circled behind him to find at least as many welts on his back.

"Just get out of here."

I couldn't take my gaze off his injuries. "What did that bastard do to you?"

"What's it look like? I came all this way to get my ass kicked. And for who? For my little brother who can't hack it. You're ruining this for us, Scott. You hear me?"

Someone gasped. I looked to the doorway, where Dina,

Beauregard, and Haltiwanger stood wearing the same expression of concern. The others jockeyed for a gossip spot just behind them. My glower forced everyone back into the bunkroom.

Jarrett slammed the shower door and keyed on the water. I gritted my teeth and watched him a moment, the rage building until I suddenly blurted out, "I don't want anything from you. Stop trying to help me."

"Don't know why I do," Jarrett answered, grinding out his words. "I guess I'm your brother, and I'm supposed to help you, but I feel like I'm wasting my time."

We lined up outside Mess Hall #3, double-checking each other's utilities for condemning lint, wrinkles, and improper fitting. Squad Corporal Lysa Gorbatova, a nineteen-year-old second year, finally met us on the line, and in Pvt. Haltiwanger's evening ritual, he muttered breathlessly, "Look at her. Just look at her."

Gorbatova was not my type. Haltiwanger opted for short, strawberry blondes, and he often described in unwelcome detail exactly what he would do to our squad corporal. He questioned my own sexual preferences since I didn't speak of women as basely as he did, but I came from Gatewood-Callista, where forty percent of the mining colony's original colonists were fundamentalist Christians of the Colonial Church of Christ. My father had separated from the church after my mother left, but he still followed many of the church's practices and had taught my brother and I to appreciate each individual's value and to adhere to a code of conduct not unlike South Point's. Sure, my father had been tough, but by sixteen I had realized that his efforts would only help me escape my heritage.

Thus, I had difficulty standing there, trying to repress a mental image of Corporal Gorbatova on all fours and barking like a dog while Haltiwanger sat on her back and slapped her bare and dimpled buttock with his riding crop. Just when I thought I had forgotten that one, I'd remember the one where he dressed her in a schoolgirl's uniform, gave her a lollipop, spanked her, then threw her on his gelrack.

"What did I miss, Mr. St. Andrew?" Gorbatova came toward me as though we had been networked to a cerebro and she had read my mind. Thankfully, she moved on to my left, to Jarrett, whose eye now resembled a bulging navel. "Have you been to the infirmary?"

"Ma'am, I'm fine, ma'am."

She suddenly craned her head toward Haltiwanger. "You . . . every night I'm out here you're looking at me like you wanna screw me. Is that right, Mr. Haltiwanger?"

"No, ma'am."

With an exaggerated frown, she sashayed up to him and caressed his pudgy cheek. "You saying I'm not desirable? You saying I'm ugly?"

"No, ma'am."

"Then why don't you wanna have sex?"

Haltiwanger's breath came raggedly, and his eyes brimmed with tears of nervousness. "Ma'am, unauthorized coitus is strictly prohibited, ma'am."

"Unauthorized coitus . . . that makes it sound more dangerous, doesn't it?"

"Ma'am, I don't know, ma'am."

Pope exited the mess hall and drew toward us. "How're we doing here, Corporal?"

Gorbatova snapped to, saluted, then stood at parade rest. "Sir, all present and accounted for, sir. Recommend Mr. Jarrett St. Andrew go to the infirmary, sir."

The sergeant cocked a brow. "Mr. St. Andrew will be just fine. Squad, fall out!"

Like a pack of starving werewolves, the others charged toward the mess hall's narrow doorway.

"Think you can handle chow without screwing up?" Jarrett asked, then blew past me.

Salisbury tofu, Cetian beans, backed potatoes, and Torosa salad were on the menu. The beans weren't that bad and had been imported from the agricultural domes on Tau Ceti XI. The colony of Aire-Wu, in the Ross 154 system, used to be the leading producer of grain, forage, fruit, and nonfood crops, but about sixteen years prior, production got cut in half by a disease that still baffled the experts. Some very sweet corn had come out of Aire-Wu, corn that had become famous throughout the colonized worlds. But even if they had been serving that corn, I wouldn't have eaten it.

The entire platoon dined together during all four mess formations, and though the second, third, and fourth years had established a supposed healthy rivalry among us that usually kept squads separated during chow, I noted with some interest that several people from the Eightieth, including Pvt. Carstaris, had come over to our side of the hall and had taken seats around Rooslin Halitov.

Ladies' man Haltiwanger, who had already fetched his tray, drifted back down the line. "That was close," he said through a sigh.

"Yeah," I said, barely interested.

"I think me and her are gonna happen," he said with a wink, then tipped his head toward Halitov and the cadets from the Eightieth. "What's that about?"

"Me, probably."

"And . . . oh, shit, there goes your brother."

I wanted to stop Jarrett, but he had already loaded his tray and now wove toward Halitov's table, looking for all the world like a battered veteran out to settle one last score. I set down my empty tray.

"Forget them," Dina said, suddenly in front of me and placing a hand on my chest. "C'mon. Sit with Paul and me." She had never come so close, and I couldn't help but imagine touching her still-wet hair.

Before I could argue, she grabbed my wrist and led me between the long tables to where Beauregard sat with Agi Narendra and Jane Clarion, who averted their gazes. The colonel's son had just launched into another of his history review sessions that would inevitably digress into a political polemic about why the colonies should secede from the alliances:

"To really understand this thing, you need to go back. I'm talking way back to 2180, to the biowars and the formation of the alliances. So we damned near killed ourselves with chemical agents. But we came back strong, declared Earth a protected planet, sent all our thugs over to Urak Sulcus, on Ganymede, then continued expansion and controlled the population by limiting colonial passports. It had to be done. So about now the alliances aren't looking too bad. They've done some pretty good things, and they're not that much different from the old Earth countries that comprise them. They're upholding democratic, capitalistic ideals, which, in my book aren't that bad. Hey, Mr. St. Andrew. Grab a seat. You eating?"

I shook my head, then glanced to Halitov's table. No war yet, though he and Jarrett were talking, their expressions strangely neutral.

Beauregard continued, not missing a beat. "So things are moving along swiftly. By 2224, Mr. St. Andrew's world, Gatewood-Callista, is set up for mining and becomes the most profitable colony in existence. Of course we colonists recognize that the alliances are becoming rich and that we're not sharing in the wealth. But thank God for Inte-Micro. In 2233 the company violates the Colonial Prudence Order and tawts out eleven-point-two light-years to Sixty-one Cygni A, Ms. Clarion's hometown."

Jane Clarion stuffed a potato into her mouth, then smiled tightly, her once-fair skin turned to tawny leather by the sun and dust. "Okay, Mr. Beauregard, you've proven your point. You'll ace the history exam."

Beauregard rolled his eyes. "So Inte-Micro claims squatter's rights for the world and establishes a precedent for independent exploration. The Colonization Ordinance of 2233 is written and approved by the alliances. Inte-Micro owns the colony, but they'll have to pay heavy taxes for the right to sell goods and services to other Alliance-held worlds. Boys and girls, the alliances began writing their epitaph with that ordinance. Exxo-Tally Corp. jumped on the bandwagon, and we hit the Racinian jackpot on Drummer-Fire."

"Not exactly," I muttered, alternating my gaze between him and Halitov. "We just found more of their abandoned tech, not anything new." I didn't feel like talking, but his cocky tone set me off. Or maybe he wasn't being cocky. Maybe it was just me. Maybe I wasn't really listening. Why weren't Jarrett and Halitov trading blows?

"Yeah, but look what it did for expansion and how it made the colonies even more valuable and exploitable to the alliances. Take Nau Dane, for instance. That incident occurred more than thirty years ago. We won't sit by for another standoff like that."

In 2273 the Exxo-Tally Corporation discovered the world of Nau Dane in the Ross 128 star system, but the right to colonize remained in dispute for nine years. Eastern Alliance explorers arrived one month after Exxo, dubbed the world Zheng He and claimed it for the alliances. The Twelve System Guard Corps had been called in and had squared off with Exxo-Tally colonists. No shots were fired, but the incident marked the beginning of the cold war between the corporations and the alliances. Yes, I knew my history, but I would not ace the exam.

"One of my uncles died on Icillica," Narendra said. "We won't sit by for anything like that again, either. You can't tell me that life support and redundancy systems go off in forty-seven of fifty-one mining facilities by accident. It wasn't the Seventeen that did it, either. Alliance Marines killed those people."

"I agree. And the tragedy *was* declared an act of sabotage," Beauregard reminded him. "But when Alliance Marines are involved, you can bet you won't find tracks. And now we've got an Alliance military outpost over in Kapteyn Beta, which, don't forget, they lied to us about for years. Called it a research station. Yeah, they were doing research all right, research into colonial weaknesses."

"Mr. Beauregard, what are you doing here if you're in favor of colonial secession?" I tapped the Guard Corps patch on my breast. "We're training for the Corps, and the alliances own the Corps. Think about article one: 'I will always remember that I am an Alliance citizen, fighting in the forces that preserve my world and our way of life. I have resigned to give my life in their defense.' Do you believe that? I do. The code is the most important thing now." I stole a look at Jarrett, who just sat quietly, eating. "The most important thing."

"My father mentioned a few details. Wish I could share them. Let's just say that when all hell breaks loose, and trust me, it will, you'll learn a few things about this Guard Corps that'll surprise you—and depress you."

"What, like there's a secret weapon on the base we've built on Tau Ceti?" Narendra asked, furrowing his thick brows. "So they told us a few secrets, figuring that we're not going anywhere soon. But I have a feeling the alliances know just as much as we first years."

"Not that much," Beauregard said. "Few pogues at the top know our location, but for the most part we're also a secret. And what they don't realize is that the Seventeen will be a potent force. Once we're all conditioned, we'll be capable of any operation. The alliances can't say the same of their troops. What Alliance Marine can pound ground, fly an atmoattack plane, serve aboard a TAWT cruiser, and even engage in the more cerebral rear echelon activities—all with the expertise of a combatant who's spent a decade training for those tasks?"

Narendra sighed. "We're cross-trained because we're a special force, but you pit us against Alliance troops and we don't stand a chance. Simple mathematics. Anyway, that's never going to happen. We're part of the Alliance military."

He shook his head. "I bet that one conditioned guardsman can take on an entire platoon."

"We haven't even seen a conditioned guardsman," said Narendra. "They go off to some other part of this rock, get conditioned, and transfer out. They won't even tell us what the conditioning is, and you can't believe all of the rumors. And they've only been conditioning people for what? A few months now?"

"Like I said, this Corps is full of surprises."

Clarion feigned a stunned look. "Whoa."

I lost track of the argument as raised voices came from Halitov's table. Carstaris had probably told Jarrett about

Halitov's paying someone to cut my rope, and now the fight would begin.

But Carstaris had left, and Jarrett and Halitov were seated next to each other and arguing with Obote and Yat-sen over an astrophysics problem involving radiation generation that had baffled all of us for the past two days. I even heard Jarrett say, "Mr. Halitov is right," which left me dumbfounded and feeling betrayed.

"What?" Dina asked, reading my expression.

I turned away. "Nothing."

"Officer on deck!" someone cried.

We shot to our feet as Platoon Leader Amber Sysvillian double-timed into the hall. Though she had just turned twenty-one, the brawny black woman bore herself with the measured steps and practiced looks of South Point's commandant, a woman twice her age. I admired how she had risen through the ranks and how she ran our platoon with equal measures of praise and criticism. She had not forgotten her days as a private.

But something with her seemed a bit off. I couldn't put my finger on it until she spoke. "Ladies and gentlemen, twenty-one days ago, Inte-Micro execs on Mars refused to allow Alliance inspectors inside the Olympus Mons Mine. Data tawted in to us just last night indicates that the standoff continues. Alliance troops are massing near Olympus Mons and in Valles Marineris. Inte-Micro has announced that it has banned inspectors from all facilities within the Sol system. The dispute doesn't stop there."

Sysvillian touched a button on her tac, and a hologram bloomed in the center of the mess. Thousands of agricultural domes, some with diameters of over two kilometers, stretched across a reddish brown plain and reared up against a gray horizon. To the west stood rows of hundreds of

Armored Troop Carriers—or "crab carriers," as we called them—silver disks resembling carapaces that curved forty-five degrees on two sides and sloped down into four segmented landing skids. Long lines of Eastern Alliance Marines shielded by combat skins set to standard khaki jogged down the carriers' gangways and joined an awesome formation that paralleled the domes. The image panned right to reveal a second detachment forming up to the east. My heart froze as two diamond formations of atmoattack jets streaked overhead, their pilots a thought, word, or thumb tap away from unloosing barrages of conventional or even nuclear weapons.

"Eighteen hours ago, a strike force numbering nearly fifty thousand Eastern Alliance infantry and air support personnel arrived at Outba, Cammil, Tau Ze, and Shefas on Tau Ceti Eleven. They're demanding access to the agridomes. Obviously someone or some group leaked information to the alliances. Now their forces are mobilizing throughout the seventeen systems. Negotiations *are* continuing. We doubt these incidents will lead to bloodshed. The commandant has established a direct line with the generals on Rexi-Calhoon. We will keep you informed as we deem necessary."

"My father's on Tau Ceti Eleven," Beauregard whispered, then raised his voice. "Ma'am? Will these events affect our program? Specifically, will our schedule be stepped up?"

"Negative. Unless you hear otherwise, it's business as usual. And if I were you, Mr. Beauregard, I would focus on improving my squad's scores. You people are in last place, aren't you?"

I searched for a hole to disappear into and found none as Beauregard answered, "Yes, ma'am. But now that we're warmed up, we'll show you what we're about."

Snickers ricocheted through the ranks, and someone behind me muttered, "Warmed up? More like burned out."

The platoon leader appeared skeptical. "I look forward to that, mister. Now, Squad Sergeant Pope will be in his office for the remainder of chow to address further questions and concerns. As you were."

Sysvillian headed for the door and most of us settled back into our seats. Beauregard broke away and jogged after the platoon leader. Dina called to him, but to my initial surprise lover boy ignored her and disappeared outside.

Beauregard had good reason to be concerned. Of the two thousand people in his father's command, only fourteen would survive.

The announcement unnerved me and brought on an appetite that had me filling a tray. As the mess hall crowd thinned out, I gorged myself with bland-tasting Salisbury tofu. Jarrett came by and warned me not to eat too much because by twenty-three hundred we'd be in our skins and back out on Whore Face. He left, I continued to eat, then, as I went to fork a piece of Torosa salad, the tray swept away.

"You're done here," Halitov said as he carried my food to the disposal chute and tossed it in.

I stood and crossed toward him. "You're right. I'm going to Pope's office and requesting my Voluntary Dust Out."

Halitov's eyes bulged even more, and I barely recognized him through his mounting rage. "You dust out, so do I."

"Not in this case. I'm withdrawing."

"What's the matter? You scared? Sometimes I can't believe you're related to Jarrett. He sees things the way they are. He's not a dreamer like you."

"And I can't believe you and I are from the same world."

"Don't you get it? Without this we're nothing."

"I don't want to quit. This is what I've always wanted to

do. The code? It means something to me. Some people are here for the wrong reasons, but I really want to be a soldier. Sure, it'll get me off Gatewood, get me an education. But I really like the idea of being a soldier. I want to know what it feels like to be courageous, to be honorable. I don't know what those things are."

"I say again, why do you want to quit?"

"I don't want to. I have to. Not for me. For you." I hurried outside.

3 ❯ The first day I arrived at South Point I had a premonition that I would not last four years. I had looked across the academy grounds, taking in the admin building's great spires, the rows and rows of barracks, and the library's domed roof, and something—I still don't know what it was—chilled me to the marrow.

As I made my way along the well-beaten path leading toward second year barracks and Pope's office, I reflected on that first day, on that premonition, and I wanted to believe that I had known all along that I would dust out. Believing that made it seem inevitable and relieved me of responsibility. Sure, I knew I could do well with my studies, but the rigors of physical training were too great, and nine people suffered because I wanted to become an officer. I couldn't bear the thought of Jarrett's taking another vicious beating on my account. Part of me said buckle down and deal with it. But a good officer realizes that doing your duty sometimes means abandoning your personal goals. I knew what I had to do. I would go back to Gatewood-Callista, marry that poor slob woman, bang out those kids, and live the best life I could until the Numox got me. I would die knowing that at least I had *tried* to improve my life. Maybe that would be enough.

I set a brutal pace, and for once even Halitov strained to keep up. He suddenly ran in front of me and seized my collar. "You can't do this. What if Pope decides to dust me out anyway?"

"Let go." I tried pulling away. "Okay. You're right. Let's head back." As I turned, I wrenched myself free. He lunged to regain his grip. I jerked back. He missed. I turned. No choice. *Run!*

"You won't make it," he shouted, charging after me.

We raced by a trio of second years whose patches IDed them as squad sergeants from the Sixty-ninth. I was so flustered that I failed to acknowledge them, though we were required to salute anyone who outranked us, including squad sergeants like this bunch.

"First years, halt!"

Halitov shouted something like "Help me stop him," but his words got lost in my panting.

The first barracks came up hard. I ducked around the corner and off the path, running between buildings and leaping over the occasional conduit that came jutting out of walls to plunge into the rocky soil. I checked the small placards posted in corners, turned right, jogged the length of another building, then broke hard to the left and dashed straight for the bleached quickcrete of billet BY27-80 as Halitov turned my name into a war cry. I reached the billet's door, sighed with relief that the entrance panel flashed green, then punched the big button. The pocket door slid away, even as Halitov charged toward me with the three sergeants plowing through his dust.

I ducked inside. Supply Sergeant Owendove sat behind a long counter, reciting a manifest to a cargo drone. Both cocked their heads as I stormed by.

Footsteps thundered behind me as I reached the main hall, an arid mausoleum lined on both sides by platoon offices where, I mused, first years held wakes for their dead careers. I had only visited Pope's little box once for a mandatory welcome conference, but I still remembered to count seven doors down on the left.

The sergeant's entrance panel glowed green. I glanced at Halitov, activated the door, then took one massive step into the office.

Pope's narrow desk faced me, and he looked up as I collided with Beauregard, who had been sitting in a chair opposite the sergeant. The strike to my groin sent me reeling back to find my own seat on the floor.

Breath ragged, drool spilling from his lips, Halitov slammed into the office but managed to stop a quarter meter from Beauregard.

"What kind of sophomoric crap is this?" Pope hollered. "What are you first years doing in my sanctuary while I'm trying to have a private conversation?"

Halitov opened his mouth, but the three sergeants plowed into the room and sent him crashing into Beauregard's lap.

Even as I experienced it, the moment seemed too absurd to be real. I sat on the floor, legs pulled into my chest, groin ablaze, as Beauregard tried to pry Halitov off his lap, the three sergeants launched into simultaneous tirades, and Pope found the top of his lungs: "Shut up! Everybody shut your holes!"

The shouting broke off into five labored breaths. Pope waited a moment more, exploiting the time to glare at each intruder, saving me for last. "Mr. St. Andrew, you were the first to come barging into my sacred den, so I'll hear from you. On your feet!"

One of the sergeants, a husky blonde towering over her male counterparts, took a step forward and said, "I'll tell you what happened, Pope."

"No, Barbie, you'll jam your thumb in your mouth and think of me."

The sergeant's fists came up, and in a blur of motion Halitov and Beauregard sprang into the most basic of fighting stances, knees and elbows slightly bent as they leaned toward their opponents. Our instruction in hand-to-hand combat had thus far involved second, third, and fourth years pummeling us as we apologized for our screw-ups. We figured they would eventually get around to teaching us aikido, karate, judo, tae kwon do, and a few of the quitunutul arts developed on lower G worlds, but even without formal training, I figured Halitov and Beauregard would give their opponents a decent run.

In the meantime, the shortest of the sergeants, an olive-skinned guy with big, glistening pores and shadowed jowls, closed the office door, then assumed his own battle stance beside Barbie.

Wincing, I finally made it to my feet and looked to Pope, who had riveted his gaze on the blond sergeant. "I was talking to Mr. St. Andrew. Once he's finished, then we'll hear from you. Mr. St. Andrew?"

My eyes itched as I scanned the others, then I stammered, "Uh, sir, I was on my way here, and I failed to recognize the sergeants. They ordered me to halt. I didn't. And here we are. I'm sorry, sir."

"Why didn't you obey them?"

"Sir, I don't know, sir." Only then did I realize that I had actually broken the code. I had failed to obey a superior officer's direct order.

"You don't know?"

"Sir, sorry, sir."

"You're gonna stand there and say you don't know why you didn't obey?"

"Sir, I guess I was scared, sir."

He snickered, then regarded the sergeants. "So he fails to salute, and you people chase him all the way here?"

"Not only did this gennyboy fail to acknowledge us, but he disobeyed a direct order to halt," Barbie said, all fire and big teeth.

Pope folded his arms over his chest. "Maybe he saluted, and you didn't see him."

My gaze lowered to Barbie's hands, which she repeatedly balled into fists. Her two flushed comrades nervously shifted their weight, and I wondered which of Pope's forthcoming remarks would unleash the trio.

But Pope pursed his lips, narrowed his gaze in thought, then took in a long, weary breath. "Sergeants, I'll handle this situation myself. You're dismissed."

Barbie stepped toward Halitov and Beauregard. "We're not going anywhere."

Pope closed his eyes, and I could almost hear the beep of his arming warhead. Three, two, one . . . "GET OUT OF MY FUCKIN' OFFICE RIGHT NOW! DO YOU FUCKIN' TRESPASSERS HEAR ME? OUT! OUT! OUT!"

At first I thought the sergeants had been unnerved by Pope's shouting, since all three scrambled for the door, but then, as the door opened, I realized why they wanted out.

Pope's vociferation had alerted Kilo Company's executive officer, First Lieutenant Jerry "Zombie" Humpfire, who now blocked the doorway like a quickcrete pylon. Rumor had it that the neckless bruiser had been pushed through physical training because he was the best hand-to-hand man in the company. Pope repeatedly referred to the redhead as a slow, fat piece of shit, but one who could turn off his skin and take ten, fifteen point-blank rounds to the extremities and still come at you like the zombie he was.

The XO's expression soured as he scrutinized the seven statues before him and pretended not to notice my birthmark. "I'm sitting over there in my office, and I'm trying to study for two exams. If I don't pass them, my average will slip, and four long years will mean nothing. So my entire career depends upon me passing those exams. And I'm in there, trying to concentrate, really trying, and I'm nervous because I'm thinking that if I don't pass these exams, well, like I said, I'll have wasted four long years. I'll be disgraced, an embarrassment." He glared at Pope. "I'll be the slow, fat piece of shit who dusted out, right?"

"Sir, no, sir," Pope snapped.

Humpfire lifted an index finger nearly twice as thick as my own. "So I want to know, what is it that's more important than my military career? WHAT IS IT?"

I knew the others wouldn't dare explain how one private's failure to salute now jeopardized the company XO's future, so I swallowed, cleared my throat, and felt a surge of reckless abandon. "Sir, it's my fault, sir. This private failed to salute these sergeants. This private failed to obey all orders and regulations of South Point and of proper authority. This private understands that honorable failure builds character, but what this private did was anything but honorable. This private apologizes for disturbing the XO's study period and accepts any and all punishments the XO wishes to dole out. This private wishes to be worthy of the sacrifices of his parents and colony, the generosity of the alliances, and the efforts of all those who teach and administer to him, sir."

"Clever, St. Andrew. You dress it in code and dance it around the room, but I still ain't buying it a drink. All of this shouting is about you failing to salute these bastards?"

I wondered, *If I agree with him, am I also agreeing that the three sergeants are bastards?* "Sir, the shouting was about my failure to salute, sir."

He checked his tac. "I've already wasted valuable minutes

of my life on this shit. Everybody out. Return to your offices or squads. NOW!"

The three sergeants shambled by the XO, as did Beauregard. I didn't move. Neither did Halitov.

"Gentlemen?"

I tensed as the XO's frown deepened. "Sir, with your permission, sir, this private wishes to speak with his squad sergeant."

"And sir, this private requests the same," Halitov added.

Humpfire raised his brow. "Sergeant?"

"Sir, the privates and I will confer *quietly*, sir," Pope answered.

"Very well. Don't disturb me again. Carry on."

We saluted, waited for the door to close, then Pope rubbed his eyes and shrank into his seat. "You damned first years, man . . . what am I gonna do with you?"

Halitov sighed. "Sir, we're sorry, sir."

"So what do you want?" Pope flicked a glance at his tac. "You got one minute. Then I want you geared up and ready for Whore Face. Skins on."

I shuddered. "Sir, I've come to request my VDO, sir."

There. I had done it. And it hadn't seemed too difficult because I knew Pope would argue with me. He would tell me that if I just kept my head low and applied myself, I would make it. He would tell me that I would regret withdrawing for the rest of my life.

"So you wanna quit, St. Andrew? No problem. Lot of people will thank you for it. You can go over to admin right now. I'll have the endorsement tapped in before you get there."

Tears welled, and I barely felt my throat. I was supposed to respond, but a thank-you didn't seem right.

"Anything else?"

I shook my head.

"Then you're dismissed."

After a crisp salute and an about-face, I started shakily for the door.

"Mr. Halitov? I'll be tapping in your VDO as well," Pope said.

"Sir?"

"Your success or failure depends upon Mr. St. Andrew's. Your memory that short?"

I whirled back to face Pope. "Sir, we both assumed that only my *involuntary* dust out would—"

"I don't give a shit what kind of dust out it is—including death. You drop, he drops. Oldest trick in the book, gentlemen. You take your weakest grunt, you pair him with your strongest, then you give 'em mutual goals to motivate 'em."

Halitov grinned. "Sir, I'm flattered, but—"

"Flattered? Mr. Halitov, you're only half a man. You got the lowest GPA in the squad. Maybe St. Andrew can't hump worth a shit over a confidence course, but he's got the second highest average in the entire platoon."

That stunned me. The code prevented us from sharing grades with each other, but I had assumed that most people scored as high as me. The news woke up that stubborn dreamer, the idiot who thought he could be an officer, the idiot who had no idea that friends would clutch his hands and bleed all over his lap.

"Way I figure it, gentlemen, I keep you two together, I get one smart, strong cadet." Pope fired up a nasty grin. "You can file for divorce *after* your conditioning."

"But, sir, St. Andrew *wants* to dust out. What am I supposed to do?"

The sergeant chuckled. "I don't know, Mr. Halitov. Like I

said, you're not the sharpest blade in our cache. But I'm you, I'm heading over to admin and getting used to my new career as a third-class miner. Or I'm dragging Mr. St. Andrew's ass back to the billet and convincing him to stay on. Of course, if you beat him, he won't do well on Whore Face, and there you are again, both dusting out." Pope rose and stepped in front of his desk. "You think we're idiots, Mr. Halitov? We got fingers on everyone. We know you paid someone to cut Mr. St. Andrew's rope. Of course, we can't prove anything since you've threatened the witnesses. But I swear to God, if you fail to get Mr. St. Andrew through this academy, your ass is IDO. You and him? You're bestest buddies for four years."

I couldn't see Halitov's face; no doubt his color had faded. "Sir," he quavered. "I understand, sir." He pivoted, and I took the cue to salute and leave.

Once in the hall, Halitov tore after me and asked, "You're from Ro, aren't you?"

Without breaking step, I replied, "Yeah. So?"

"I'm from Vosk. You ever been there?"

Why the oaf wanted to talk about subterranean cities on Gatewood-Callista I didn't know. "I haven't been to Vosk. Have you ever been to South Point's admin building?"

He seized my neck in both hands and drove me against the wall. "We're going back to the billet. See, if I dust out, then I got nothing to lose, which means you're dead. So tonight you'll be the second-best cadet out there. You'll climb and rappel so fast you didn't know you could."

Though I told myself that he wouldn't kill me, that he needed me to graduate, I had never seen a face more rigid, more possessed. I nodded, gasped, and the echo of distant footsteps triggered my release.

As we moved on, and I massaged my sore throat, Halitov smirked and said, "You wouldn't have made it in Vosk. They would've got you. I hate that place. It killed my real father, and it's been working real hard on my mother and stepdad."

The door slid aside, and we stepped into the cool night air. *Shraxi* issued baritone hoots, and a strange night odor, a kind of postcoital stench, wafted in from the distant mesas. Insects, some accidentally imported, some indigenous and none too large, hid in the outlying scrub. One bug we called a "triplet" sang out *ta-ta-ta . . . ta-ta-ta . . .* in the silence between hoots.

We hurried onto the trail, and Halitov slapped a paw on my shoulder. "I can't go back. No way."

"Will this be a guilt trip, a beating, or both?"

"I can't go back. Way it is."

"Know what? Neither can I."

"Then why'd you ask Pope for your withdrawal?"

I swore under my breath. "I told you. For my brother. For the rest of you."

"See, that's the kind of shit I need to learn. How do you think of that shit? You make decisions that'll benefit the team rather than yourself. This whole thing is a competition to me. But it really isn't, right?"

"We're only competing with ourselves—which is why I keep losing."

"Not tonight. I'll never be your bestest buddy like little Pope says, but you and I, we'll make it. And we're going to live on worlds with skies, and people will respect us because we earned what we have. No fuckin' Alliance trader will ever give me a dirty look again. I'm not just some colo. I'm with the Seventeen. You fuckin' look at me like that again, and I'll fuckin' break your fuckin' face. Do you hear me? DO YOU HEAR ME?"

It took me a moment to realize he wasn't yelling at me. "I

hear you," I said, hoping to wrench him from the memory. "We need to haul ass."

Squad Corporal Gorbatova stood outside our billet, speaking quietly into her tac. She bit back a curse as we hustled past her and keyed open the door. Everyone else had already headed up to Whore Face.

"Ten seconds," Halitov cried as we reached our gelracks.

I fetched my backup rope, then lifted my pack and double-checked my tac to make sure skin status stood in the green.

Halitov shouldered his own rope and pack, read his tac, then huffed. "Ready?"

"Ready."

He led the way out, and we spotted Gorbatova jogging about twenty meters ahead on the south trail that snaked along the gorge and emptied into the talus and scree at Whore Face's foot. The corporal's skin had been set to night green and cast a bioluminescent glow over the rocky countryside. In a few minutes, she would tap a command into her tac and dissolve from view as protein microprocessors shifted skin energy to mirror the terrain.

"Let's skin," I suggested.

"Let's wait till we get up there."

"Why?"

He didn't answer. I shrugged and matched his sprint, though I couldn't help but wonder about his reservations. Pope had warned us about the claustrophobia associated with first-time skinning, but he had also reassured us that in time we would get used to it. Coming from a world of closed spaces had allowed me to accept my skin without complications. Jarrett had equal success.

Within ten minutes, my rope and pack seemed to double in weight. Thankfully, we had reached the forty-five-degree slope of Whore Face's back. We began our ascent, and once more I asked Halitov if he'd like to skin. No, he wouldn't. Without protection or proper visibility, we might step into a hole or trip over a sharp piece of debris. I stopped and pulled a light stick from my pack. Halitov ignored my shout to wait up, so I hurled the light stick ahead of him. He scooped it up and forged on as I veered into his path.

The rest of the squad waited up top, eight or nine young first years shimmering like emeralds and milling about the gloomy mound. As I reached the summit, I wanted to fall to my knees and catch my breath, but as Pope had told us, cadets never get tired and are never out of breath—meaning you'd better not ever gasp or drool in front him. I allowed myself no more than a straight-shouldered pause, a wise decision since Pope was already up top, having caught a lift to the summit. His face blurred in and out of focus from behind his skin, which rose nine centimeters from his utilities. His voice came with the usual whir, as though he were speaking into a rotating fan. "Mr. St. Andrew?" He approached with a bounce in his step indicative of his skin's lower gravity setting. "Fall in!"

"Sir, aye-aye, sir!" Three taps on my tac, and the energy skin spread from my wrist to envelope me. "Vitals and AO," I ordered the tac's Artificial Intelligence. Heads Up Viewers materialized about a quarter meter ahead, the left reflecting my pulse, respiration, and blood pressure, the right feeding me a real-time, overhead shot of the Area of Operations and the personnel operating therein.

For centuries, conventional wisdom behind combat suit technology had held that you should shield the combatant in a bulky, heavyweight material while providing armaments, life support, and a power source. Maybe you increased physical strength through hydraulics or some other method, maybe you didn't. Either way, all of that bulk and firepower usually posed more dangers to the user than to the enemy. I had read stories about old United States Marines who had been operating on Mars. One guy wearing what they used to call a "thunder suit" got disoriented and accidentally took out his whole company before someone greased him. Another soldier simply tripped and decapitated herself as she reached up to block her fall.

So the geniuses in Alliance Research finally abandoned the conventional. Instead of bringing the shield to the user, they posed the question: What if the user *produced* the shield? We're supposed to be nothing but energy, and energy never dies. How much of that energy is required to sustain a life? Is there any left over that we can harness?

Inspired by Racinian technology, our tacs tap directly into the heat and electrical output of our bodies, then they enhance it. I've read the physics behind them over twenty times, and it still hasn't clicked, but the end result is a very convenient and potent power source. You figure out a way to have it controlled by the user and discover ways in which to utilize that power by, say, harnessing the quantum bond between particles to create a seemingly impenetrable skin around life-forms, a skin capable of producing its own enzymes and phosphorus-containing molecules, a skin that can mimic or ward off nearly every environment. Then you develop recycling capabilities that include air, waste products, and a rudimentary, self-contained medical system. What you get is a stunningly easy to use and effective combat suit with few drawbacks. Still, early pundits found the idea laughable, called it rubber science bounding into mysticism. They warned supporters that they could ruin their careers by endorsing such technology. Those same pundits predicted the collapse of the Inte-Micro and Exxo-Tally corporations.

I took a deep breath of recycled air, lowered my skin's temperature a few degrees, and decreased humidity by ten percent. The skin status bar along the bottom of my HUD confirmed that the changes had been made. Following Pope's lead, I lightened my own gravity, bringing myself to .9968 of Earth standard. Exeter's 1.0007 had never posed much of a problem, but my new setting would increase my endurance—

And alert Pope, who now spoke via our direct tac links. "Mr. St. Andrew," he called, his voice resonating directly from my own skin. "Gee setting is default for this exercise."

"Sir, yes, sir. Sorry, sir."

"I catch anyone else trying to lighten up, and I'll send you over this cliff myself," Pope threatened on the open channel.

Though I wanted to tell the sergeant that I hadn't intended to cheat, I knew I'd be wasting my time. I moved to the line, fell in beside Halitov, then ordered my tac's comm system to patch me into his private channel. "You all right?"

"Shut up. And be ready."

Halitov's skin had been set to night green like everyone else's, but his glowed much paler, an indication that something severely taxed his life force and now weakened his defenses. Dina and Beauregard leaned back and stared down the line at Halitov's skin. My mouth grew dry as I realized that Pvt. Rooslin Halitov, supposedly my new lifeline, might not be any help. "Mr. Halitov? What's wrong?"

He swung his head to face me, and at that proximity my tac filtered out the distortion so that I could see him as clearly as if we weren't wearing skins. "Told you to shut up."

"All right, squad, here it is," Pope began, poised in front of the line with Gorbatova at his side and Staff Sergeant Rodriguez down below in her tent. "On my mark you will set your pitons, clip in, and begin rappelling down this face. Remember, the hardest part's at the beginning. Focus on smooth takeoffs. You get euphoric, and you're bound to fuck up. And oh, yeah, you'll be timed. Now, don't get any bright ideas of just jumping off and resetting your gravity like a couple of first years from the Seventy-ninth did last night. They survived the fall and made the best time on the course. But they kept bouncing like a couple of basketballs. We found 'em nearly a klick away. Their skins weakened, and they broke a couple dozen bones apiece. We IDOed 'em before they regained consciousness. So like I say, no superhero bullshit. Use your skin as a cloak and a safety net, nothing more."

"Scott," Dina called, and I liked the way she used my first name. "Paul thinks they're up to something. We're not just rappelling. Watch yourself, okay?"

"Yeah. Thanks."

With my rope slung over one shoulder and my pack slung over the other, I watched as Pope shifted down the line, making his required last inspection before he sent us over the edge. As he neared me, I locked my gaze forward. The shadows of the gorge intersected in dozens of oily channels that tilted back toward the surrounding mesas. During my elementary education, I had stepped through a few holographs of Earth's Grand Canyon, but northwestern Arizona's terrain seemed diminutive when compared to Exeter's great formations, some of which dropped off for three kilometers. Whore Face was one of the smallest formations, the "first year hill" of climbing, but it could kill you.

"Something on your mind, Mr. Halitov?" Pope asked, as he broke through the line for a rear assault.

"Sir, no, sir."

"Your skin's down to eighty percent and falling."

"Sir, I don't know why, sir."

"Well, you've got five seconds to figure it out." The sergeant brushed by Halitov, their skins crackling and heaving white-hot webs that stitched over their shoulders. Pope reached the end of the line and shouted, "Are you ready?"

"Sir, we're ready, sir!" everyone but Halitov shouted.

"Very well. Eighty-first Squad? Go! Go! Go!"

4 **Sergeant Pope's cries** echoed off toward the mesas as I ran to Whore Face's edge and found my climbing mark between the flashing cones. Trembling, I sloughed off the pack and rope, then dropped to my knees and dug out my hammer and one of the steel pitons. "Bring shield down to ten percent around my hands," I ordered my tac's AI, then dug my bare hand into a crevice, checking for stability. The crack would have to do. I dug the piton into the seam and began pounding the spike's looped end with my hammer as nine other first years did likewise in a chaotic rhythm that reverberated madly through the night. Traditional rappelling dictated that you should never trust your life to just one bolt or piton, but the urgency of combat training and the protection of our skins ruled against that. We would survive a fall, but as Pope had indicated, the rebounding might turn us into rag dolls if we failed to properly gauge the first impact.

Somewhere down the line, Narendra and Obote groaned and called the exercise a low-tech joke, but I knew otherwise. One of the wisest assumptions the Guard Corps brass had made involved the reliability of tech. We had already been taught to assume that for every new weapon you have, your enemy will either have or develop a device that renders your toy useless. Bayonets and standard-issue K-bars would never go out of fashion. And neither would old-fashioned climbing and rappelling.

With my piton set, I found the end of the nylon rope to which I had attached a locking carabiner clip. I had knotted the rope's other end to prevent rappelling off the end; unfortunately, I had learned that precaution from experience. Our ropes were only fifty meters long, and we would have to switch lines six times during our descent. Eventually, we would work with a single rope and temporary pitons equipped with small explosives. We would anchor in, descend to the end of our line, set a new anchor beside us, remote detonate the anchor above, then clip our rope to the new anchor. We would repeat the laborious process five times. For now, five other ropes had already been anchored into the strata, and we climbed in neat little lanes to prevent someone from accidentally clipping in to the wrong rope. Of course, my first time down I had inadvertently grabbed Halitov's. And my second time down, well, someone had express-mailed me to the bottom.

I slapped the carabiner clip around the piton's looped end, stood, then tossed my rope over the edge. Dammit. Dina and Beauregard were already descending. I shook off the thought and concentrated on my own climb. "Skin to zero," I ordered as I retrieved the sit-harness from my pack and strapped it on, wishing that we could have geared up before the clock had started. When Pope had said, "Gear up," he had meant that you should have your rope and pack in hand. The first time he had given that order, all ten of us had stood on the summit with sit-harnesses buckled tight and ropes ready to be clipped in. Pope had gone down the line, removing each of our harnesses and screaming about how you didn't rappel when everything was hunky-dory and that you had to establish a self-belay with particle fire kicking dirt in your field of view. After that, he had piled up our harnesses, then had sent us on a mad search through the pile for our own. Pretty juvenile stuff, but we needed it.

I clipped the rope to my sit-harness, then checked the lock-off of my traditional figure-eight belay, a solid piece of steel with two loops that would allow me to pay out the line smoothly and gradually. Equipment set, I stole a look at my squadmates. Only Obote, Narendra, Halitov, and myself remained up top, and Halitov still hadn't clipped in to his line. "Hey, I'm supposed to be the second-fastest first year up here," I told him.

"I'll be done in a second," he snapped. "Just go."

Drawing a deep breath, I reactivated my skin and thinned it to twenty percent over my braking hand at the top of the line, thirty over the trailing hand. With my back to the gorge, I eased over the edge, hearing one of Pope's lectures thunder up from the past: "Check your rappel setup before you head down. But don't stand there for more than a few seconds doin' that. If you're not skinned, you need a glove on your braking hand, unless you got a fetish for rope burns. Bounding rappels shock-load your pitons and your rope. The greater the takeoff, the harder the brake."

Once my elbows had cleared the edge, I planted my boots on the face, feeling the dull, repelling force of my skin as it slipped into the cracks and helped me establish good purchase.

"You gonna takeoff or take in the view, Mr. St. Andrew?"

"Sir, I'm heading down, sir!" I pushed off hard and loosened my grip on the rope. Strata rolled up as I dropped two, four, six meters before my boots thudded once more on the rock. *Smooth takeoff and brake. I can do this. Eight or nine more, and I'll reach the first rope.*

Carabiner clips jingled, and I glanced up as Halitov swung out into his first takeoff. My jaw fell open. He had pushed off way too hard and now plummeted by me, descending some twelve meters before the impact of his boots knocked him into a spin. His right shoulder, bicep, and hip connected with the rock, and were it not for his skin, he might have broken his arm. Then again, I thought I had seen his skin flicker at the point of contact. He grunted as he struggled to return his boots to the face.

"Mr. Halitov?"

"Worry about yourself," he said in a rapid fire that had me bracing for my next takeoff. "And don't waste time clipping in to your next line. Just grab it with both hands up top, push off, and fall."

An airjeep whizzed by, its running lights flashing brightly enough to illuminate Pope, who sat in the passenger's seat of the open compartment, with Corporal Gorbatova at the stick. He looked pissed off. "Mr. St. Andrew, your brother's already on his third line. You're still on your first."

"That's right," Jarrett said over the private channel. "But don't worry, my brother will make it down—maybe sometime next week—but he'll make it down."

"Scott?" Dina called from somewhere below. "Check your HUV. Here they come!"

A line of twenty first years—the Seventy-ninth and Eightieth Squadrons, to be precise—charged up Whore Face's back, boots rumbling, war cries overpowering even the triplets and *shraxi*.

"Eighty-first?" Pope called to us. "Pursuit force in the zone. Their job is to prevent you from rappelling to the bottom. You fall, you're out."

"Twenty-x mag on pursuit force," I said, and the tac zoomed in on Carstaris, Fayvette, and a few others I knew from the Eightieth as they pulled big K-bars from their packs and dropped to their knees before our pitons. The image panned left to reveal Anson, Cotto, Enlia, and Xiao-pong from the Seventy-ninth doing likewise.

"If you're still on your first line, get off," Beauregard hollered. "They're cutting 'em! They're cutting 'em!"

I lost my breath as I took off, dropped another ten meters, then came crashing onto the face. Another push, and I bought five more meters.

"Scott! Damn you! Come on!" Jarrett cried.

The cliff top now bore an undulating halo as ropes to my left tumbled down toward Dina, Beauregard, Clarion, and Narendra. Our pursuers clipped into our anchors and began their descents.

Tucking myself tightly into the cliff, I sprang into another takeoff—

"They're on your rope!" Halitov warned. "Here!"

I gasped.

The rope gave.

I dropped.

One, two, three seconds and the line crashed down and skittered across the skin protecting my head. I shuddered with the déjà vu of falling. Once again, I had failed them and myself.

"Mr. Scott St. Andrew is off the course," Pope announced.

Halitov looked up at me, his face scrunched into a thick knot as I hurtled toward the canyon floor. I hadn't realized it, but he had swung his first line into my lane, and only then did it brush against my shoulder. I reached for it—

—missed—

as he clung to his second line and pushed off horizontally to swing into my lane. Given my weight, momentum, and the fact that our skins would repel each other, I figured that if he had a plan, it sure didn't involve catching me. I would blow him down to the end of his rope, which would then jerk so hard that it would probably break his back.

No, he didn't plan on catching me. He reached for my line, which had remained clipped to my sit-harness and tumbled ahead of me. His first attempt missed, but he followed with a second swipe, caught the rope, then coiled it three times around his hand as I sailed past him. The slack in my rope began whipping through the carabiner at my waist. In another few seconds, the knot would slam against the clip, the rope would snap taut as a bowstring, and Halitov's arm would rip from the socket.

Knowing that, he loosened his grip on his own rope and descended with me. My rope did snap taut, but with a much weaker jerk than if Halitov had remained stationary. I slapped both hands on the line and remembered to breathe.

But we both kept plunging toward our appointment with Whore Face's lap, me clinging for dear life, he bracing my line with one hand, trying to slow our descent with his other. I spotted another piton, my third maybe, with a rope dangling from it. We drifted closer to the face, and I seized the rope in one hand, applying as much pressure as I could to slow myself and ease Halitov's burden.

Another jerk sent us into the face, but I clung to that other line.

"I'm out," rasped Halitov. "And I can't reach my next rope without letting you go."

"I got another one down here," I said. "Give me a second I'll clip in, then release."

Willing myself into being of pure muscle, I released the hand on my original line. With all of my weight on one arm, I shifted to clip in to the new line. I sighed as the carabiner slapped in place. I worked the rope into my belay, then slapped my free hand home. "I'm in!"

"And I'm fucked."

Pvt. Val d'Or from the Eightieth swooped down in an inverted rappel and braked about two meters above Halitov. Like a scrawny blond diver from a Pacific island, Val d'Or removed the K-bar from his mouth and began sawing into Halitov's line.

Now that Halitov was free, he should be able to swing out and reach his next rope, which hung from a piton a few meters away and at shoulder height. But he didn't. He released my rope, two-handed his own, and ascended toward Val d'Or.

"What are you doing?"

"This fucker's going down the hard way," he shouted, then reached Val d'Or and slapped a hand on the cadet's cutting wrist. Skins flickered and crackled, but fortunately for both they had set their shields at five percent near their hands to increase sensitivity, otherwise both would have been repelled in a fierce rebound.

But even with Halitov's hand on his wrist, Val d'Or kept working his knife, and as Halitov reached up with his other hand to block the blade, his rope fell away. Now only his grip on Val d'Or's wrist stood between him and the bottom.

"This a circus act or what, Halitov?"

Were I Halitov, I might not have answered Pope, considering that my boots dangled in midair and I clutched a cadet who wanted nothing more than to see me fall. But once again my guardian demon surprised me. "Sir, no, sir. I've just temporarily lost my line, sir."

A malicious grin carved Val d'Or's youthful face, and suddenly I knew his plan. "Mr. Halitov! Let go!"

Too late.

"Skin up to one hundred," Val d'Or cried. The shield around Val d'Or's hand throbbed with light and blasted Halitov away as though he had just touched a billion-volt fence.

As he whirred by me, I made a pathetic attempt to toss my line near him, not that he could have caught it. A somersaulting freefall tends to disorient you. Halitov vanished into a gaping maw of shadows far below.

I shivered and waited for his scream, though I should have been paying attention to the AO above.

Val d'Or sunk his blade into my rope and whooped. I had seen what a hand-to-hand confrontation would win me, so I threw myself away from the wall, letting the rope whip through my braking hand. I had damned near made it to my next piton and was about to congratulate myself when Val d'Or sang out, "Good-bye, Mr. St. Andrew."

Three ropes cut in a single day of training. Pope would later tell me that I had set a new South Point record for incompetence. Nothing like being remembered.

"You can all thank Mr. Rooslin Halitov for tonight's exercise," Pope said, sitting on the hood of his airjeep and framed by Whore Face and the other two squadrons being debriefed. He regarded Halitov, who stood in line next to me, and spat through the gap in his teeth. "Yeah, Mr. Halitov gave us the idea for tonight's course. Did you like having your rope cut, mister?"

"Sir, no, sir."

"So how many of you scumbags did Corporal Gorbatova have to save?"

Every hand raised except for Beauregard's.

Pope hauled himself from the airjeep and targeted the colonel's son. "You're the only one?"

"Sir, yes, sir."

"Why is that, Mr. Beauregard?"

"Sir, I received a tip from someone in the Seventy-ninth, sir. That cadet would not tell me what they were planning but that we should watch out for them and the Eightieth, sir."

"Mr. Beauregard, do you believe it's ethical for you to be privy to such information prior to an exercise? Or does it constitute cheating?"

"Sir, it does not constitute cheating, sir." For the first time since I'd known him, Beauregard's voice cracked.

"What makes you say that? After all, *you're the only one* who made it down."

"Sir, I shared the information with the rest of the squad, sir."

"You mean you wanted to implicate them?"

"Sir, no, sir. I only wanted them to be aware of the danger and prepare for it, sir. You taught us yourself that the side with the best information usually wins."

"But you didn't win tonight."

"Sir, no, sir. We were outnumbered two-to-one, sir."

Pope steered himself front and center. "That's right, Eighty-first, you were outnumbered. Get used to it. Now then, Mr. Beauregard? Report to Lieutenant Humpfire's office. Mr. Halitov and Mr. Scott St. Andrew remain here. The rest of you? Dismissed."

Eight dejected first years dragged themselves away. Jarrett squeezed the back of my neck and whispered, "Still think you can hack it?" Without waiting for an answer, he jogged after the others.

I turned into a bag of rattling bones as Pope neared me and Halitov. For a second, an odd trace of sadness seeped into the sergeant's expression. That night I would dream of his death, a dream that would have nothing to do with what really happened, save for the end. "Gentlemen, I think it's time we stopped living in denial."

Halitov's frown matched mine. "Sir?" he asked.

"You two should head over to admin."

I froze. "Sir, are you dusting us out, sir?"

"I am."

"Why? We didn't do any worse than anyone else—except for Beauregard." The edge in Halitov's voice and the lack of a "sir" before and after his reply ignited Pope's gaze.

"Seems like you now got a problem skinning, Mr. Halitov. That, coupled with your poor scholarship and selfishness make you a perfect candidate for dust out."

"But sir, we had an agreement!"

While I shivered over Halitov's insubordination, Pope charged toward the much larger man, deftly slid a leg behind Halitov's, then tripped him to the ground. "Don't you raise your voice to me, Private. I say you're IDO, then you're IDO."

"Sir, no, sir!"

I crossed in front of Pope. "Sir, this private requests another opportunity for himself and Mr. Halitov, sir."

"Get the fuck outta my way, gennyboy."

Ironic that I had placed myself between them to prevent Halitov from doing something he would regret. No, my squadmate did not take a swing at Pope.

I did.

Caught him squarely in the chin with a solid jab that sent bolts of pain writhing up my arm as he tottered back, reached for his chin, then dropped like a drunk, heaving a small dust cloud.

Anyone watching us might have seen a portrait of three stunned cadets bound to the canvas of the moment; three young men, each contemplating his immediate future and waiting for one another to move but not a one daring to initiate until—

"Solid strike there, Mr. St. Andrew. First class."

I stammered. "Sir, uh, I'm sorry, sir. Are you all right, sir?"

"Yeah, I'm all right." He wiped his hands on his hips, then rose. "You're aware of the penalty for striking me, are you not?"

I focused on his reddening chin. "I am, sir. IDO, sir."

"And are you aware of the penalty for using a word like *gennyboy*?"

"I am, sir. IDO, sir. But that rule isn't enforced here, or so it seems, sir."

Pope glanced over my shoulder at Halitov, who now stood and swatted the dirt from his utilities. "Mr. Halitov, did you hear me call Mr. St. Andrew a gennyboy?"

"No, sir, I did not, sir."

Pope drew in a long breath and closed his eyes. "I want the truth, Halitov!"

"Sir, I did hear you call him that, sir."

"Well then, gentlemen. The situation has become interesting." He poked me with his index finger. "I drop you for striking me"—he stabbed Halitov with the same finger—"and you IDO automatically. But then you first years turn around and report my comment, and I'm IDOing with you. This'll work out just right. We're all gonna take a walk to admin."

I recoiled in confusion. "Sir, you want to drop, sir?"

Pope just stared at me.

"Well, we're not dropping with you," Halitov said, then tacked on a vehement *"Sir."*

"We're not?" I asked.

Halitov showed his teeth. "No one's dropping. Far as I'm concerned, this never happened. With your permission, sir, I'd like to head back to the billet and prepare for lights-out."

Pope swore under his breath. "You two bastards, you don't get it. And I can't tell you. But one day you're gonna look back on this moment, and you're gonna wish you had listened." He swung back toward his airjeep. "Dismissed."

Sharing the same puzzled look, Halitov and I saluted Pope, though he faced away, then we retrieved our gear and started for the trail back.

We didn't realize that Pope had been trying to save us. Platoon Leader Sysvillian had not told us everything regarding the crises in the Sol and Tau Ceti systems. In fact, the war had already started, and Pope had known. As usual, we first years had been given the mushroom treatment: kept full of shit and in the dark. I guess the commandant had feared that our worrying about our families would interfere with our studies and training. But she owed us the truth, and I've never forgiven her for that. Pope had wanted to tell us, but the code forbade him. I still wonder what I would have done if he had.

5 **During the next** week, we returned only once to Whore Face for a mundane ascent without being attacked. We hiked a lot, so much that I don't even remember how many kilometers per day. Pope introduced us to a new confidence course, one that required skins and had us at one point hurtling the knee-high laser beams of a conventional minefield. Jarrett broke a beam and launched twenty meters in what Pope called a beautiful arc. My brother timed his drop and adjusted his skin's gravity so that it would absorb nearly all of his impact. He suffered only sprained ankles and swore off my help. Each day he seemed more cynical, more unwilling to talk. The classes bored him. He went mindlessly through the confidence courses. He distanced himself from everyone except Jane Clarion. I once saw him slip out of his bunk in the middle of the night. A glance to Clarion's empty bunk confirmed my suspicions. My brother had stooped to the lowest of the low. I wondered if he really cared about the code, and if he really understood why we were at South Point.

One evening near week's end, Pope divided us into two lines of five and had us lying prone on the dusty parade deck. Halitov's boots rested on my shoulders, my boots rested on Clarion's, and so on. The sergeant instructed us to remain in position, then climbed into his airjeep. He flew off and wheeled back to dive. The airjeep's engine brayed like a mule on fire as he drew closer. I tried to steal a look, but the engine wash blinded me. That engine, though, I heard it so distinctly that my paranoia consumed me. Pope had finally gone insane and had decided that he would crash his airjeep into us, killing some and himself. The not knowing drove me to my feet. I wandered into the dust storm, which quickly thinned as Pope's engine died. The sergeant emerged from the dust, eyes narrowed, index finger coming to bear. "I told you to remain in position!"

"Sir, yes, sir."

"Then what are you doing?"

I considered telling him the truth. Considered it for the better part of a millisecond. "Sir, I have to use the latrine, sir."

Hoots and guffaws rose behind me.

"That what you're gonna tell the enemy, Mr. St. Andrew? Can you hold off on that attack until I take a leak?"

"Sir, no, sir."

"You think this is some petty little exercise? Here's some irony for you: your life depends upon your being able to play dead—no matter what's going on around you. You got it?"

"Sir, yes, sir."

"Now we'll do it again. And I don't care if you piss your pants, Mr. St. Andrew. Do you read me?"

"Sir, loud and clear, sir."

"Fall in!"

"Sir, aye-aye, sir!"

That night, hugged by the cool gel of my rack, I stared at the billet's ceiling and tried to think of ways to build my courage. I reasoned that I needed to learn to risk my life as freely as the others did. Why did I have so much trouble with that? Why was I always so scared?

And that's when Halitov leaned into view, his face a waning, sweaty moon in the half-light, his eyes vanishing into their sockets as his lips came together to shush me. He clutched my throat with one hand, covered my mouth and nose with the other. "I'm not going to kill you. I'll just take you real close 'cause that's what you're doing to me every time you screw up. You gotta know what it's like not to breathe, to be closed in—I mean really closed in—and there's no one to help. There's just me, laughing at you, the way they laughed at me."

With my hands locked firmly around his wrists, I tried to pull him off. Tears welled. I shuddered, tried sucking air through his fingers, gasped—

Then Haltiwanger, of all people, jumped on Halitov's back, slung an arm under the bruiser's chin, and got him in a headlock that lasted a surprising three seconds before Halitov ripped free and the lights snapped on.

Squad Corporal Gorbatova stood at the end of the billet, her expression remarkably serene as I struggled for breath, Halitov snapped to, and Haltiwanger sat on the floor, rubbing his arm. She called us outside and ordered Halitov and me to jog barefoot in a tight circle while she went off behind the billet with Haltiwanger.

"We get punished, and he gets laid," Halitov spat, his breath trailing up into the frosty air.

"Who laughed at you?"

"What?"

"You said you would laugh at me the way they laughed at you. Who were they?"

"Nobody. Forget it."

We spent twenty minutes digging a furrow until Corporal Gorbatova and Haltiwanger returned, their faces full of color. The corporal ordered us back to our gelracks, and I made sure to thank Haltiwanger before we turned in.

"For what?" he asked. "I should be thanking you. And tomorrow I'll issue my report." He winked and headed off to his bunk.

I fell into my own rack, my disillusionment threatening to stifle me as effectively as Halitov had. Cadets cursing, sleeping with each other, trying to kill each other, all of it made me nauseous. I had come to South Point to rise above that kind of behavior, to—as the code stated—cultivate poise and a quiet, firm demeanor; to be helpful to others and restrain them from wrongdoing; to take pride in the academy's noble traditions and never commit an act that would compromise them. That was the kind of behavior that would help save me from my colonial roots.

What I failed to realize was that, like Pope, many of the upperclassmen knew that the war had begun, and a powerful sense of reckless abandon had already infected them. They expected that the moment they graduated they would be shipped right out to the lines and that they should savor every moment at the academy and live life as fiercely as they could. I should have recognized what was happening, but not dusting out and remaining one step ahead of Halitov consumed most of my time.

The next night, I spent the first hour of evening study period stealing looks at Dina. I ached to be with her, and I'd settle for just talking. Another half hour passed before I found the nerve to get up and pretend to walk casually toward her rack. "Hey."

She lay sprawled out and glanced over the rim of her tablet. "Hey."

"My eyes hurt."

"Mine, too." She lowered the tablet. "Sometimes you can overstudy."

"Yeah, I know."

She met my gaze, smiled, but it wasn't the kind of smile I saw Clarion give Jarrett. Her grin seemed reserved, even sisterly. Damn it.

"Need something?" she asked.

"Just wondering. Want to, uh, go for a run?"

Her gaze averted. "I don't know. I'm pretty tired."

"All right. Maybe we can . . ." I headed back for my rack. "Sorry I bothered you."

"Scott? I guess a run wouldn't be too bad."

I returned to her rack, proffered my hand, and helped her up. As we passed Halitov's rack, he lowered his own tablet and smirked. I simply nodded and kept tight on Dina's heels.

We walked in silence, me planning our entire lives together for so long that my vacant gaze must have unsettled her. "Hello? Anyone home?" she asked.

"Sorry."

"You do that a lot," she said, her hair gleaming in the twilight. "Where do you go?"

"I don't know," I lied, realizing we had already reached the perimeter of the barracks sector and now stood on a scenic lookout.

Ahead lay the towering buttes, mesas, and valleys of Virginis Canyon, the largest formation on Exeter at over nine hundred kilometers long, up to forty kilometers wide, and fifteen hundred kilometers deep. Though we faced the canyon's most shallow, most narrow section, with crimson walls standing just a quarter klick apart and rising just two hundred meters, you had to marvel at how that ancient river had so forcefully cut through the plateau. "How 'bout we go down? Talus and scree will break it up a little."

She nodded and led the way on a trail winding along a forty-five-degree incline. It took us about fifteen minutes to reach bottom. Pope would not have been happy with that time, but we had descended without a single slip.

I felt entombed by the great walls on either side of us, walls capped off by a sky slowly washing off to bare the stars. Boulders of every size and shape imaginable dotted the dried-up riverbed, and the smaller rubble would disrupt our footing and make our run a bit more perilous and exciting.

Dina consulted her tac. "Not too far, okay?"

"Just a couple of klicks. Take us to that second lookout. I've never seen this place at night."

"It's beautiful. Paul and I came here the night before he left. He really loves me."

"So that's where you were."

"Didn't know you were checking up on me."

My cheeks warmed. "When is he coming back?"

"They didn't say. Right now he's leading a training recon on the other side of the moon. He got a temp transfer to First Battalion, Comet Company, and that's all I know."

"Pretty rare for a first year to become Op Commander."

"Yeah, I know. I read on the appointment page that only once in the academy's history was a first year recommended for the rank of corporal."

"That was Bryant, the regimental commander."

"Right. Pope thinks Paul might be the second. But I don't know. He keeps telling me he can't do it without me."

While the colonel's son probably deserved the honor, I'd be lying if I said I was happy for him.

"What's wrong?"

"Nothing. You ready? This is a race."

Her lips curled in a look so alluring that I couldn't bear it for more than a few seconds. "Ready? Ready? Go!"

Of course she beat me off the mark because she had signaled the start, but she could outrun me either way.

We snaked through the gorge, leaping over small mounds of shattered shale and limestone. She widened the gap by ducking behind a columnlike boulder, then darted right to find a much smoother course than the one I had chosen.

Frustrated, I thought of skinning, but she would never let me live that down. So I kept on, trying to keep her in sight but eventually losing her to a gloom descending like thunderheads into the gorge.

"I beat you by exactly three minutes, fourteen seconds," Dina said, tanking down air.

I slapped palms on my hips and fought for my own breath. "Fourteen? My tac says ten."

We stood on the second lookout, girdled by mesas resembling the flat-topped waves of a black sea quick-frozen and coruscating with starlight. I hadn't realized we had ventured so far from the academy grounds, now glowing dimly on the horizon. I stood, crossed to within a meter of the cliff edge, then sat, pulling my knees into my chest. "You'd never see anything like this on my world. All we get are holo artists' renderings. They never look like this."

She pulled up a rocky seat next to me. "I keep telling myself I don't have to worry about you. But I'm wrong, right?"

"I'll probably IDO one of these days. I'll try not to bring you down. I'm sorry, I—"

"I wasn't talking about that. I don't want to hurt you."

No, I wouldn't look at her. I had heard the old "we should just be friends" line more times than I cared to remember.

Then she touched me, traced my birthmark with her index finger.

I pulled away. "Don't."

"Must be hard."

"Sometimes. Ready to head back?"

"Not yet. You know, I have a mark, too. On my hip. It's not from epi, though. And no, I won't show it to you."

"One of my teachers told me that birthmarks relate to experiences of a remembered past life."

"You talking about reincarnation?"

"Yeah. They represent a violent death in your previous life."

"Cheerful stuff."

"I'm sorry, I just—"

"Thought you had a chance with me?"

"No. I mean, I don't know anything about you. I don't even know what colo you're from."

"I'm from Indicity on Rexi-Calhoon. Ever been there?"

I shook my head.

"You'd like it. Far less provincial than the other colos. I mean, it's even got a theater district."

"Explains why you're so, I don't know, *worldly*."

"Never been called that. Thanks."

After a deep sigh, I groaned and pushed myself up.

"Whoa," she uttered, nearly out of breath.

"What?"

She sprang to her feet. "There."

In the distance, a streak of blue-green light cut straight up into the sky. Another streak followed, then a third, a fourth. They kept coming at two-second intervals to create an eerily beautiful light show. I pricked up my ears, searching for some accompanying repercussion, but detected none.

"Tracers?" I asked.

"No. I don't know what they are."

"Could be conventional artillery."

"Nope. Wrong signature. I'm skinning for a better look."

As she reached for her tac, I reached for mine. We skinned up and focused our scans on the lights.

And came smack against a wall of disruption that turned our HUVs to static.

"Something's going on," Dina said, her voice echoing in a thin warble.

Sergeant Pope had left his door open, and as we arrived at his office, he spun in his chair to face us, his eyes a little red. Two tablets sat on his desk, both on.

"Sir? The privates request a word with you, sir."

"Come in. Speak."

"Sir, we were at the second lookout, sir," said Dina. "We saw something out there—blue lights shooting upward, sir. We skinned to check them out, but something jammed us."

"You were at the second lookout?"

"Sir, yes, sir," I answered. "We took a break from studying and jogged out there."

He made a face. "You probably just beat the *shraxi*."

"Sir, do you know what those lights were?" Dina asked firmly.

"Negative. Anything else?"

I softened my voice. "Sir, are you all right, sir?"

He rubbed the corners of his eyes. "Just been studying too much. And the dust's getting to me again. Good evening. And dismissed."

We saluted and left. On the way back to the billet, Dina muttered anxiously to herself about the lights.

"Don't worry about them. Probably just some training exercise," I said. "Jamming is just part of the event."

"I don't think so. Before he left, Paul told me that the Guard Corps's been mining more ruins with the help of the Wardens. Rumor has it they found something. Maybe those lights have something to do with it. Want to go out there? We have that two-day R&R coming up. We could pack some gear, hike out, see what we can see."

"That's beyond the perimeter," I said, unnerved by such talk. "Out near the Minsalo Caves. We'd be breaking the code. If we get caught—"

"We won't. And I'm thinking this might have something to do with all those rumors about the caves."

Apparently, several people on Roger Minsalo's speleological team had gone into the caves with minor ailments like strained muscles and scratches. Team members reported emerging from the cave healed of those afflictions. If further studies had been made, we weren't able to access them through our tablets, so no one really knew whether Minsalo's people had actually been healed or the whole "miracle" was just a series of coincidences.

I had to admit that I was probably as suspicious and curious as she was—but not enough to break the code. "Sorry, Dina. A hiking trip is not worth the risk. No way."

"Maybe you're right. But it would be fun."

"Yeah, it would."

I wanted to spend more time with her, and I could—if I was willing to break the code. Why was there always a price?

We reached our billet, and she paused before going inside. "Can I tell you something?"

I gave a slight shrug.

"There's something about you. I don't know what it is. I just get this feeling that I was meant to know you. And that mark on your face? I think it's a blessing. You just don't recognize it."

"Aw, that's sweet," Halitov cooed, coming through the door. "If you two are gonna . . . you know . . . you mind if I watch?"

"You wouldn't understand what you were seeing," Dina said, then strutted past him and into the billet.

"I'm telling Beauregard on you," he cried after her, then faced me with his devilish grin. "I'm such a kidder. Hey, you hear about your brother?"

"What?"

"Jarrett's gonna VDO."

"What? How do you know?"

"He's in there now. He just said good-bye to all of us. He's been waiting for you."

I snorted and hustled into the billet. Jarrett stood near Dina's rack, speaking quickly to her. As I neared them, he broke off and raised his chin. "Let's talk."

"You quitting?"

"Let's go talk."

"Is he quitting?" I asked Dina.

She retreated to her locker.

Jarrett gestured to the door, then ambled off. I followed in confusion. I knew he was growing more disillusioned, but I never thought he would actually want to quit. He led me outside and between billets, where we leaned against the wall and listened to the triplets for a few moments before I finally said, "So?"

"I'll tell Pope tomorrow," he answered.

"Why? You said your grades are good. You're keeping up with PT and the rest of it. I mean, we're just getting used to this life, right? If anyone should be VDOing—"

"It should be me," he finished. "You always wanted this, not me. It was your idea."

"It didn't take much to convince you."

"I just wanted to get away. Being a soldier? What a joke. This whole Guard Corps is nothing more than a cheap copy of the Alliance Army."

"You're wrong."

"Scott, you're going to give them ten years of your life to wind up no better than you would be back home."

"I'll never be an officer back home."

"You think becoming an officer will change anything?"

"Yes, I do."

He smiled bitterly. "Scott, you'll always be a gennyboy. No matter what you do, they'll talk behind your back. You're kidding yourself. A commission won't help you."

"I'll make it help. Whatever it takes. I won't go home."

"So you'll get trained, get shipped out to some hole, and die. That's how you'll make it help. You're a goddamned idiot. And I can't believe I let you talk me into this bullshit."

"You agreed to come."

"And now I want out."

"Why don't you just suck it up? Get the degree. You do the ten years, then you take it anywhere you want—even Earth. For God's sake, they're giving you a thirty-three-million-dollar education for free. You're telling me that won't change who you are?"

"No, it won't. And you were going to throw it all away, too."

"Yeah, I was—for you and the others. I know I've been holding you back. I wanted to make it easier."

"Okay, maybe you did. You've always bought into that honor crap. But I never have, and I won't pretend anymore. I can see right through this whole academy. It's a big scam. And we're all suckers who believed their promises. Wake up, Scott. Look around. I thought this would make me better, too.

But it won't. They're just using us. Cheap labor." He snorted. "Courage? Honor? Duty? Loyalty? You won't find 'em here."

I realized then that he had made up his mind, and knowing Jarrett, nothing I could say would sway him. I started to choke up. "You can't leave me."

His voice broke, and I thought I heard real emotion. "I'm sorry. That's the worst part of it, the hardest part. But I hate it here."

"Why didn't we talk sooner? Maybe we—"

"What? Could've figured this out? I'm all screwed up. That's why I have to leave."

"No, it's why you have to stay."

He just looked at me, shook his head, then turned his gaze to the barracks. "C'mon. Lights-out pretty soon."

We returned to our billet, and despite everything I had been through, nothing hurt or scared me more than knowing my brother was leaving. His presence had reminded me that I had never left home, that I had brought home with me, that as long as he was there, I would be safe.

6 ❯ **The next morning,** just after first call, I asked Jarrett if I could go with him to see Pope.

"Why? You need to talk to him yourself?" my brother asked, freshly showered and zipping into his utilities.

"No, I just want to hear you say it. Voluntary Dust Out."

"I'd like to go, too," said Halitov, muscling up beside me and cocking a brow at Jarrett. "I have a stake in this. You leave your brother, and he gets all emotionally messed up, well, I IDO myself."

"Sorry," Jarrett snapped. "It's my show." He unconsciously checked his uniform, then pounded off to tell our sergeant that he no longer wished to wear that uniform.

Halitov grunted. "You two must have had problems when you were kids."

I turned my back, and with a consuming numbness, busied myself with my own utilities.

A few minutes later we all marched out and formed on the line, shivering against the crisp air. Obote and Narendra closed in the gap where Jarrett would have stood. Corporal Gorbatova gave us her usual once-over, telling Haltiwanger that his uniform had light years to go before it would be ready for inspection. She had said those exact words the morning prior, though we all knew she would not punish him for his wrinkles since she was partly responsible for them. She queried me regarding my brother's whereabouts, and I told her evenly that he had requested a meeting with the squad sergeant.

"To VDO, right?" she asked.

"Ma'am, I believe so, ma'am."

"And how does that make you feel, Private?"

I wasn't in the mood to have my already raw emotions poked and prodded. "Ma'am, this private doesn't understand the question, ma'am."

"Don't want to talk about it, huh?"

"Ma'am, no, ma'am."

"Very well. Squad! Fall out to the exercise field."

Morning physical training lasted a grueling two hours, your basic stretching, running, jumping, rolling, and crawling with a little tai chi thrown in for good measure. As we completed the last of our exercises, Jarrett and Sergeant Pope jogged onto the field. Pope veered toward Gorbatova, and Jarrett approached me, wearing an expression that I couldn't place. Shock? Annoyance? Fear? "What happened?"

"Nothing."

"What're you doing here? Thought they'd put you up in admin until the next shuttle tawts in. You change your mind?"

"No."

"Then what happened? You were with Pope for two hours."

"Nothing."

Gorbatova ordered us to fall in, and we marched back to the billet for second, third, and fourth year reveille. Every gaze trained on Jarrett as he joined us, acting, well, as if nothing had happened. Since he wouldn't talk, I wanted to ask Pope what had transpired, but my next opportunity wouldn't come until morning mess—that is, if Pope chose to eat with us, which, unfortunately, he did not. When I finally did get the chance to ask him, his reply was equally curt. All

I knew was that Jarrett had not VDOed, and while my brother would not voice what had happened, you could not mistake the resentment in his tone.

For three solid days I worked on Jarrett, trying to pry out the details of the meeting, but he only spoke with Clarion. She wouldn't talk, either. What was he hiding? Had he asked for his VDO and been denied? That wasn't possible. Our contracts explicitly stated that we had the option to Voluntary Dust Out at any time.

On the third night, I tried to pull up my contract, but my tablet just flashed error messages. I asked Dina and Halitov to do likewise, and they met the same wall. In fact, no one in our squad could access personnel files. Some people shrugged it off as a temporary error, but I had feeling it was quite deliberate. I was right.

At last, our hard-won R&R arrived, and I tried to forget about the mystery of my brother and the personnel files. As the last dregs of night seeped from the sky, I returned from the mess to find Jarrett, Dina, and Clarion packing their knapsacks. "What's going on?"

"Nothing," Jarrett snapped.

"Where are you going?"

"Nowhere."

I crossed to Dina. "You're not going out to—"

"Yes, we are."

Jarrett glared at her.

She glared back. "He should come with us."

"He won't. Trust me."

"But Dina, we talked about this," I said. "It's not worth the risk. Those lights are probably nothing."

She lowered her voice. "They're hiding something from

us, and if I'm going to give them ten years of my life, I want to know what it is."

"And if we do find something, then I'm going to use it to blackmail my ass out of here," Jarrett added. "So that's the plan, little brother."

"You think they'll let you leave after you discover classified information?"

"If I learn something really terrible about this place, I'm thinking they'll want me as far away as possible from the other cadets."

"Or they'll just purge that memory from your mind."

"That's illegal."

"You think they'll care?"

He grew more flustered. "You know what? Even if we don't find anything, I win because then I'll do something so bad that they'll have to kick me out. Since you know the code so well, maybe you can help me think of an act that'll break as many articles as possible."

"You're telling me they won't let you VDO?"

He zipped up his sack. "Wish I had more time to chat. But we have to go."

Dina took my hand. "Come with us. We're not really breaking the code—just stretching it a little."

"I can't."

"You need to"—she eyed my brother—"for him. Now c'mon. I'll help you pack."

"No."

"Scott, if they're lying to us, then how much is the code worth?"

"But what if they're not?"

"Wouldn't you rather know or just be a slave?"

"Maybe this sounds corny, but I'd rather be a slave to honor."

"But you don't know if it's honor. And right now, you're a slave to ignorance."

Under Dina's constant urging, I finally surrendered. We slipped out of the barracks and made it all the way out to the perimeter. Had we skinned up, the fourth years on sentry duty would have spotted us in an instant via our tacs. Still reeling with regret, I asked Jarrett how we were supposed to get past the perimeter guards, but he refused to answer. When we reached their post, he activated his tac and transferred orders to their tablets. They let us pass.

"Fake orders?" I asked. "You got us by with fake orders? Where'd you get 'em? How much did they cost? I don't believe this. Do you know what they're going to do to us when we get back?"

"What? Kick us out?"

"Not all of us want to leave!"

"Scott, shuddup."

We headed out for the long, ten-hour hike to the Minsalo Caves. I knew why Jarrett and Dina wanted to go, but Clarion had just said that if Jarrett was going, she was. I thought that a rather poor excuse to risk her career. Maybe their sex had turned into love; I wasn't sure. In any event, we kept out of the open and dared not skin.

Meanwhile, cadets who obeyed the code were spending their two days at the Latitude, the only R&R facility on Exeter and located within admin. Equipped with three Olympic-size swimming pools amid a South American hydroponic jungle and encompassed by hotels, restaurants, bars, a shopping mall, an infirmary, and half a dozen other facilities, the place infected you with a temporary case of amnesia so that all those endless hours of studying had never happened. Holo and micro-G sports gyms were the most popular, followed closely by the Immersion Rooms, where virtual reality seemed anything but and you could easily spend your entire break in one of those chairs.

All of which argued against we four traipsing out into the dry wasteland when we could be sipping drinks and living in some serious denial.

Five hours into our hike, Virginis Canyon opened to nearly half a kilometer and dropped to just over twice that. Even the nearby table mountains seemed to cower from the great trench. We dodged from boulder to boulder along the canyon's top, never venturing closer than fifteen meters to the edge. Clarion kept an eye out for airjeeps whose pilots would depend upon infrared to distinguish us from that tremendous backdrop of varicolored dust and rock.

I worked up a pretty good sweat, and the straps of my heavy pack dug grooves in my shoulders. We took several short breaks to dip into our canteens and chew on nutrient bars, otherwise Jarrett led us in a relentless pace. Soon our path descended at a ten-degree, twenty-degree, then thirty-degree angle, as though some massive being had set down its foot and we trekked across the print. According to my tac, we were just five hundred meters away from the Minsalo Caves' huge, amphitheaterlike entrance. Virginis Canyon's ancient river, entrenched in the steep-walled canyon, had eroded away a portion of the canyon wall against which the current was strongest. The river had excavated large quantities of limestone to form a complex network of hundreds of chambers and galleries. Then, as the riverbed had lowered, it had left the cave entrance high on the side of the canyon wall, some six hundred meters above the bed, meaning we would have to rappel down about four hundred meters to reach the entrance.

As we drew closer to the site, the ground became much more uneven, with depressions, narrow sinkholes, and troughs increasing in number and indicating the collapse of the roofs of large caverns. Jarrett finally raised his hand, then crawled on his belly toward the cliff's edge for a peek. "I can see it," he yelled.

My brother's proximity to the edge left me breathless. You humbled yourself before a thousand-kilometer drop, especially when you couldn't skin.

Shielding her eyes from the glare, Dina studied the horizon. "There's a whole lot of nothing out here. Lots of nothing. Nothing everywhere."

"Maybe your little light show originates down there," said Jarrett. "Let's gear out and get down."

Clarion gazed sympathetically at Jarrett, then approached and whispered something. He brightened as he dropped his pack, then broke out his climbing gear.

Dina came over, looking tired, sweaty, and still squinting against the sun. "We'd better hurry. I'm sure the next patrol is on its way."

"I'm surprised we didn't get picked up already. We'll probably get arrested inside."

"Maybe you're right. But we have to try." She closed her eyes. "I wonder how Paul's doing. I'm worried about him."

I turned away and rifled through my pack.

"You know, they could have taken him away," she said, her voice cracking. "Imagine that?"

"He isn't ready. Neither are we."

"If a war really does break out, then I don't know if I can spend four years knowing that I'll be shipped off to die."

"That's our job. You didn't come here to be a soldier?"

"I'm not sure."

"No wonder you get along with my brother. If you don't know for sure, then you don't belong here."

Dina huffed. "How can you be so certain?"

"I just am."

"That's no answer."

"I wish I could explain it."

"But you can't because you're just like me—you're not sure."

I shrugged and crossed to the edge.

The canyon wall posed no more of a challenge than old Whore Face did. Sans the nerve-rattling presence of Gorbatova, Pope, and Rodriguez, we lowered ourselves toward the mouth of stone without a slip. I knew I could thank Halitov's "coaching" for my success. The only real challenge came as we neared the entrance and had to build up enough momentum to swing ourselves onto the ledge. Jarrett made the first landing, anchored himself to the wall, then caught each of us as we pendulumed inside.

"Caves of solution," Clarion said, as she unfastened her sit-harness, then gazed up at the entrance's towering ceiling. "Remember that on the first exam?"

"How 'bout this one," Dina challenged. "Minsalo and his team discovered this place. What was his first name and his occupation?"

I knew the answers, but I looked to Clarion, who smiled through her ignorance.

"Who cares about that shit?" groaned Jarrett. "Let's move out and see what we can find. And what about the rumor?"

"His first name was Roger," I said to Dina. "He was a speleologist with the Seventeen's corps of engineers. And Jarrett? There's nothing left down there. The rumors are, well, who knows about them."

"We'll know—if I have anything to say about it."

Wishing we could skin and use infrared to navigate through the cave system, we thumbed on our searchlights, which, if nothing else, allowed us to better enjoy the red, brown, and alabaster-white walls, as well as the dozens of textures of dissolved lime carbonate. Somewhere far below us came an eerie dripping sound, and as the entrance funneled into a narrow gallery that lazily curved down about thirty-five degrees, the temperature began to drop and a whistling wind resounded from above. We spotted several markers that had been affixed to the walls by the various speleological teams. You could cover the metallic hemispheres with your palm, and they pulsed with light as we neared them. I had read that they could be removed from the wall without causing damage. Their presence made me feel a bit more comfortable about descending a kilometer into the ground. We couldn't pinpoint our location through our tacs without alerting the academy guards, so without the markers, we could easily get lost. Sure, we had all studied several 3-D maps of the caves because they held historical significance: within them explorers had discovered the first signs of Racinian technology on Exeter, but I assumed most of us had forgotten those lessons.

The tunnel continued to drop, the bumpy ceiling just a few meters above us. Jarrett walked point, with Clarion just behind to admire his ass. That dripping sound droned on, and the whistling wind grew fainter. A damp, sweet smell wafted toward us as we slowly emerged into an extraordinary hall with vaulted ceilings and enough dripstone to make us feel like we stared up a hundred meters at the teeth of the thing that had swallowed us. Those teeth—or, more precisely, stalactites—arrowed down from the roof and tapered off into sharp points, while others met up with the stalagmites to our right that rose from the floor to form a score of pillars with diameters of fifty meters or more. Just beyond them hung a cluster of helicitie—twisted, flowerlike varieties of stalactite that were much more common in the Minsalo Caves than in any others in colonized territory. Humbled by the sight, we shuffled slowly across the damp floor, the hall extending well beyond our lights.

"They called this one the Great Hall," said Jarrett, his voice echoing off with such clarity that it startled me. And lo and behold, he remembered something from class. "Boring name for such an impressive formation. I think we're getting close to the first hangar. Anybody feel anything?" He waved his light back at us.

Clarion and Dina shook their heads.

"Maybe it just takes time," I guessed.

"Or it's bullshit," said Clarion. "The kind of superstition that helps entertain scientists with boring lives. Caves with healing properties? Oh, yes, they're over there, next to the Fountain of Youth and the picture of the Virgin Mary that cries. For a small donation, we'll show 'em to you."

Jarrett unsheathed his K-bar, nicked his middle finger, then squeezed out a little blood. "Let's see if this place heals me without paying the donation. Hey, what was that?" The beam of his searchlight focused on the back of a figure in the distance, a figure with long, white hair and dressed in academy utilities. The person flitted off.

Jarrett hollered again, and I shouted for him to wait, but he'd already charged off in pursuit, towing Dina and Clarion.

Aiming my light for the rock-strewn path ahead, I reluctantly jogged toward reverberating footfalls and flickering beams that made the whole course about as surreal as a Callistan nightclub.

We chased the figure through the entire Great Hall and

into a tunnel shaped like a ragged triangle barely two meters wide at the base, three high. I figured that once we reached the Racinian hangar on the other side, a contingent of fourth years would be waiting for us.

"Where'd he go?" Clarion cried as we came into a hexagonal room so wide and so tall that I could not see the opposite metallic walls nor pick out the domed ceiling which I guessed was there.

Jarrett, Dina, and Clarion spread out, their lights playing over shiny walls and a stone floor buffed so smooth that I swore I double-timed over marble. My little tablet had barely hinted at the immensity of the hangar, nor had it fully revealed the seamless congruity of where metal met metal or where metal met stone. Despite being in near-darkness in a vast, empty chamber, I still appreciated the fact that I'd never been so close to anything Racinian, even if it were just a room. I wanted to touch the wall, but I had fallen too far behind to stop.

"Halt!" Jarrett shouted as the figure darted through his light.

I shivered and saw my breath as we ran on and on, the darkness barely yielding to our lights. Perhaps fifteen minutes later, we reached the other side of the hangar, where the metal walls poured into a perfectly circular conduit of stone. We bent down and rushed into the tube as a quavering, feminine voice ahead repeatedly shouted, "No."

For another ten long minutes we followed the tube as it curved right, left, then angled ninety degrees to our left or right, I wasn't sure. Our pace coupled with the poor light left me utterly disoriented. Twice I banged my head on the damp ceiling and swore.

"If there are people down here," Dina called back. "They're baiting us right into their trap."

"Which won't surprise me one bit," I muttered, seeing my career flash before my eyes.

"Whoa," Jarrett said. "I don't remember anything about this . . ."

The tunnel opened up on a cavity about five hundred meters across and ringed by a natural catwalk about three meters wide. I directed my beam at the ceiling, and once more it was not powerful enough to pick out the distant overhead; however, I did spot something down in the pit, a curving metallic surface like the nose cone of a missile. In the meantime, the others had already hustled onto the walk, still in pursuit of the woman, who now shadowhugged the wall and somehow navigated without a light. I squinted at her but spotted no evidence of a skin's telltale fluctuation.

Even as I shifted my attention to the catwalk, the woman screamed, and the others captured her in their beams. She had collapsed at the entrance of another gallery curving off from the cavity and slowly rolled onto her back, her chest rising and falling so rapidly that she had to be hyperventilating. Jarrett got to her first, and she crawled a little away from him before surrendering.

I came up beside Dina. The woman's skin appeared so sallow and wrinkled that it seemed more like tissue paper than flesh. Her eyes widened, the irises a weird, deep shade of red, her head haloed by that mop of coarse, white hair. She shifted her gaze a little, inspected us, then spoke in a rapid fire that we could barely follow. "Toroidal Curvature of the containment field allows the formation of the mediators and the establishment of a stable family of Primal Space Time Matter particles. The main TAWT drive computers, networked in a Quantum Communication Array allow the so-called faster-than-light computations to be made, which in turn collapse the wave function of any and all present conditions. As the ship's computer observes the conditions, it in effect can answer questions before they are posed."

Jarrett frowned at me.

"Why is she reciting a page from colonial history?" asked Dina.

"And why is she wearing our utilities?" Clarion added. "Unless—"

"You're not them?" the woman cried, then grabbed Jarrett's wrist with a bony hand. "You haven't come to take me back?"

Jarrett tugged himself free. "Take you back where?"

"Better yet, who're you talking about?" I asked.

"Twenty-two-sixty-six. Mining of bauxite begins on fifth planet in Ross Two-forty-eight solar system," the woman replied, her ruby eyes going vacant. "Inte-Micro Corporation CEO Tamer Yatanaya names planet Allah-Trope and declares it retreat for Muslims being persecuted by Eastern Alliance powers. Allah-Trope becomes first offworld colony with predominately one religion. By year's end, floating research operations are dropped onto planet Epsilon Eri Three—a world entirely covered by warm oceans whose salt content is only slightly higher than Terra's. Thousands of new microorganisms discovered. Aquacultural experiments yield new food sources for a human population that now numbers twenty billion, with six billion living in Sol system colonies and nearly five billion in extrasolar settlements."

"What's the matter with you?" Jarrett asked.

"I . . . it won't . . . I can't . . ."

"Are you a cadet?" Clarion demanded.

Dina crouched down and took the woman's hand in her own. "Are you a third year? A fourth year?"

The woman's eyes glossed with tears, and as she tried to answer, Jarrett checked her pockets for anything that might reveal her identity.

I slid back her sleeve. "No tac," I announced. If she was a cadet, she had managed to get the thing off. I had been told that only the brass could remove your tac. So why had they taken hers?

"You're first years, aren't you," she finally said. "How did you get down here? Did they ask you to help them?"

"So you're a cadet," Clarion said, apparently too amazed to realize she had been asked a question. "What happened to you? Did you get the Racinian conditioning? Is this what it does?"

"I don't know," the woman answered. "I remember that I escaped. And I came here because I thought the caves would help. You know? The rumors?" She touched her cheek. "But they haven't."

"They took you off for the conditioning, then?" I asked.

She began to nod but flinched in severe pain. "I'm . . . I'm . . ."

"You're what?" demanded Jarrett.

"I'm twenty-two years old."

No one gasped. I think we felt more pity than anything else.

"If she got the conditioning, then something obviously went wrong," I said. There had always been talk about the dangers of alien technology. Most of that talk had come from the alliances' armies, and we'd all dismissed it as due to jealousy. Their soldiers could not be conditioned because of their cerebroed educations, and we could. Of course they would try to make us colos feel bad about getting something good.

"What's your name?" Dina asked.

"I don't know," the woman responded with a shiver. "I try to remember, but I can't." She took a deep breath. "Twenty-eighty-five. Oberon Mountain mines yield five hundred trillion dollars in resources during first six months of operation. Profits dubbed by media as 'Shakespeare's Blessing,' since moon was named after character in *A Midsummer Night's Dream*. Need for skilled workers creates job rush among lower and middle classes, who leave Terra in droves. Physically challenged persons seek freedom of zero-G living environments."

"She's like a living, breathing cerebro gone haywire," Jarrett said. "What the hell did they do to her?"

"Don't worry, you'll be okay now," Dina said. "We'll help you. And we won't turn you over to them."

"I'm going to skin up," I said. "I'll use my med unit on her. That should stabilize her vitals and get some fluids in her."

"You do that, you'll bring 'em all here," said Jarrett.

I leveled my gaze on him and spoke slowly, evenly. "I don't care. Let 'em pick us up for trying to help someone." I reached for my tac—

He grabbed my wrist. "Do not fuck with me, Scott."

"Let go."

He grinned. "Now you're the tough guy? I've spent most of my life kicking your ass. You're going to kick mine now?"

"Let go."

"You hit that tac and I'm going to make you pay right here, right now, for all the bullshit you've put me through. Are you listening to me?"

Without warning, the woman sprang to her feet and retreated to the wall, where she stood, back firmly pressed on the ocher rock, palms down, fingers extended. She glanced at us with fear and without recognition. "Twenty-three hundred. The Twelve System Guard Corps renamed the Seventeen System Guard Corps. Representatives from all offworld systems make formal announcement of formation of new Colonial Alliance. East and West Alliances fail to recognize new government. Colonial expansion halts. Following year, I die."

"No, don't—"

Dina's cry came too late.

The woman kicked off from the wall, and with a few inhumanly powerful strides, she vaulted into the cavity, even as I broke free from Jarrett and reached for her.

"Oh, my god," Clarion gasped.

Without a fading scream—or any other sound, for that matter—the woman vanished. I waited for the distant thud of her impact. None came.

"Oh, my god," Clarion repeated.

I don't remember how long we stood there, but eventually Jarrett suggested that we move on.

"We could have helped her," I told him. "You think about that."

"Forget it, Scott. If you think that makes me feel guilty, it doesn't. Who knows what she was. And if she died, that would've happened anyway."

"This was a mistake," Clarion said. "I want to go back."

"You know we can't," Jarrett told her. "You know that."

She thought about it, finally nodded. "Maybe they wanted us to meet her. Maybe the fourth years knew we were coming and staged this whole thing to scare us. Maybe Pope was in on it, too. That woman wasn't really old or messed up. Right now they're watching us and laughing their asses off."

"I hope you're right," Dina said. "Otherwise, I'm not feeling real happy about Racinian conditioning. Maybe I'm VDO right behind you, Jarrett."

He sighed. "Good luck."

"For once and for all tell us: can we VDO?" she asked. "It's our right. It's in the contract."

"I'm still here. What does that tell you? Let's go." He spun and started along the catwalk, one hand dragging along the wall.

We threaded our way through a half-dozen more tunnels joined by modest-sized chambers with modest collections of flow- and dripstone. Dina kept prying Jarrett for more information, but he ignored her. About two hours later, we entered another hexagonal chamber identical to the earlier one, it too devoid of any Racinian tech.

"Did they store aircraft down here?" I thought aloud. "And if so, how'd they get 'em out? Does this chamber extend all the way to the surface? I still can't see the roof."

"Look at this," Jarrett beckoned, his light shining on a trio of tunnel entrances. "I remember the instructor telling us about this fork in the tunnel, but I don't remember that third one on the far right. I don't see any markers inside."

"This is some R&R," Clarion moaned. "I'm getting cold. I'm hungry. And what do you think we'll find that'll help you, Jarrett?" She turned to Dina. "You saw some lights. So what. Anything Racinian has obviously been moved out, and if there's anything here that the brass doesn't want us to see, you think they'll leave it lying around?"

"Maybe," argued Dina. "The same way we walked right up to that woman. I don't think the fourth years staged that. They conditioned her. Something went wrong. I believe what she said."

Jarrett held up his middle finger as though he were flipping us the bird. "This cave exploring is getting pretty interesting."

"Whoa." I rushed up and examined the cut—or, rather, the absence of a cut.

He pulled back. "All right, fuck it. They catch us, they catch us. Everyone skin up. Full scan. All emissions. There's gotta be something down here."

We complied, and I skimmed a data strip in my HUV, reading nothing out of the ordinary.

"What are we looking for?" asked Dina.

"Weird stuff," Jarrett answered. "Must be emissions or something that healed my finger."

"Maybe this is a holy place," Clarion suggested. "Maybe we're in the presence of a powerful being."

"Then why didn't this powerful being save that woman?" I asked. "It healed my brother's finger but wouldn't help her?"

"Whatever happened to her could've been beyond the capabilities of this being or these caves," said Dina. "Maybe there are rules we just don't understand."

Jarrett pulled out his K-bar and held it tightly in one hand, the blade jutting from the bottom of his fist and balanced over his heart. "Let's see what happens if I do this." He reared back.

I froze, wanted to shout for him to stop as Dina and Clarion suddenly screamed.

"Just kidding," he said to our joint swearing. "I nearly cried cutting my finger back there." He winked and shuffled off toward the unmapped tunnel.

"If your brother didn't have such a nice ass, I'd kick it for him," Clarion said.

We de-skinned, and for about another half hour we hustled through the mystery tunnel, following a sinuous route and listening to Jarrett bemoan the fact that he couldn't take a long-range scan to reveal the tunnel's terminus. The natural conduit stretched well beyond our lights. We did know from our last skin-up that we were heading back toward the academy and had descended about nine hundred and fifty meters into the ground. We had probably already alerted the authorities, but just in case we hadn't, we wouldn't skin again. The icy air made us long for those warm coats of energy.

At one point the tunnel dropped off into a chamber about twenty meters below. Jarrett took one look at it and announced, "Ladies and gentlemen, we have us a bivvy."

"We're stopping?" I asked incredulously.

"The ladies look tired. So we're stopping. You want to go on, that's fine with me."

I threw my hands in the air. "Fine. There's probably a team in here searching for us, but we'll stop."

Jarrett was first into the chamber, and he teased us as we rappelled toward him. I was last down the line, and my damned piton blew loose from the fissure I had chosen. Why I continued to have no luck with climbing I didn't know, but at least Clarion was there to spot my fall and guide me through the first rebound. Still, I hit the floor a second time and came to a tumbling halt. Jarrett applauded. I cursed.

After we ate, I made two unsuccessful attempts to strike up conversation with Dina and Clarion. Trouble was, we had hiked so much that both were too exhausted to do anything but sleep.

For several hours I just watched Dina and invented new reasons to hate Paul Beauregard. Somewhere far off, the wind bellowed, and sometime later I fell asleep, since Jarrett had volunteered to take the first watch.

I wish I could say that I dreamed that night, that I reached some kind of epiphany in the cave, that the spirits of Racinians visited me and exposed the military's treachery. But the world had been set to pause until Jarrett shook me awake. He backhanded tears from his cheeks as he told me that I had slept seven hours and that it was time to leave.

"What's wrong?"

"Everything. Come on."

Looking as groggy as a pair of first years who had slept in a cave, Dina and Clarion gathered their packs and fell in with us, Dina muttering, "Let us find something. Please let us find something."

But we would do no more than travel through the endless tunnel for five more hours until a blinding shaft of light carved its way toward us. Jarrett hustled for the light, and the discrete hum of an airjeep grew louder as we followed him and neared the exit.

We emerged on a bluff opposite old Whore Face. The tunnel had led us all the way back within South Point's perimeter. I had never noticed the tunnel's entrance because it lay behind a wide lip of rock that concealed it from view unless you came at it from the exact angle in an airjeep. You couldn't see it from the riverbed below.

"Get away from the entrance," Jarrett ordered. "We don't want them to know where it is."

We hustled along the bluff, seeing that it followed a rocky path down toward the riverbed. I continually scanned the sky for that airjeep, but I guess I had mistaken the hum. A boomerang-shaped C-129 Guard Corps Transport on final approach toward South Point's small spaceport cut a white ribbon overhead. We all knew that the next shuttle wouldn't arrive for nearly a month, so the presence of that aircraft took most of us aback. Jarrett seemed unfazed.

By the time we reached the riverbed, an airjeep did finally arrive, piloted by Pope himself, with Gorbatova strapped into the co-pilot's seat. We snapped to as the sergeant slid out and seemed to grow a meter taller as he brought his glare toward us.

"Sir, I'm sorry, sir, but the mission was unsuccessful," Jarrett said.

"We went through a lot of trouble for you, Private. Don't tell me the mission was unsuccessful."

"Sir, I'm sorry, sir. I did cut my finger, and it did heal in a very short time, sir. We met an old woman who might've been a cadet; we weren't sure. We lost her. She might be dead. If there's anything else there, we missed it."

"And that's it?"

"Sir, that's it, sir."

Pope's cheeks flushed as he exchanged a look with the squad corporal. "Ms. Gorbatova and I broke the code. We lied to buy you time. We did that for nothing?"

"Sir, can I VDO now, sir?"

"No."

"But sir, you promised that if I—"

"What's going on?" I shifted between them.

"Mr. St. Andrew, I assume your brother hasn't mentioned the fact that we're already at war with the alliances?"

"No, sir, he has not, sir."

"And I assume he hasn't told you that your option to VDO is no longer valid during wartime?"

"No, sir, he has not, sir."

"Well, ladies and gentlemen, there it is. And in about two hours, our beloved regimental commander is going to recall everyone from R&R, then assemble the entire regiment to make the announcement. If the Guard Corps is hiding anything, we're gonna find out the hard way. And you, Jarrett St. Andrew, will be with us."

Jarrett's eyes burned. "Sir, no, sir!"

"You'll do what they say, Private. Otherwise when they

get through with you, you won't even remember wanting to VDO. Understand?"

My brother swore and turned his back.

"All right. Everybody into the jeep. And if you're the praying sort, then go ahead—because at this time tomorrow, we'll all be on line to be conditioned, cerebroed, then shipped off to war."

PART 2

‹ ›

Quantum Bonds

On cool summer nights, when the moons are full and the tide is low and lapping quietly at the shore, when I've found numb relief in a bottle of expensive bourbon and lounge on a chair with my feet dug deeply into the sand, then, and only then, can I consider those days from the time we learned of war until the time we left Exeter.

General Julia J. Marxi, South Point's commandant, tawted out on the C-129 Guard Corps Transport, bound for Rexi-Calhoon's Columbia Colony, where she would attend an emergency meeting of the new Colonial Alliance's congress.

The regimental commander, Colonel Michael James Bryant, assumed control of the regiment and, as Pope had predicted, ordered all fifteen hundred of us to report to admin's primary assembly hall, an act that already foreshadowed the importance of what he had to say since we infrequently convened as an entire regiment.

I had only seen Bryant from afar, and my seat in the third row next to my stone-faced brother afforded me a clear view of the South Point alumnus who, despite his remarkable reputation, appeared remarkably nondescript. I had half expected to find him a sinewy tank of a middle-aged man, squarely built and well scrubbed, a walking advertisement for the cadre. But Bryant appeared more an academic than an athlete, surprisingly rawboned, even somewhat undernourished. He wore his sandy hair slightly longer than most of us, and his lips seemed too small and permanently in conflict with his smile. He wrung his hands at least ten times before mounting the dais and silencing the murmurs by his mere presence. We rose, snapped to, and waited for his release. As we returned to our seats, I glanced down the row. A tear slipped from Dina's eye.

"Ladies and gentlemen, on March seventeenth, twenty-three-oh-one, at nine A.M. Colonial Standard Time, the Colonial Congress of the new Seventeen System Alliance issued to Sol's Eastern and Western Alliances a formal declaration of war."

Absolute silence in the hall.

"We regret not being able to issue this statement to you sooner, but the commandant felt that premature announcements would be more harmful than helpful. We had all hoped that by now hostilities would have ended. Unfortunately, the situation on Mars kindled the other conflicts. I have the unenviable duty to inform you that on Tau Ceti Eleven, a contingent of Colonial Wardens took on an Eastern Alliance regiment at Shefas. Intel indicates that of the approximately two thousand personnel, only fourteen managed to withdraw and escape. The others were *not* taken as POWs. They were massacred."

Bryant's words stunned me. He seemed in favor of the new colo government, but the Seventeen was part of the Eastern and Western Alliances, and those kinds of sentiments were no less than treacherous.

"Within the next hour I'll be uploading a detailed report to your tablets. I'll supply you with everything I can within clearance. Now, for those of you unfamiliar with her, I'd like to introduce Ms. Mary Brooks, chief of the Colonial Alliance Security Council."

I hadn't noticed the smartly dressed woman seated in the

front row until she climbed gracefully onto the dais. Dark-haired and about thirty-five, Ms. Brooks chaired a council of colonial senators who, along with military representatives, advised the new Colonial Congress on security and military matters. More important, the council was instrumental in approving and overseeing military policy and served as the colonial president's principal arm for negotiating with the Terran Alliances. Although Ms. Brooks wasn't part of the military, when she spoke, the brass listened. She scrutinized us a moment, then nodded to Bryant. "Thank you, Colonel. Ladies and gentlemen, first let me express my sincere sympathy for you and your families. Know that our thoughts and prayers are with you. I've come all the way from Columbia Colony, where, as you know, the Colonial Congress has convened to meet with the Seventeen's generals and plot our next move. I say our next move because I must inform you that General Yllar Juvhixa has, along with her advisory committee, decreed that the Corps no longer serves the Eastern and Western Alliances but now operates under the auspices of the new Colonial Alliance. The Seventeen, has, in effect, seceded from the Terran Alliances and is no longer part of the Western and Eastern Alliance Navy."

Rumors of colonial secession had been circulating for most of our lives, and most of us had shrugged them off. We had often discussed in the mess that the colonies could never take on the alliances and win. But it had happened. And they would try. We would try.

"What does this mean to you?" Ms. Brooks went on. "It means you have a decision to make. You may remain here, where you'll be immediately conditioned, then commissioned and assigned to a combat unit. With Racinian conditioning, you'll be qualified to lead raw recruits into battle. I'm not mincing words here. Those recruits will be raw. Or, you may choose to leave. Three transports will arrive at nineteen hundred tomorrow. They'll take you to the Terran Alliances' Kapteyn Beta Outpost. To be honest, we have no idea what'll happen to you once you reach that ring station. You might return to the Terran Alliance military, or they might hold you as a POW. They might kill you. In any case, the commandant wants you to have the option to fight with us or leave. We know we're asking you to break the code to join the colonial cause, but it's the only way to defend our systems. If you can't do that, by all means, go. Now, I plan on being here until late tomorrow, and I urge any of you who wish to speak with me to come to admin. Thank you."

I was in shock, my life turned upside down in the course of a three-minute speech.

"Anybody who gets on those transports is dead," Jarrett said.

"No," I argued. "They won't do that. We're too valuable."

"Were you listening? They massacred the Wardens, and those people are a hell of lot more valuable than we are. The alliances want to demoralize us as quickly as possible. Killing a whole lot of young sons and daughters is exactly what they'll do." His expression grew long. "Shit. There goes another ticket out of here. But I'll tell you this much: I won't let them condition me."

"All right, South Point Regiment," Bryant said. "All R&R activities have been cancelled. We'll set condition Fire Marx One, full alert. Check with your COs for your watch stations and times. You'll also be receiving your individual conditioning schedules. They'll tell you where and when to report. We'll get off as many communiqués as we can, and if you'd like your messages to be part of the master chip tawted out, make your requests ASAP. Once again, check your tablets for that update. And may your God or Gods be with you all. Dismissed."

I rose, but so many cadets flooded the aisles behind me that it would take several minutes to exit. A familiar face materialized in the crowd and shouldered his way forward. "Mr. St. Andrew," Paul Beauregard called. "Thought I saw you down here."

"Hard to miss me," I said bitterly, tapping my birthmark.

"They just sent word. My father was among those fourteen who made it." Beauregard's gaze found Dina, and he nearly trampled me to get to her.

I started into the aisle, then looked back for my brother. He had already gone.

Back at our billet, Pope told us that we would be confined for the next six hours, after which we would be issued QQ90 particle rifles, a variant on the conventional slugshooter with a tiny, synchrotron particle accelerator used to propel the ammo. While a fully powered skin could repel the slug, twenty or thirty strikes to the same zone would weaken the shield and allow a bullet through. Problem was, none of us had received advance rifle training (reserved for second years), just the introductory courses that Pope and Gorbatova had rushed us through in the last few weeks.

So, with minimal training, we would stand outside our billet for a six-hour watch, after which we would be relieved by the Seventy-ninth.

All ten of us lay on our gelracks, and I guessed that the others were like me, working out their futures in silence. I thought we'd be talking furiously, but the shock had finally settled in.

Paul Beauregard rose and crossed at the end of billet, his

face hard, gaze unflinching. "The articles of the Code of Conduct are no longer valid. We're not Alliance citizens anymore. We're colonists, and that's where our loyalties should lie. We've been exploited for long enough. Maybe history is repeating itself here, but if it doesn't, then our families are doomed. I want to know right now who will stand with me."

Dina left her gelrack and shifted behind Beauregard, as did Jarrett and Halitov. It took but another few seconds for Clarion to join my brother.

I figured that Agi Narendra, who believed that his uncle had been killed by Alliance Marines, would rise and add himself to the group. But he shifted to the opposite end of the billet, drawing a murmur from his friend, Too Yat-sen. "Hey, I'm not a traitor," Narendra said under Beauregard's accusing gaze. "But they've already killed most of my family. I can't let 'em take me."

"That's your reason?" asked Beauregard.

"You people are going to lose."

"We people?"

"A lot of us wanted to come here because we knew service in the Corps would give us a better life than one on our homeworlds. If we join the Seventeen, then we're back where we started. Maybe even worse. Isn't that right, Scott?"

I shuddered as he dumped the argument on me.

"Do you agree with him?" Beauregard asked.

"I don't know. I thought that coming here would give me another chance. The whole idea was to escape colo life." My cheek flinched.

"Scott, come on," Jarrett said impatiently.

Mario Obote, Too Yat-sen, and Joey Haltiwanger now stood beside Narendra. My breath grew shallow. "Joey?"

He averted his gaze. "If I'm going to fight, I want to fight on a winning team."

"We're colonists," Beauregard said. "That's our heritage. That's who we are. You can't escape that."

"I think we can," said Narendra.

"What is this?" hollered Pope as he burst into the billet, a tablet tucked under his arm. Since I was the only one not in a group, Pope set his crosshairs over me. "Mr. St. Andrew? Explain."

"Sir, we were just having a conversation, sir."

Pope eyed Beauregard's crew, then Narendra's. "Picked your sides already, huh? Thought it would take a little longer. For anyone who cares, Staff Sergeant Rodriguez and, to my great dismay, Squad Corporal Gorbatova have elected to ship out and return to the Terran Alliances. Guess you, Mr. Narendra, along with Mr. Yat-sen, Mr. Obote, and Mr. Haltiwanger will be joining them. I'm remaining with the Seventeen."

"Sir, I hope there aren't any hard feelings, sir. It's just—"

Pope cut off Narendra with snorting laughter. "No hard feelings, Private? This is a fuckin' war. I want you scumbags out of my sight. Report to admin right now. You'll remain there in First Battalion's custody until those transports arrive. Move out!" A ball of energy seemed to swell inside Pope, stiffening his joints and turning his cheeks crimson as he watched them file out.

I wanted to call after Joey, but what do you say to a friend who, in a heartbeat, has chosen to become your enemy?

"And what about you, Mr. St. Andrew?" Pope asked. "Are you with us? Or against us?"

"Sir, do I have to tell you right now, sir?"

"As irony would have it, you do. I came in here to take

that vote." He slid out his tablet, ran a finger across the illu-minated display. "They've stepped up the conditioning schedule. Those who are with us are going within the hour."

Jarrett flinched.

"Sir, if I go, do you think I'll really be ready? They're throwing away four years of assimilation time. How can they just condition us and send us off, sir?"

"We're heavily outnumbered. The only way we have a chance is to get as many conditioned officers out there as we can. There's no time to wait until you *feel* you've assimi-lated."

"But sir, do you think we have a chance?"

"The colos have been planning this for a long time, and they have more resources than you think."

That might have been true, but I couldn't help thinking about how we'd been slaughtered at Tau Ceti Eleven. Rumors were already circulating that we had deliberately fired the first shot and that Beauregard's father had been the one responsible. Of course, Paul had downplayed the whole thing by saying that even if his father had fired the first shot, he had only been following orders.

Pope hardened his gaze. "So, I ask again, Mr. St. Andrew. Are you with us or against us?"

I looked to Jarrett, Dina, and Clarion. "What about the woman? You're okay with the conditioning—even after see-ing that?"

The woman shrugged. Jarrett looked away.

Pope nodded, unmoved. "It's alien tech. And it's old. Of course it's going to be dangerous. Of course there'll be risks. And mistakes. Coming here in the first place was a risk. This is just one more. And if it makes you feel better, we're all going together. Mr. St. Andrew, are you in?"

"Scott . . ." Jarrett warned.

"Sir, this private does, in fact, wish to be commissioned as a member of the Seventeen System Guard Corps, sir."

Pope rolled his eyes. "A simple yes would have sufficed."

I didn't tell any of them then, but I needed to say that. I needed to believe that I wasn't just joining a rebellion but keeping a dream alive.

After Pope left to set up our conditioning schedule, Jarrett came up to me, looked me straight in the eye, and said, "I should tell you I'm sorry. But I don't feel that. I just feel . . . I don't know. Bye."

"Where are you going?"

"I won't let them condition me."

"But you said if you get on a transport— So where are you going?"

"Anywhere but here. Maybe back to the caves. I have some food in my pack. Maybe I can wait this out."

I tensed. "Know what? I'm not even going to stop you."

A half hour later they picked up my brother, out near the perimeter. They beat him into submission, brought him back, then crammed him, along with the rest of us, into a pair of airjeeps and flew us out to a region about a kilometer north of the Minsalo Caves. Dina clutched Beauregard's hand, and I felt Clarion shivering next to me. A battered Jarrett rode in the other jeep, along with Halitov, Carstaris, Fayvette, and my old nemesis from Whore Face, Mr. Val d'Or. A pair of second lieutenants from our own Third Battalion met us on a narrow tarmac whose straight lines stood in sharp relief against the heavily fissured plain. We descended into a camouflaged bunker, passed through the ribs of the DNA identification scanners, then climbed aboard a wide lift. We rode that elevator for at least ten minutes, dropping so far into the earth that I noticed a decrease in temperature despite the recyclers.

The doors opened up on another of the those colossal hexagonal chambers we had seen in the caves, this one aglow in spotlights hanging from tremendous booms. More striking still were the five hundred or more antigrav stretchers hovering in neat rows and forming white-sheeted avenues blurring off into the shadows and silhouettes of bustling figures. A gray-haired man dressed in a pale green medical jumpsuit tapped something into his tablet, then regarded us with a distracted glance. He turned to one of his twenty or so assistants standing nearby and said, "Next group ready for prep."

Then he noticed my face and pointed. "You? Come with me."

My brother seized my hand and shook it firmly. "We're going to be okay." Then he caught me off guard with a quick embrace, one we should have held much longer.

I swallowed and followed the doctor or whatever he was as my nerves found my voice. "Is there a problem? They told me there wouldn't be a problem. My mark's just the residual effect of epineuropathy."

"We know," he said curtly, then paused before a stretcher. "Strip and lie down. Place your clothes between your legs." He removed a watchlike instrument from one of the stretcher's side compartments. "You'll put this on. You'll feel sleepy. When you wake up, you'll be back in your gel-rack, and this will all be over. You might remember the cerebro hookup, you might not." He set the band on the sheet, then walked back toward the lift.

Far across the chamber, Dina, Jarrett, Beauregard, and Halitov began unzipping their utilities. Another group of about fifteen exited the lift, and the reception continued. I removed my clothing, scooped up the band, and quickly slid onto the stretcher, one leg draped over my crotch. I hadn't realized that the band would weigh so much and pondered exactly what was inside the six thick metal ampoules attached to it. I slid the thing over my wrist, which suddenly went numb. I guessed they were drugging me as part of the preparation, and I felt disappointed that I would not get to see the Racinian conditioning machines, hulking wonders of physics gleaming in artificial light—or so I imagined them.

Truth was, I *would* get to see the conditioning chamber, though it would hardly live up to the engineering of my imagination. I wouldn't have time to consider my disillusionment. I was not supposed to see that place.

It's hard for me to state with any certainty how much of the conditioning and cerebro hookup I actually remember because the memories of those moments burn brilliantly for one second, usher in new ones, then all of them vanish in the next second. At this particular moment I remember feeling the ground quake. I remember those voices, so many voices. And the screams.

I awoke in a dimly lit black tube with a diameter of just over a meter. Though my eyes would open only to slits, I glimpsed thousands of translucent leads impaling my nude body and stretching away like finely furred gossamers that attached me to the tube. I realized I was pissing, but another lead caught my urine. The tube's bottom irised open with a whir, and a mild electric shock sent me rigid, then relaxed, then rigid again. The tube suddenly peeled back in two metallic rinds that severed gossamers as they whirred.

Bursts of light or electricity, I wasn't sure, leapt from the severed leads as I staggered forward on numb legs. Through intermittent flashes, another chamber came into focus, this one a perfect circle with low, domed ceiling spanned by billions of throbbing gossamers similar to the ones attached to me. Scores of naked cadets swayed forward from open tubes like mine, their leads sparking and writhing. A pressure on my head brought my hands there, where I felt the thin, C-shaped cerebro cupping my now cleanly shaven scalp. I cocked my head at a sudden weight on my shoulder, and there was Private Carstaris from the Eightieth, her face a monstrosity of twisted flesh, the gossamers affixed to her breasts squirming with lives of their own. "St. Andrew," she whispered, her voice severely warped. She removed her hand, dropped to her knees, then released a strangled cry answered by another tremor that sent me toppling beside her.

With no strength to haul myself up and my cheek planted squarely on the smooth metal floor, I lay there, just staring across the chamber, watching my comrades squirm, listening to them shriek, and fighting to feel something familiar—even the simple rise and fall of my chest.

"This one's still alive," someone said behind me.

"Excellent. That's the gennyboy. Let's get him out of here."

I couldn't see their faces, but I did sense that they were transferring me to a stretcher. My wrist tingled.

Feeling as though someone had just removed a heavy, dark blanket from my face, I woke with a chill in my gelrack, the ceiling's grainy quickcrete never a more welcome sight. Tiny red marks dotted my arms like a carefully planned rash, and I shivered as I touched them. I slid back my covers, saw more crimson speckles on my legs, then lifted my cotton shirt, revealing another symmetrical freckling on my abdomen. I remembered the gossamers, though at that moment I did not recall my terrifying encounter with Carstaris. I had no idea that anything had gone wrong.

Strangely enough, I did know that I would be okay, although I should rest easy for another hour or so. I knew that the shock to my body would take about that long to heal and any grogginess I might be feeling would taper off. But I didn't know how I knew this.

I turned my head. Halitov lay supine in his rack, his eyes closed, his arms and face bearing the blotches of conditioning. I strained to see past him, but my eyes stung with the effort. That pain would wear off, and my vocal cords would soon function.

Darkness lay beyond the window opposite my rack, and I wondered how long the conditioning process had taken. My tac would not turn on. Had those transports already arrived to whisk off Haltiwanger and the rest? What if they came and told me I had been out for a century? I smiled inwardly. The conditioning had not affected my imagination.

"Private Scott St. Andrew?" came a feminine voice.

"Ma'am, yes, ma'am," I whispered to Platoon Leader Amber Sysvillian, whose entrance had been as quiet as it was surprising. She stood at the foot of my gelrack, gazing grimly at a tablet.

"How're you feeling?" she asked.

"Ma'am, I feeling fine, ma'am," I answered with false enthusiasm.

"Private, I have some unfortunate news for you. There was an accident during the conditioning process. Seismic activity resulted in the premature jettisoning of many cadets, including yourself."

I closed my eyes. "I don't remember."

"Some of it's still in your long-term, but we had to purge a sizable portion of your short-term. Your memory's going to be undependable until your brain adjusts to the mnemosyne."

"Mnemosyne?"

"I don't know much about them yet. Racinian biotech introduced into your brain. They help with subatomic perception, with information storage, and work in conjunction with your cerebro. We can access our memories as efficiently as we access, say, a tablet. And once we learn something, we never forget it. I teach you to repair a tawt drive. Twenty years later you remember every word I said and the schematics are as clear in your mind's eye as they were the day I showed them to you. But like I said, there was an accident."

It was not like Sysvillian to adopt such a sympathetic tone, be so forthcoming, or take such a special interest in a lowly private. I should have seen it coming.

"Ma'am, is there something wrong with me?" I asked.

"Not exactly. But Mr. St. Andrew, some of your colleagues didn't make it. And your brother, well, he—"

"Didn't make it. They're dead? What about my brother?"

"I'm sorry."

I sprang from my gelrack. "Jarrett?"

"Your brother was among twenty-two cadets whose bodies were severely burned. The list has just been uploaded to your slates. On behalf of South Point and the Seventeen System Guard Corps, I'd like to express our most sincere condolences. I understand your brother was a fine first year and would have made an even finer officer. But you'll still carry the torch for your family."

"I want to see him."

"That's not possible. The corpses are still out at the site. They're being prepped for shipment. Your parents will be notified via the next chip tawted out. Right now you should get ready for watch and Accelerated Assimilation Training. Check your tac; it should be working. And don't be late for anything. Remember, we're at war now." She started to leave. "And Mr. St. Andrew? I apologize if my beside manner isn't any good. I lost a lot of friends today myself."

At that moment I could not accept that someone so full of life could be snuffed out so easily and with such impunity. And I heard my brother tell me how he would not be conditioned, as though he had known something would go wrong.

No, he couldn't be dead. He would come through the billet door at any minute. That's right. He would. And I thought that seeing the casualty list might confirm Sysvillian's lie. Jarrett's name wound *not* be on the list. I retrieved my tablet from my footlocker and tapped to the latest announcements page:

SOUTH POINT REGIMENT 3RD BATTALION, KILO COMPANY, 27TH PLATOON
FILTER FIVE BRAVO SIERRA
ANNOUNCEMENT #2301.90R7097097498949
SUBJECT: RACINIAN CONDITIONING FATALITY REPORT

PVT Anson, Z. 09230098	PVT Ague, P. 09380980983
PVT Cotto, P. 09238	PVT Carstaris, V. 098081
PVT Enlai, R. 497466	PVT Fayvette, L. 9872967
PVT Guy, T. 98792862	PVT Garrison, T. 9822664
PVT Jones, M. 9867676	PVT Ji, J. 9827979
PVT Kahn, J. 8788685	PVT Kalvin, R. 098279792
PVT Omans, S. 87638769	PVT Rousseau, M. 9629869

PVT St. Andrew, J. 89749273   PVT Padante, B. 98629662
PVT Telford, A. 58696202   PVT Watkins, L. 65653883
PVT Val d'Or, E. 87629869   PVT Xiaoping, I. 7637678
PVT Yaobang, T. 86397613311   CPL Yosemite, C. 5425426

I stared at my brother's name until the letters smeared into a single, bloody stripe.

"What're you doing?" Halitov called as he picked sleep grit from the corners of his eyes.

"Nothing." I rose and crossed to the end of my gelrack, where I began smashing my tablet against the bar.

"What are you doing?" Halitov cried.

I continued banging the tablet until Dina and Beauregard, who had been sleeping, woke abruptly and held me while Clarion pulled the shattered computer from my hand.

I was eighteen years old. No one close to me had ever died. And I had no idea how many more would. I fell on my gelrack, buried my head, and sobbed.

"He was looking at something when he did that," Halitov said, gripping his own tablet. "And here's what. Have a look."

"Oh, no," Clarion said.

"Accident?" asked Beauregard. "I don't remember anything about an accident."

"Scott, I'm so sorry," Dina said, resting her hand on my back. "I'm just . . . so sorry."

8 ❯ **Since two thirds** of Third Battalion had been wiped out by the conditioning accident, including all first years in the Seventy-ninth and Eightieth Squads and my brother from the Eighty-first, those of us who remained in the Eighty-first were immediately reassigned to Fourth Battalion, Nova Company, Thirty-ninth Platoon, 111th Squad. We were rushed off to one of the library's underground classrooms for the first class in our Accelerated Assimilation Training program. Though I understood why they thrust us into training, they owed a memorial service—if only a short one—to those who had died. They owed that to my brother. While I seethed over that, I got a chance to ask Sysvillian if there was something wrong with me. "Not exactly," she had said. Well, I sure as hell wanted that part explained.

We had all commented on the problems we were having with our memories. Simple things like forgetting where you stowed that brush or even long-term items like the name of an old friend. We still felt fatigued, with frequent stabs of pain at the gossamer connection points. Sergeant Pope kept close at my side and twice reassured me that I could overcome any loss. I thanked him for his faith but warned him not to say my brother's name again. Secretly, I felt overjoyed that he cared. I needed him, needed them, just to remain sane. Jarrett, the brother who had taught me how to build cave forts, kiss girls, and come home late without getting caught—yet the same brother who had picked on me, taunted me, and had tried to toughen me up, was dead. I had heard that during war, time speeds up, that a weekend is like a year, a year like a lifetime, but Jarrett's death slowed it all down, made it come at me so distinctly that during my AAT classes I did not suffer the kind of information overload that agitated the others. I learned my lessons carefully, dutifully, and forgot nothing. Later, I discovered there was another reason for my success.

During that first lesson, the instructor, Lieutenant Colonel Victoria Bayshore from Second Battalion, had listed some of the side effects of conditioning and had mentioned the Racinian biotech in an annoyingly marginal way, saying only that we had labeled them "mnemosyne" after the Greek goddess of memory and that they were a species of eidetic parasite found aboard Racinian spacecraft. She would have made a wonderful politician, her gray temples and solid frame radiating wisdom, sensibility, and plausible deniability. She made us exercise our memories by recalling specific long- and short-term events. After three hours, they ushered us into another classroom.

There, we griped about our hunger until Major Yokito Yakata, a rapier of a man and Second Battalion's XO, came running into the room, ran up the opposite wall, then ran across the ceiling as we assumed the fly-catching position with our mouths. He pushed off the ceiling, did a back flip, and landed easily on his feet, his utilities immaculate. "Who's next?" he asked curtly.

Halitov raised his hand. "Sir? I don't want to be next, sir. I just want to know how you did that."

"Private, there's a bond in nature, a bond much stronger than gravity, a quantum bond between particles that allows our tacs to operate and allows us to tawt in and out of systems. My job is to teach you how to manipulate this bond with your minds. In the beginning, all matter was one. Can you take yourself back to that time? If you can, you'll discover the profound changes in quantum theory. Now then. I wish we had time for a more traditional approach, but this is war. You will learn. You must learn. Yes, throwing you into this could be risky, but it's far less dangerous than your *not* having the conditioning. Who's next?"

I raised my hand, more out of a desire to torture myself than to learn. Jarrett had died. Why did I deserve to live?

"No, not you," Yakata said. "Not yet. We don't want to intimidate the others, do we?"

"Sir?"

"Oh," he answered me with a cryptic smile. "I see." His gaze swept the others. "Come on, now. Who will be next?"

Beauregard raised his hand.

"You, Private? Very good. To the doorway."

Once Beauregard reached his position, Yakata marched up and fixed him with an icy stare. "When you run on the ground, you know you can do that. You are confident. But when I ask you to run up the wall, everything you know about the laws of nature tells you that it's not possible. That's because you only feel yourself, your own body. You don't even consider trying to feel the wall."

"*Feel* the wall?"

"Exactly. When your foot hits the wall, don't think about your foot on the wall. Just think about the wall. What connections can you make to it? What bonds do you seek?"

"Sir, I, uh . . . okay, sir. I'll give it a try." Beauregard swallowed. He sprinted across the room, hit the wall with one boot, and I nearly fell out of my chair as his other boot came up and he scaled the quickcrete to a height of about three meters before pushing away to drop feet-first in a respectable landing.

"Very good first try, Private Beauregard. Who's next?"

Every hand went up.

Yakata's gaze fell on Dina. As she hastened toward the doorway, Beauregard sat beside me and whispered breathlessly, "I don't believe it. I thought about the wall, and when my boot hit it, it was like some kind of magnetism or glue or something held it there."

"Not glue or magnetism," Yakata interjected, having somehow overheard us. "A quantum bond." He cocked his head to Dina. "Ready, Private?"

She nodded. "Feel the wall. Got it."

I held my breath as she darted by, reached the wall, then took one, two, three, four steps until her body shifted horizontal. Then with five, six, seven more steps, she placed a foot on the ceiling before she came sailing down in a chaotic landing that drove Yakata forward in a lightning display to spot her. I had never seen a human being move so quickly.

"Excellent," Yakata said. "You felt the ceiling for a moment before the old fears came."

"Sir, I'm sorry, sir," Dina said. "I did feel the ceiling for a second. But how? How can we do this?"

"The mnemosyne help to activate another sense in our brains: the ability to manipulate the quantum bond between particles. We're no more than particles ourselves. Matter experiencing itself, no? Distances and time mean nothing. Other forces of nature—the strong and weak nuclear forces, gravity, electromagnetism—we're all of these, and we're only beginning to discover the potential power here. One day, we'll abandon our tawt drives and will ourselves across the galaxy."

"Sir, meaning no disrespect, sir, but this is getting a little too metaphysical for me," Halitov said. "The conditioning has screwed around with my brain and allowed me to detect quantum bonds and exploit them. Why do we have to engage in all of this touchy-feely stuff? Just tell me how to flip it on and off, and I'll do it."

Yakata drew in a long breath, closed his eyes. "To the doorway, Private."

Wearing a tired smirk, Halitov dragged himself to our makeshift starting gate. "Sir, I'm ready, sir."

"Go."

Sprinting about as quickly as Beauregard had, Halitov reached the wall, threw up one foot, the other, realized he wasn't going any farther, then slapped a hand on his tac. His skin quick-sealed him in a saffron glow a second before he rebounded three times off the floor and came to an embarrassing, if not physically painful, halt. He scrambled to his feet, de-skinned, then faced Yakata with an accusing stare. "Why doesn't it work for me?"

"Because you haven't surrendered your intellect," Yakata said, though he seemed a little stunned by Halitov's failure. "We're not getting touchy-feely here. The relationship between mind and matter is quite physical." He thought a moment. "Sit down, Mr. Halitov. Mr. St. Andrew? I think we can show them now."

"Sir, I'm not sure what you mean, sir," I said, striding to the doorway. "You think I can do this?"

"We'll see. Ready? Go."

As I dashed toward the wall, I remembered Yakata's instructions. I projected myself into the stone, and for a moment I saw myself running forward, saw my boots connect with quickcrete and felt their impacts, saw how I moved across the vertical surface as though it were horizontal. Then, as I stepped onto the ceiling, I returned to myself and ran over the class, who, from my point of view, hung miraculously from the ceiling. I did not feel the blood rush to my head or any other indication that gravity wanted to splatter me on the deck. My bindings were much more powerful. I stopped, looked "up" at them, their faces paling, then I turned back to Yakata. "How can I do this?"

"Come down, and I'll tell you."

I shifted back across the ceiling, descended the wall, then felt something give as I took a concentrated hop onto the deck. The squad eyed me with a kind of weird reverence. The feat hadn't been easy, but it had been possible.

"Mr. St. Andrew, the mnemosyne respond positively to the residuum of your epineuropathy, which, in layman's terms, simply means that you can access them far more intimately and efficiently than any of us. Your response to the conditioning is estimated to be three times greater than ours. With practice, you won't need your tac for defense. You'll feel the particles of an incoming round and manipulate the bond to deflect them." He tapped his cheek to indicate my birthmark. "Guess this is the universe's way of paying you back."

"So now I know why they put so much pressure on me to make sure he didn't IDO," Pope said heatedly. "Why didn't they just tell me, *sir*?"

Yakata cocked a brow. "Because you might've pushed him through when he wasn't ready. Sure, they didn't want him to fail, but they didn't want him to have any special allowances. If he couldn't pack the gear before the conditioning, he most certainly wouldn't pack it afterward." Yakata waved a finger at me. "Mr. St. Andrew, people with extraordinary abilities are asked to put out extraordinary efforts. Your burden will be far greater than theirs, and the price you'll pay will be even steeper. You'll rely on every lesson you've learned, and you won't have the luxury of dusting out."

"Yes, sir." I turned to Pope. "Sir, I'm sorry about this, sir."

"It ain't your fault. And you can quit calling me 'sir.' Far as I know, we'll all be commissioned as second lieutenants."

"That's correct," said Yakata. "You may return to your seat, Mr. St. Andrew. Now then, Mr. Pope. Let's talk about things you don't know you know. For example, why don't you tell me about the quitunutul arts."

"Sir, I don't know anything about . . . well, I guess I do. There are seven quitunutul fighting arts, sir, each one focusing on a particular move and all developed on lower-G worlds. *Chak* is the art of the turn. *Ai* is the floating kick, counterkick. *Ixta* is the fist, elbow, fist. *Biza* is the head drive. *Dirc* is the somersault and kick. *Gozt* is the bullet thrust. And *shoru* is the slide and drop. There are hundreds more, but they are all variations on these seven."

"Where did you learn this information?"

"I don't know, sir. I can't remember."

"Do you remember our practice sessions?"

"No, sir."

Yakata frowned. "As far as I know, all of you were cerebroed. Four years' worth of data and training was uploaded into your long-term memories—as enhanced by the mnemosyne. All those classes, the confidence courses, all of those experiences should be distinct memories. Each one of you should remember practicing the quitunutul arts with me. How many remember?"

Not a single hand split the air.

"Sir, the accident—"

"I know all about the accident," Yakata snapped, then

looked lost for a second. "The verbal triggers should still be working."

Beauregard cleared his throat. "Sir, if I may ask, sir. Is there a problem with our conditioning? Something go wrong with our cerebros? Are we all right? I think we have a right to know, sir."

The classroom's light flicked off to a chorus of moans.

After a pocketful of seconds, an alarm drummed rapidly through the intercom, an alarm I had heard only once in my time at the academy—and that was during a drill. A violet light stick above the doorway clicked on.

"On your line!" cried Yakata. "We're under attack."

"But our location's classified," said Halitov.

"Yeah, it's been classified as a target," Beauregard answered. "The alliances know who and where we are. And they'll do anything to get their hands on us."

"All right! Listen up! We'll circle around the back of the library, then cross over to admin," Yakata said. "I'll get us into the armory. Let's move."

As the others sprinted out, Dina held back me, Pope, Beauregard, Halitov, and Clarion. "I don't know about you, but I have no intention of being captured," Dina said. "If it looks like we're not going to win this, I say we meet up at the cave entrance by Whore Face."

"Believe me, we're not going to win this," Beauregard said. "We'll go to the armory with Yakata, then I say we head straight for that cave."

"You first years think you got a plan, huh?" Pope said, twisting his lip. "Well, I'll tell you what. It doesn't sound too bad. I'm in."

"And so are we," Halitov said, slapping my back.

"We're falling behind," Clarion urged from the doorway.

We sprinted through the poorly lit hall, found the lift out

of power, then ducked into the stairwell. Two flights later, we emerged on the library's ground level, stole along the walls of another corridor, then bolted past a rear exit that Yakata had already keyed open.

The powerful stench of cooling heatshields clogged the night air and drove my gaze skyward, where a half dozen Western Alliance crab carriers, their silver carapaces gleaming in planetlight, their landing gear unfolding like anxious talons, rumbled down in vertical landings toward the field in front of admin, about a quarter of a kilometer away.

It was a perfect night for an attack. Magnificent visibility. Little wind. Unusually warm. Even the *shraxi* and the triplets had gone silent, as though they knew what was happening and would conceal themselves until humanity's madness had passed.

I hesitated outside the library door, just watching Dina, Halitov, Clarion, and Pope dematerialize into speckles of darkness. I imagined my whole life playing out like a surreal film directed by a psychotic and edited by a drunk. Too much imagery all too soon. Not enough development of what really matters. *One brother dead. Barely time to grieve. The war has started. The war has come here.*

Halitov came running back for me. "Asshole? Come on!" He jerked me by the wrist.

I guess I would have stayed there and got shot to alleviate that deep, warm ache of my brother's death.

We caught up with Yakata and the rest, who led us along the broken hogbacks behind admin. By the time we reached a position opposite the triangular arch of the rear entrance, two squads of Alliance Marines had already surrounded the building, their skins set to a dark-green camo pattern, their QQ90 particle rifles held high, at the ready, and functioning only for authorized users. We looked

down on them from a height of about fifty meters, with
about two hundred meters between us—a dangerously
wide gap.

"Shit, they beat us," Pope said, peering furtively at the
troops. "No way in there now."

"Count seven posted along our side," said Yakata. "Wait
here. When they fall, all of you run to that door."

"When they fall?" Halitov asked, unable to douse his grin.
"Those are Alliance Marines, Q'ed and skinned. Isn't an
extrasolar force anywhere that can touch 'em."

"What I'm going to do, Mr. Halitov, is make you believe."
Yakata skinned up, then charged over the hill.

All seven Marines whipped toward Yakata. Proximity
alarms rang out in their Heads Up Viewers, and infrared
converted the night into a transparent, target-rich environment with a single silhouette glittering against curtains of
cold stone.

It would take only one Marine to set her QQ90 to auto-
track, then squeeze the trigger. The weapon would automatically fire ten rounds per second, while its AI focused those
rounds on a distinct location of Yakata's skin. Considering
the level of training most Alliance Marines received, that
target zone would probably be very close to if not exactly
over, Yakata's heart. Perfect kill shot. Two to three seconds,
and it would all be over.

The two Marines to Yakata's right opened fire first, joined
a half second later by the other five. Seven streams of white-
hot incoming converged on the XO, even as he dropped into
an amazingly swift somersault as though he were floating in
zero G.

Dirc is the somersault and kick.

I still wondered how the move would help. Wouldn't the
rounds still lock on and penetrate his skin?

"Oh, my god," someone muttered as those seven streams came within a quarter meter of Yakata's tumbling form, then abruptly curled back toward their masters.

You'll feel the particles of an incoming round and manipulate the bond to deflect them.

Even as Yakata came out of the somersault and performed the ritual dropkick for good measure, seven glowing skins faded and seven guards collapsed to the dusty earth, victims of their own weapons.

"I don't believe it," Halitov muttered.

Yakata charged to the door, then looked up and waved us down. As we skinned, fanned out, then sidestepped across the steep grade, I noticed a bright speck in the corner of my HUV. There, just rounding the corner of the building, was another Marine, who raised his weapon and trained it on an unsuspecting Yakata.

I charged toward that Marine, giving myself to whatever the hell they had put in my brain, those mnemosynes, those things, whatever they were, I begged for their help. I swore there was about seventy-five meters between me and that soldier. I bridged the distance in two heartbeats, but not before the bastard opened fire.

While his salvo tore into Yakata's skin, I placed my arms over my head, the backs of my forearms serving as a battering ram as I launched myself headfirst toward the Marine.

Gozt is the bullet thrust.

I felt weightless as I hurtled toward him, and when our skins touched, we rebounded with a force ten times greater than the one that had repelled Halitov from Val d'Or, back on old Whore Face. The Marine struck the quickcrete and dug himself a vertical grave as I sailed fifty meters back and dug a trench of my own with my rump.

Dina and Beauregard crouched over Yakata, who lay on

his back, just outside the door. His mouth moved, but I couldn't hear him. By the time I made it over there, he had died. He wasn't the first dead person I had ever seen, just the bloodiest.

"What did he say?" I asked Beauregard.

The colonel's son grimaced. "He told us to follow you."

"He was delirious, dying. Forget it," I said.

"Forgotten," Beauregard replied—just a little too quickly. "I'm off an Op command. I know this drill. Let's get down there, Q up, then we fall back to the caves."

"What about them?" Dina asked, tipping her head to the other four members of the 111th Squad, three young men and one young woman whose names I had only recently learned. They huddled close to the door, waiting for Pope to finish keying in the code.

"Hey, Beauregard?" the woman whispered. "We'll take our chances back in the hills. If you people think you're going to get to the armory, you're sadly mistaken. The Marines are inside." She lifted her chin to the other three, and they bounded off, toward the hogbacks.

"Is that desertion?" Halitov asked, gaping at the fleeing half of our squad.

"I don't know," Pope said. "Why don't you ask Mr. Beauregard. They were under *his* self-appointed command."

Halitov would have no time to debate the point. Pope finished his work on the keypad and the door opened. We hustled into a maintenance tunnel that, according to a small map of the zone gleaming in my HUV, wound its way behind the Latitude. The beauty of our entry was that we could take a series of these tunnels directly to the armory. Yakata had planned it that way. Any other entrance into admin would have forced us to pass through some of the facilities within the Latitude or through the academy's administration offices. No doubt the Marines had already secured those areas. Too bad our squadmates didn't have as much faith in Yakata's plan as we had. I never heard what happened to them.

"Question," Beauregard shouted, sprinting at the front of the pack. "When we get down there, how do we get in? Guards on? Codes? What?"

"No guards," Pope answered. "I know the entrance code."

"Now that you mention it, so do I," Halitov said.

I shuddered. A verbal trigger clicked in my thoughts. I knew the code, too.

"Shit, I don't wanna know how much stuff they put in my head," Halitov said. "If something as stupid as an armory door code is in there, I'm afraid to think what else."

"Maybe we have full access to the academy now. Got a tablet and then some in our heads," Clarion said. "Just have to figure out how to retrieve that information." Her words echoed away as we rounded a corner and our skins automatically switched to infrared. The power had died.

I ordered up my skin's external volume, which enhanced my own hearing by a factor of about two, and the distant thudding became the distinct pinging of QQ90 rounds, with the faint cries of the dying behind them. An explosion rattled the overhead and tossed down a confetti of dust as we nearly collided with each other at the stairwell. We took it all the way down to the armory level, but the security door leading to the hallway beyond had automatically locked during the first alarm.

"Let's prove your theory, Ms. Clarion," Pope said. "I'm thinking about the code to this hatch, and I got nothing. If it's in our heads, how do we get to it? What's the verbal trigger?"

"Are we gonna get past this door or fuck around with

magic tricks," cried Halitov. "Get out the way!" He bolted forward, parting Clarion, Dina, Pope, and Beauregard with his arms. Then he jogged to the back of the stairwell, putting himself about five meters from the door. I blinked because I thought my eyes or my skin was playing one of Halitov's aforementioned tricks. In a display of magnificent motion, the brawny cadet took four massive strides toward the door, pulled his arms into his chest, then coiled into a flying somersault, coming out of it with his boots perpendicular to and about a quarter meter from the door. When those boots hit to finish the *dirc*, one that would've made Yakata proud, the entire wall rippled with a force that blew all of us back onto the floor. Even as I sat up, the door snapped off its tracks and slapped with a heavy thud to the deck as Halitov coiled into a second somersault over it. The son of a bitch landed on his feet, turned back to us, and smirked. "Well, I sure as shit didn't *feel* the door." He started into the hall.

We picked ourselves up and charged in behind him, drummed on by the continuing explosions and gunfire. I broke into a path parallel to the others and caught up with Halitov. "So what *did* you feel?" I asked him on his private channel.

"Wish I knew. I started running at the door, and for some reason I got real calm. The rest? I don't know. It's weird. Just when I think I can compare it to something, it just doesn't seem right." He pointed to twin hatches ahead. "Armory."

"You want to try that again?" I challenged.

But Pope hauled past us and let his finger glide over the keypad. The doors hissed aside to reveal a vast, librarylike chamber with row after row of weapons stored in locked, transparent cases that had been set into the numbered shelving system. The shelves rose over three meters and stretched to the far end of the armory—50.87 meters away, as reported by my HUV.

As we stepped into the place, our aloneness gnawed at me. I couldn't believe that Yakata was the only person who had had the bright idea of getting to a weapon as the attack began. Those already in admin should have come down and loaded up, and surely others would still be doing so.

Then it all became clear as I neared the first shelf. All of those transparent cases sat empty. There was, in fact, not a single weapon to be found among a cache that had originally numbered ten thousand.

"Well, this ruins my day," yelled Halitov.

"Somebody beat us here?" Pope asked, nonplussed.

Beauregard glanced up to the ceiling, mumbled something to himself, swore, then swore again. "Bryant sided with the Seventeen, but our old friend Lieutenant Colonel Darien Butler went with the alliances. So you've got a regimental commander on one side, an XO on the other. You're the XO, you make sure the academy can fall easily to an attack. He must've cleared out this place behind Bryant's back. God, I wish Marxi was still here."

"I'm sorry, I just . . . I just can't do this anymore," Clarion said. Her skin darkened, winked out. She rubbed her eyes, then looked at me, and I got the feeling that she wanted something, I didn't know what. She suddenly fled.

Dina started after her.

"Let her go," Beauregard cried.

"That's right, Ms. Forrest," Pope added. "She chooses. Not us."

"She can't choose to die," Dina argued, hesitating in the hallway.

"If I'm an Alliance CO, I give the order to spare anyone running around with a shaved head," retorted Beauregard. "Probably means that person was recently conditioned, and conditioned individuals are the ones I want to capture alive."

"What now?" Halitov asked, abruptly de-skinning and scratching his arms and legs as though he were crawling with insects.

"Plan doesn't change. We head out to Whore Face," Beauregard said. "And to the caves. You, Mr. Halitov, are walking point."

"Put St. Andrew up there," Halitov spat. "You heard what Yakata said about him."

Beauregard shifted toward me, his face growing distinct through the skin. I pretended that I didn't see the worry in his eyes. "You want it?" he asked

"I'm your point man." I mouthed for him to switch to the private channel. "Let Halitov pull up the rear. He's got a problem with skinning."

"I know. He's got a lot of problems, but he knows how to take down a door, eh?" The colonel's son spared a quick grin. "All right, Mr. St. Andrew. Lead on. Dina? You stay with me."

9 > **As we neared** the same door we had used to enter the administration building, two Marines dropped down through a gaping hole they had blown in the ceiling. They trained their particle rifles on the point man, which, at the moment, I wished were Halitov. I surrendered to the notion that in a bat of the lashes I'd be lying on the deck, spilling my bowels amid the flickering glow of my dying skin.

"Halt! We won't fire if you come peacefully," said one of the Marines, a tall woman whose dark features came into focus as she weakened her skin. She seemed determined but nervous.

"Are you people deaf?" asked the Marine's partner, a husky Asian man with an indistinct tattoo on his neck.

I raised my arm, signaling everyone to stop. We stood in the middle of the hall, squaring off with the Marines. I looked to Beauregard.

"Yakata told me to follow you," he whispered over the channel. "Give me a reason."

Without a nanosecond's thought, I raced toward the Marines so quickly that I beat the shift in their expressions. Odd thing was, the sprint seemed no faster to me than my average run. Only their slow movements indicated that my body surfed the quantum bond between particles. I reached the woman, who still stared after my ghost, then finally reacted to me standing in front of her, but by then, of course, it was too late. I slapped my palms on her shoulders, and our skins rebounded, blasting her into her partner and blasting me back toward Beauregard.

"That's it," Halitov shouted. "Everybody run! All we have to do is run like St. Andrew! They can't catch us!" He charged past the group. "Look at me. See how fast?" As he stomped by, I noticed that he wasn't running any faster than he had before the conditioning.

Beauregard proffered a de-skinned hand, which I took. Back on my feet, I joined the others at the door, where beside us the guards were just sitting up to aim their rifles. Beauregard shoved Dina outside, and Pope slid out after her.

My gaze traveled up to the hole in the ceiling, then down to meet Beauregard's. He took the cue. "On three," I said.

"Don't make me fire," the woman gritted out.

"One, two, three!"

Despite being newly conditioned, we must have made an impressive sight, Beauregard impossibly scaling a vertical door frame, me mirroring the impossible next to him. I don't remember if the Marines fired or not, but I've always assumed they were too stunned to take aim. The colonel's son and I jogged onto the ceiling. He stepped inverted into the hole. I took my step, but dropped straight down from the ceiling like a spider on a faulty tether. I hit the floor, rebounded two meters, tried to roll upright, lost control, then rebounded off the wall and belly-flopped onto the floor. I rolled over, nauseous from the fall and shocked that for some reason the bond had been severed. Of course the Marines were on me. Of course I stared up the barrels of their particle rifles. I could try another run, but if the conditioning failed me, I knew the Marines would shoot, if only in retaliation for their bruised egos.

I de-skinned to let them know I would come peacefully,

and they waved me through the door and outside, where we trudged in cold shadows around the building. I looked for Dina, Pope, and Halitov, but they were gone.

During our first week at the academy, they made us memorize the Articles of the Code of Conduct, part of the overall academy code, and I remember Pope telling us to recite them to ourselves if we were ever captured. Most of us had thought that was a pretty ridiculous thing to ask. At the moment of capture, most people will not think particularly rational thoughts. But, perhaps with the help of my conditioning, some of the articles came to me, though a bit jumbled as my memory struggled to adjust: *I will never surrender of my own volition. If in command, I will never surrender the members of my command while they still have the will and/or means to resist.*

"So the Seventeen's conditioning gennyboys?" said the Asian Marine behind me. "They harness all this Racinian tech and waste it on genetically impure colos. Now you're telling me they're wasting it on the lowest of the low?"

"These mining kids all think they can come here, slap on a uniform, and everybody's gonna forget that they're mining kids," answered the woman. "The Seventeen's become a joke. And this conditioning is just a little bandage. Looks like your alien magic isn't so reliable, eh, gennyboy?"

I want to say that I turned and ground those two Marines into pulp. Truth was that as they ridiculed me, I continually tried to feel the dusty soil, the smooth wall of a tower to our right, even the hillocks and hogbacks across the field. Nothing.

Once we reached the front of the building, the Marines met up with their squad sergeant, a well-groomed young man in his late twenties who had de-skinned, shivered against the wind, and directed a half dozen other personnel, who shouted and ran off toward the growing chaos of invasion. Beyond us lay the six crab carriers, their powerful spotlights illuminating a full battalion of troops that had spread out to cordon off the area. To the east stood two ragged lines of cadets, three hundred maybe, none of them with shaved heads, all under the vigilance of the crab carriers' gunners, who sat in their domed nests, triple-barreled particle cannons aimed at the lines. I assumed that Halti-wanger, Obote, Yat-sen, and the others of my squad who had rejected the Seventeen were among the group. The cadets were checked in by a trio of officers who passed pen scanners over their tacs, consulted tablets, then ordered them on toward the loading ramp of the nearest carrier.

"Show me your tac," said the squad sergeant, jolting my attention away from the spectacle.

I held up my wrist. He waved his pen scanner over my band and cocked a brow as he read his tablet. "This one gets you two an extra day of R&R," he told his troops. "Take him over to the conditioning line for final check-in and processing." He turned a warning gaze on me. "I just deactivated your tac, so running is a really bad idea."

"Sir, I understand, sir."

"Don't worry, gennyboy. I'm sure the alliances can tweak your loyalty and find a place for you. You'll still get to fight for us."

I just eyed the sergeant, not bothering to temper my disgust.

"Get him out of here."

Twin turbines boomed through the surrounding mesas as a C-129 Guard Corps Transport rose dangerously fast from the spaceport on the opposite end of the field. The silver boomerang wagged its wings in vertical takeoff, then banked sharply to the west as it gained altitude.

A higher-pitched whine resounded behind me, grew

louder, then materialized into a pair of atmoattack jets with T-shaped bows attached to bewinged spherical fuselages. The two fighters charged overhead and opened up with conventional guns on the fleeing transport.

With nearly every gaze stolen by the sudden air battle, I dug the tip of my boot into the dirt, felt the dirt the way I had felt that classroom wall, and knew the time had come.

Even the fighters seemed to rip through the air in a weird, water-slow ballet as I ran from the sergeant and his two Marines. I headed out, across the field, weaving between the crab carriers and spotting another line of cadets being loaded into a ship to the rear. I recognized Staff Sergeant Claudia Rodriguez among the dour-looking cadets. Her gaze lit on me. "St. Andrew?" she screamed, then wrenched herself from the line and came dashing toward me.

Behind her, one of the Marines guarding the line brought his rifle to bear.

Still running, I held out my palm, motioning her to go back, but she didn't stop, and I guessed that she had changed her mind about abandoning the Seventeen and had found a way to act on that in me.

The first salvo ripped into her shoulders, the second into her bowels as she screamed, doubled over, then dropped to her knees as a final salvo booted her onto her chest.

As she died, my wrist itched in remembrance of her powerful grip on the day she had come between me and Halitov.

With a shudder that reached my voice, I ran with everything I had away from there. The Marine fired again, but he either missed or I had outrun his rounds.

In the meantime, the transport had taken a pummeling from the two atmoattack fighters, and, drawing a gray ribbon across the starry sky, plunged in a rough emergency landing behind a pair of mesas just south of Whore Face.

I should have ignored that damned transport and just hauled my ass to the cave. My timing would have been much better, my life much simpler, had I done that. But guilt got the better of me. The people in that transport were obviously still loyal to the Seventeen, and if the mnemosyne didn't bail out on me, I knew I was the only one who could get to them before troops arrived. Leaving the crab carriers' lights behind, I headed off for the gloomy canyons.

About a kilometer had stood between me and the crash site. As I ran, I imagined myself already there, felt the particles of the ship's hull, and I realized with a chill that I was, in fact, standing in front of the smoldering ship, its bow sunk about eight meters into the ground at the base of a cliff wall about five hundred meters high. I fell onto my rump, shaking, overwhelmed. I touched my chest, my arms, then the ground. I had merely thought about reaching the ship. I would need to be very careful about what I imagined and where I projected myself.

A belly hatch located near the ship's stern abruptly blew open, and a woman in pilot's jumpsuit fell two meters to the dust. I scrambled to her, rolled her onto her back. A dark stain had spread over the suit, extending from her collar and wrapping around her left side. I slid a hand behind her head, held her up, and right then and there she heaved a last breath and died on me, her tongue falling limp to one side in the Q pattern of lifelessness.

"Is there anyone who can help?" came another woman's voice from within the transport.

I gently lowered the dead pilot's head to the ground, then stood and pulled myself up into the ship, the deck tipped nearly forty-five degrees, forcing me to cling to the backs of jumpseats bolted to the floor. The C-129 was capable of transporting about one hundred troops, but even in the dim crimson of emergency lights marking the center aisle, I could see that nearly all of those seats were unoccupied. A shifting silhouette drew me to the front of the hold, and I came upon a woman who had sat in the front row and whose jumpseat had ripped from its bolts to fall forward, pinning her to the deck. I realized with a start the woman with the laceration across her forehead and blood splattered down her face was Ms. Brooks, the powerful chief of the Security Council and the woman who had charged us with making one of the most important decisions of our lives.

"Ma'am? I'm Private Scott St. Andrew. And don't worry. I'm loyal to the Seventeen."

"It's too heavy," she said, her palms on the deck. "I can't push it up. My leg's caught, and it's killing me. I think it's broken. Damn. I cut my arm, too."

I braced myself between the seat opposite hers, gripped the back of her chair, and drove it upright with a terrific groan.

She panted, cursed, then unbuckled her straps and leaned down to massage her swelling left ankle. "Yeah, it's broken," she gasped. "Closed fracture. My brother's a doctor. Wish he were here."

"Anyone else on board?" I asked.

"Another pilot in the cockpit. We wanted to take more. Please believe me, we did. But there wasn't time to get them across the field. And I have to get back to Columbia. You don't understand. *I have to get back.*"

I staggered my way through a narrow passage and found the second pilot slumped in her chair. Particle cannon fire had torn through the ship's shield, through the canopy, and pierced the pilot where she sat. Three gaping holes had been torn right through the back of her seat, and I didn't dare cross in front of her to view the damage.

Back in the hold, I yanked a small medical kit from the bulkhead, threw it outside, then helped Ms. Brooks out of her chair. I slung one of her arms over my shoulders and guided her gingerly toward the exit. There, I jumped down first, then she lowered herself to me and made the jump on one leg, with me bracing her fall.

"What were you doing way out here?" she asked as we struggled away, her arm once again slung over my shoulders.

"I saw you were about to crash, so I came out. I'm meeting up with some friends in the Minsalo Caves. I hope they make it. Ma'am, I'd like to take you there. There's an entrance not far from here, and it's not on the maps."

"Wait. You have to go back to the cockpit. There's a nav chip in there, a transparent ROM card. There's no way to navigate away from this moon without it. We're too far out for conventional AIs to accurately calculate the distance. And like I said, I have to get back."

"I know what the chip is. Those chips were supposed to help keep this place a secret."

"Yeah, well, the alliances have obviously acquired some. If we don't have one of our own, then we can only leave on one of their carriers."

A growing rumble from behind the cliff drove my legs into motion. "Sorry, ma'am. We'll have to come back for it."

"They'll take it."

"Then let 'em have it. There's no time."

I forced her along the cliff's base, plotting a course along a stand of boulders that might afford us decent cover. Once there, we paused a moment for me to apply disinfectant to her cuts and do a poor job of bandaging. She found some painkillers in the kit and popped four even though the warning label said to take no more than two within six hours. I felt naked without my tac and swore over my inability to pinpoint our location and plot the exact distance to the cave entrance. I could once more propel myself there via the bond, but what about Ms. Brooks? Could she come along for the ride? I wondered if there might be a field produced around my body that allowed matter within it to exploit the bond with me. After all, my utilities, boots, and tac had come along during every attempt. But what if I was wrong? Could I abandon Ms. Brooks? I could try, then come back for her, but at any time the mnemosyne could fail.

"With your tac deactivated, so too is your locator, they can only track us through motion and infrared," Ms. Brooks said.

"Yeah, but we're easy to spot against all this cold rock," I pointed out.

"Just keep moving."

And that's exactly what we did. I found a rough trail that paralleled the cliff base and braced Ms. Brooks as the grade rose and eventually wandered into a pass between two fifty-meter-high outcroppings. We followed a ridgeline for about an hour, then worked our way down until the familiar wall of Whore Face appeared about a quarter kilometer away, with the bluff opposite it just a hundred meters ahead. The natural trail vanished around the headland, leading toward the cave entrance.

"It's right on the other side of that bluff," I assured Ms. Brooks, my lips chapping, my voice ragged. I hazarded a look at her. She had been crying. "You all right?"

"Yes," she managed, her ankle so swollen now that it appeared as thick as her calf. "If we get out of this, I'll be recommending you for several medals."

"I don't want medals, ma'am. Just my hair back."

"It'll grow."

We reached the natural trail, probably formed by an ancient tributary, and began our curving descent toward the bluff's face. Fresh surges of adrenaline pushed me on, and I increased our pace until we drew within a few meters of the wide lip of rock shielding an arrowhead-shaped wedge of darkness: the cave entrance. I tossed a look back at the admin building, just a sprinkling of lights below a sky washed out by the crab carriers' beams. Dozens of airjeeps buzzed over the area, assumedly carrying Western Alliance officers.

"Scott? Is that you?"

I jolted toward the familiar voice. Jane Clarion emerged from the cave entrance.

"You came back. . . ." I said, warming with relief and grinning broadly. "Who else made it?"

"I did, Scott," said Joey Haltiwanger, stepping out of the shadows.

"But Joey, I thought you . . ."

"Nothing's changed, Scott. We can't let you throw your life away."

"Look what they did to Jarrett," Clarion said. "Don't let that happen to you."

"What do you people want?" Brooks asked.

"They want you to stand down," said a skinned Marine as he edged out of the cave, his particle rifle fixed on Ms. Brooks. A second Marine jogged out behind the first and aimed at me.

"Jane, what did you do?" I asked. "Where are the others?"

"We couldn't find them in the caves, so I guess they're still coming," she answered. "We'll wait for them."

My mouth fell open. "Why?"

"Don't you get it? I'm doing this to help you, to help everybody. If we don't turn ourselves in, we'll die."

"She's right," said Haltiwanger. "Scott, I still want to serve with you. You're the only friend I ever had here. You just picked the wrong side. Stand down. Forget about trying to escape. We're so outnumbered. You have no idea. And remember, we swore our allegiance to this force. Remember the code."

"So all of that hiking to walk right into this," Ms. Brooks snapped, glowering at me. "Your caring friends . . ."

"I'm sorry." I removed Ms. Brooks's arm from my shoulder, then lowered her carefully to the ground. As I turned to face the nearest Marine, I felt his weapon.

And abruptly stood in front of him with both hands wrapped around the barrel. I shoved the weapon hard to the right, driving him with it, then released the barrel. He and his rifle began the long descent toward the riverbed below.

Even as I finished with him, I ran toward the lip of rock, scaled it to a height of four meters, as though I were back in Yakata's classroom, then launched into the first part of an *ai*, the floating kick, counterkick. Elbows bent, hands balled into fists, one leg fully extended, the other pulled up toward my chest, I dropped down on the unsuspecting Marine. My boot penetrated his glowing skin as though it were not there, and I connected with his neck and came down, driving him facefirst toward the soil. His rifle went off, stitching a line about a finger's width away from Haltiwanger's boots.

After rolling off the Marine, I tore the particle rifle out of his hands and flung it over the cliff.

Two hands slapped on my back and dragged me up by my utilities. I cocked my head, caught a glimpse of Clarion, then realized that she had slid a leg over mine and intended to trip me to the ground.

"Scott, don't make me do this," she warned.

Though dazed, the Marine I had knocked down rose to his hands and knees. I figured that in a few seconds he would be up to assist Clarion. In the meantime, Haltiwanger stood near Ms. Brooks, wary that she, despite her ankle, might very well lunge to assist.

I whirled, tearing one of Clarion's hands off my utilities and reaching up to wrap my own fingers around her throat.

She released her other hand and two-handed my wrist, fighting for breath and digging nails into my skin.

"Jane, just look the other way. Let us go," I said.

"I . . . can't."

And with that, she kneed me in the abdomen with a force that severed my grip on her throat and hurled me onto my butt. The dust settled to unveil the remaining Marine now up on his knees and flashing the business end of his QQ780 particle pistol. "Eye for an eye, motherfucker," he said.

Clarion, seeing that the Marine was about to pull the trigger, stepped into his line of fire, shouting for him to stop.

The first round blew off Clarion's right leg; the second round amputated her left in a fountain of blood and pulverized bone that splashed over me. Her body dropped to the stumps, and the Marine punched her with a final round to the heart—

As I rolled left and kept rolling with a strong sense of the bonds between me and the cliff wall. Clarion's body dropped, and the Marine fired into my memory. My roll gained me altitude, and by the time I came out of it I was floating about four meters in the air and about three meters away from the rock wall. I tilted upright and drove myself down in the *shoru*, feet locked together, elbows bent, arms locked to my sides. The slide and drop is meant to disorient an opponent. He sees you coming at him like a bullet whose course will not change. He does not realize that you will flip onto your stomach and drop suddenly to his knees. In standard low G, this is performed by a sudden thrust of the legs, but I only needed to consider the bonds I wished to exploit.

A triplet of rounds exploded from the Marine's gun. The scintillating orbs streaked over my legs and chest a nanosecond before I flipped onto my stomach for the drop. He fired again, but I wasn't paying attention to the rounds. I thrust out my fists and smashed into him, the gun still going off, he trying to force me back with his free hand, me letting inertia bend him so far back that I heard the bones in his legs pop. He wailed in agony as I dropped fully on top of him, wrenched the pistol from his grip, tossed it over the cliff, then drew back a fist.

"Hey! Watch out!" Ms. Brooks cried.

When Joey Haltiwanger had retrieved the Marine's K-bar I didn't know, and exactly why he had resorted to such brutality is a question that still haunts me. Maybe after witnessing my conditioning, he figured I had the power to kill him and would. Maybe he was truly loyal to the alliances and that loyalty had dissolved our friendship.

A sudden stinging coiled through my shoulder as Haltiwanger drove in the blade.

The rest came reflexively. I reached back over my head with both hands, locked on to his head, and whipped him over me like a rag doll. Still wielding him by the head, I thrashed the Marine beneath me until I had broken Joey's neck and back and had beaten the Marine into unconsciousness. The bonds of the universe had become my dark ally.

"I can't feel anything," Haltiwanger said as I dumped him onto the ground. "Scott? What did you do me?"

I crawled around to face him, his eyes shifting in and out of focus. I choked up and suddenly felt the blade in my shoulder. "Joey? I'm sorry." I touched his cheek. His head fell slack, his gaze absent. God help me, I had done my duty.

"Hold your breath," came a voice just behind me, a voice that took me a second to recognize as Ms. Brooks's.

A fresh bolt of pain shot across my shoulders and into my heart. I suddenly felt my pulse raging in one shoulder and cocked my head to see Ms. Brooks holding the blood-slick blade she had just pulled from my back.

Given the mental anguish of killing a friend and seeing another one die and the physical torment of my shoulder, I was at first not much help to Ms. Brooks, who searched in vain for the medical kit, then shoved a balled-up piece of Clarion's utilities under mine to serve as bandage and compress. She helped me to my feet. I found a small light in the unconscious Marine's pack, then braced Ms. Brooks as we crossed to the cave entrance. We hobbled about fifty meters down the dark shaft, then sat to catch our breaths.

After about five minutes, all of it came bubbling out. I cried like a five-year-old, and Ms. Brooks pulled my head into her shoulder.

10 › **After an hour's** travel through the tunnel, Ms. Brooks and I began to feel nauseous. We paused in a section where the tunnel widened to twenty meters.

"It's probably a posttraumatic reaction," she said, grimacing through a swallow. "God, I have to get back."

"You're pretty dedicated to your job."

"You could say that. You could also say my coming here wasn't an accident. And my leaving is imperative." She tapped her temple. "I came to exchange tawting codes. My people at Columbia need them. We could lose the war if I don't get back."

"Why didn't you just send a courier? I mean, you had to know this place was a prime target."

"It was a risk I was willing to take. There are at least two traitors in the Security Council. My mission here was part of a ploy to ferret them out and obtain the codes."

"Codes that could decide the war," I said dubiously.

"Tawting codes. The secret is where they'll take us, and the secret stays with me until I get back to Columbia."

"All right. So if you ever get back you'll upload those codes directly into a cerebro."

"Very good. It's old tech, but it still works."

A tingle fanned across my back. Something was happening. "You feel that?"

"I don't know. I feel something."

"There's a rumor about these caves. They're supposed to

have healing properties. My brother—" I broke off as an image of Jarrett lit so clearly in my mind. "Sorry. My brother cut his finger down here, and it healed the same day."

"Then maybe . . ." She never finished her sentence. An odd look came over her face. She swallowed again, shuddered, then her eyes rolled back, and she passed out.

I leaned forward, wanting to get up and attend to her, but I felt warm and weightless, aware of no more than a speckled void whose current swept me away.

"I'd like to know how he escaped."

"You still think Yakata was a liar? You saw it with your own eyes."

"So how did he wind up with her and make it to the tunnel?"

"That part he'll have to explain."

"Yeah, and the part where he killed Haltiwanger and Clarion. That's what interests me the most."

Dina and Halitov were talking about me, but I still felt too weak to open my eyes and react. I knew I lay flat on my back on hard stone, and I felt the cave's icy air sting my cheeks and numb the tip of my nose. Beauregard was there as well, along with Pope, who whispered a litany of the events that had occurred and the Western Alliance resources he had observed, his voice growing more intense with each repetition.

"Ma'am, are you all right?" I heard Dina ask.

"I don't know," answered Ms. Brooks. "Oh . . . oh . . . I don't believe it. It can't . . . This is . . ."

"What's wrong, ma'am?" asked Beauregard.

"My ankle was broken. . . . It's . . . healed."

I forced open my eyes. Darkness. Shafts of light. Indistinct images. Sideways people. And the cave finally sharpened into the view. We were in the Great Hall, hours away from the academy. I had no idea how I had arrived there.

"St. Andrew's awake," Halitov said, offering the barest of nods.

Dina abruptly hovered over me. "Hey, there. Long sleep, huh? Didn't even feel us carrying you?"

"No." I reached back to the wound in my shoulder.

"I saw the tear in your utilities. By the time we found you, your back was already healed," she said. "How do you feel?"

"Still a little groggy. But all right, I guess."

She proffered her hand, which I took and sat up.

Ms. Brooks stood across from me, and she broke away from her conversation with Beauregard. "Mr. St. Andrew, you were right about this place. I can't understand why no one in our intelligence community ever reported this."

"It wasn't reported because it's so damned hard to believe," said Halitov. "A cave with healing properties? It's just nuts."

"I've been thinking about this," Beauregard said, shaking a finger into his thought. "What if everything's linked? The Racinian tech, this place, the quantum bond, everything. Maybe this isn't a natural cave system at all—it was just meant to look like one. Maybe this is a place were bonds that have been broken can be restored. Original configurations of particles are returned. There's a kind of symmetry going on here, and when the asymmetrical enters, it is addressed—or healed, if you will."

"I won't," retorted Halitov. "There's a scientific explanation behind this. Period. It's alien shit or something. No miracle."

Beauregard sighed. "I never said it was a miracle. I'm going for the science myself. Just trying to understand it."

"This is something too important to go unnoticed," said Ms. Brooks. "This effect has obviously been a kept a secret from the Security Council and the congress, probably by traitors in the Seventeen who'll turn over these caves to the alliances."

"And that turning-over process has already begun," Halitov reminded her. "We can't hide here indefinitely."

Ms. Brooks stepped up on a long raft of stone about knee high, pursed her lips, then said, "Well, people, I'm taking charge of this group. We'll begin planning our next move—which should involve getting us off this moon."

"Ma'am, I mean no disrespect, but do you have any experience commanding a combat unit?" Pope asked. "Maybe right now we don't look like one, but that's what we are."

Her dark brows rose. "I may be a politician, but I have been out in the field, Mr.—"

"Pope, ma'am. Judiah Pope. And like I said, I mean no disrespect. Just like to know where we stand."

"I accompanied an inspection force to Kapteyn Beta in 'ninety-nine. Those were combat-ready troops, guardsmen all the way. Five hundred under my jurisdiction. And we almost got into it on that ring. And I've been on over a dozen more similar missions. So stand easy, Mr. Pope. I'm not completely out of my element. The only problem I have is that I'm not conditioned. I'll be holding you back. Nevertheless, it's vital that I get off this moon. As I told Mr. St. Andrew, I'm carrying tawting codes that must be delivered to Columbia Colony."

"We'll get you off, ma'am," said Beauregard. "Whatever it takes. And I have a couple of ideas. I was with First Battalion, Comet Company on the other side of the moon. I led a training recon to establish covert locations for storing some of the academy's ordnance, including a number of spacecraft. We moved a couple of C-one-twenties, four twenty-nines, and a couple of smaller non-tawt satellite deployers into some canyons we camouflaged with skins powered by solar batteries. If the alliances haven't found them yet, I know we can get to one of the twenty-nines and launch via autopilot before they can get fighters out to us. The access codes to those ships were cerebroed into every one of us, so that's not a problem. And I'm pretty sure they've all got nav chips to get us out of Seventy Virginis."

"You said those spacecraft are on the other side of the moon?" Pope asked. "Dumb question: How do we get there without being spotted?"

"There's a string of tunnels we can use as a shortcut. It'll take us about two days. The last klick will be the most dangerous 'cause we'll be out in the open. Once we're under the skin, we'll be all right. There's a huge cache of food and water there as well. Seems to me that at least Commandant Marxi saw this coming."

"Which is why she got her ass off planet just before the attack," said Halitov. "And if the ships are gone, I'm betting we can blame her."

"They're calling us traitors right now," Ms. Brooks pointed out. "And if I make it back to Rexi-Calhoon, I'll go to Columbia Colony and question the commandant myself. So, Mr. Beauregard, do you know the way from here?"

"I think so, ma'am. If you're ready, we can move out now."

"I am. And given your insight, I'm placing you in command of this evacuation."

"Yes, ma'am." Beauregard faced me. "What about you? You ready?"

Yes, I was ready to vent. Beauregard had nothing to do with exploring the caves, had *not* saved Ms. Brooks, and had now earned himself a command. I was jealous. And then, as every muscle tensed, I felt ashamed. Beauregard could help us escape. My duty was to consider the group over myself. "I'm ready. But if you want, I can save us some time and run a recon first."

"You kidding? We can't wait for you."

"Maybe I'll need a couple of hours. I won't need the tunnels. You just need to point me in the right direction and give me a few landmarks. I won't be spotted."

Beauregard snorted. "You're serious."

"You want to hump out there for nothing?" I sighed. "Look, I can't explain how it happens, it's just the conditioning, I guess."

"Yeah, the same conditioning that we can't rely on," Halitov said. "One minute it's there, the next it ain't. And Yakata said we're supposed to know more than we know. They screwed us up—and you were no exception."

"You're right, we shouldn't depend on the conditioning. But why not risk just me instead of all of us? We lose a little time, that's all."

"If St. Andrew wants to go, I say let him go," Pope interjected.

"Let him go," Dina echoed.

"I've seen what he can do firsthand," Ms. Brooks added. "Mr. Beauregard, I strongly suggest you allow him to go."

Halitov wove by the others to get in my face. "So tell me, Scotty boy, you kill Clarion and Haltiwanger?"

Ms. Brooks hopped down from the stone dais to stand beside me. "What he did was save my life."

"I didn't kill Clarion. She was trying to turn us in. One of the Marines got her."

"So you killed Haltiwanger."

I lowered my gaze and nodded.

Halitov slapped me on the back. "Good work. They probably would've reeducated him and stuck him back on the line. That's one less we gotta worry about."

I knew he was right, but I had difficulty getting past his ruthlessness. We had both come to know Clarion and Haltiwanger like siblings, yet he had offhandedly dismissed their deaths. How could he ignore a past we had so intimately shared together? Fact was, he hadn't. His angst would emerge years later, on a day when both of us could not help but remember.

"Hold up your tac," Beauregard instructed me, then produced a pen scanner identical to the ones used by the Marines. "I'll reactivate it."

The band's tiny panel lit as he waved the scanner. Local time popped up, and my gaze widened. It was already late morning. "All right, I'm set. I know the way out from here," I told them. "Be back soon."

"If we have to move, I'll encrypt and contact you on a local freq. They'll be monitoring, so the message will be brief," Beauregard said. "My tac's got maps of the terrain we reconned. Uploading to yours now." He skinned, then mumbled a series of commands. An upload message winked on my display.

"Scott, be careful," Dina said, and even with her shaved scalp, she quickened my pulse and warmed my cheeks.

I closed my eyes for a moment, concentrated on the tunnel winding out, on the cliff face that lumbered up to the pockmarked mesa we had traversed the first time we had come to the caves. I opened my eyes, skinned to a setting that would mirror the landscape, rendering me invisible to the casual observer, and ran.

Vague sections of peat-colored rock shot by. Sunlight pierced my gaze. I sprinted straight up the cliff face and leapt onto the mesa. I pivoted, scanning all three hundred and sixty degrees of the terrain, then, assured that there were no patrols nearby, I took off. Even if Alliance troops patched in to my locator or locked on to my skin emissions, they would still not catch me. My Heads Up Viewer indicated that I ran across the broken plain at an implausible rate of one hundred and eleven kilometers per hour.

The ordnance site lay about fifty kilometers from the cave's main entrance, so it took me about thirty minutes to near the scene. As I ran parallel to a gorge about a hundred meters wide, three hundred deep, I contemplated the abilities I had gained from my conditioning and struggled with the inconsistencies. My exploitation of the bond felt regulated by something. Maybe tapping too deeply into the bond was dangerous and activated some kind of fail-safe system. Or maybe I still didn't know how to fully manipulate the bond. It seemed more instinctual than anything else. Maybe I never would realize my full potential.

After about five minutes of travel, the gorge divided into three narrower, shallower chasms, and my HUV superimposed a short-range scanner image of the invisible skins draped over the openings and concealing four spacecraft, as well as long rows of silver storage containers.

I climbed down the gorge via a series of small cliffs until, about ten meters from the energy skin, I ran out of road. All or nothing now. I thought of closing my eyes, thought of trying to find another way down, thought of how time was running out, then jumped.

Sans the characteristic rebound I would have felt had I not

been conditioned, I impaled the energy barrier and plummeted another fifteen meters to a mottled bed of fluvial pebbles produced by an ancient river. The impact felt the same as if I had leapt from a height of one meter. I laughed aloud as I looked up at the distant ledge, one that could easily have been on old Whore Face.

The C-129s Beauregard had mentioned sat in a neat row, a quartet of silver boomerangs waiting for us. I guessed that somewhere in that huge wall of containers were the foodstuffs Beauregard had also mentioned. He would have to point us to them. Before leaving to report my find, I jogged over to the nearest ship and stood on tiptoe to reach the belly panel near the stern. "C-One-twenty-nine transport, South Point Academy, Exeter. Seventy Virginis star system. Unit number one-seven-nine-five-five, Alpha, Sierra, Bravo, six." I read the ID panel aloud, hoping to spark the access code which lay hidden in my memory.

And there it was, a ridiculously large number to memorize, yet one I somehow just knew: 98274091847091609610 978987. I remembered reading that the brain does not store memories like computer files but often spreads them throughout itself. Sometimes all parts of our brains work in concert to produce a single memory. I had read case studies of people who had suffered strokes or blood loss to certain regions of the brain. Some had forgotten how to read, yet they could still write. Ten minutes later, they couldn't read what they had written. At least they knew they had forgotten something. I wasn't sure what was inside me that I couldn't remember, and I wished I had a quiet moment to learn what I knew. Confused? I sure was.

With a slight hiss and thud, the hatch opened, and the loading ramp began to descend. I climbed into the transport, dashed through the hold, then dropped into the pilot's chair.

"I need the access code to this cockpit. It's in there, somewhere. Unit number one-seven-nine-five-five, Alpha, Sierra, Bravo, six. Cockpit code is . . ."

I plugged in the numbers on a tablet mounted to the center console: 9990-86868-11-11-001. A code-accept message shimmered for a few seconds, then a main menu popped up. I tapped for preflight, then bolted out of the cockpit.

Outside, I drew in a long breath, pointed myself for the gorge wall, sensed the bonds between particles, and beat a subatomic retreat up to the nearest ledge.

Halfway back to the caves, I got a call from Beauregard, who said that Alliance troops were picking their way through the caves and that he and the others were moving into that string of tunnels. I confirmed that the transports were still in place and that I had preflighted one. He suggested that I head to an arroyo where the tunnels let out. It was just a kilometer away. We would meet up inside.

Considering the chaos of recent days, I was taken aback when the next few steps went off without a hitch. I found the arroyo, met up with the group about twenty minutes later, then began the long hike via conventional travel back to the ordnance site. We bridged more than half the distance before settling down for the night.

We woke early the next morning and hiked hard. Pope spurred us on with well-honed barbs that reminded me of just how fine a squad sergeant he had been. He knew exactly how to push your buttons, and whispered things to me like, "I know you wanna fuck Dina, you idiot. Ain't ever gonna happen, enhanced conditioning or not. Beauregard's got a lock on her, so you'd best square away your feelings and find some other woman to star in your wet dreams."

Always the brilliant and classy orator, Pope probably had a lot of experience with being rejected by women. To be fair, I had heard that he and a second lieutenant from the Sixty-seventh had had a little tryst before I had arrived at South Point. Haltiwanger had heard that woman was a full head taller than Pope, with the kind of looks that made everyone say, "What the hell is *she* doing with *him*?"

Despite Pope's digs, I enjoyed talking with him. Since our conditioning, his demeanor had somewhat softened. More often than not, he spoke to me as a peer, listened to what I had to say, and commented on it without his customary terseness or derision. I learned that he was an only child, that he hailed from Rockwa on Kennedy-Centauri, and that his parents had owned a popular souvenir franchise at the space-port.

"So what made you want to come here?" I asked.

"You know people have all of these complex answers for wanting to become an officer. They'll recite you all of this highfalutin stuff about honor, loyalty, courage, determination, and nine other intangibles that sound real pretty but don't mean jack shit. Truth is, I was at my parents' shop one day about four years ago, and this couple comes in, elderly couple, and they wanna buy something for their grandkids, who, it turns out, actually live on Earth. So my dad's all excited, figuring these old people got some money if they got grandkids who are real Terrans. So he's out there on the sales floor, helping them, but what he doesn't realize is that there's some fuckin' gunner from L-town on Drummer-Fire, and he's got a pistol jammed in my mother's mouth and wants the sodo gas we keep locked up in the case. Guy's a big fuckin' bastard, twice as tall as me, with this long, braided beard, I'll never forget it. So I sneak along the counter, 'cause I think the gunner doesn't see me, and I'm trying to get my father's attention, but someone else sees me, it's this captain from the Seventeen System Guard Corps. Guy has just gotten off the shuttle, come home to see his wife and little kid, and he looks at me with these big, blue, shiny eyes, looks past me and at my mother, and then he comes running into the store, drawing his pistol."

We walked for another ten, maybe twenty meters. I asked Pope what had happened. "Just give me a minute," he said.

"You don't have to tell me. It's all right."

"So the gunner, he just, you know, reacts, puts the slug in my mother's head. Then he trains his weapon on the captain, who starts firing. I mean this fuckin' guy wants to empty the whole fuckin' clip into this scumbag gunner's head. But even as he's pumping off rounds, the gunner gets one off. Kill shot. Between the eyes. They drop together. My father? He's screaming. The old people run out of the store, and you wanna laugh? They fuckin' stole the rubaka egg my father was showing them. Anyway, we rushed my mother to hospital, but she was long gone. So I guess I shoulda given you the short answer on why I came to the academy. Bottom line: I owe that captain."

"You don't blame him for your mother's death?"

"That gunner would've killed her either way. That's the way they operate in L-town. A couple of days later, I met that captain's wife and kid. I knew then that I wanted to be someone like him, someone who rises above humanity's sorry ass state, someone who could do what he did."

"Well, sir, for what it's worth—"

He shook his head vigorously. "No, Mr. St. Andrew, I'll never be that captain. I won't even come close. But I'll be damned if I don't try."

"Yes, sir."

Pushing ahead of me, he said, "Mr. St. Andrew, I appreciate your company, if not your pace. Move out, scumbag! Move out!"

We neared the main gorge. Beauregard signaled a halt, then we got down on our bellies behind a jagged row of reddish brown rocks rising no more than calf height. Me, Pope, and Halitov kept close to Ms. Brooks, since she was not skinned and could be more easily spotted. Our own skins would help to conceal her.

"Crab carrier out there," Beauregard reported. "Just past the third gully. You see it? Shit. It was only a matter of time—time we pissed away getting here."

"Don't sweat it," said Pope. "Remember, we're conditioned. They're not."

"Yeah, if it works," Halitov groaned. "My memory's screwed up, I can do amazing shit one second, nothing the next, and now we stake our lives on this half-ass process. Anybody read about this in our cadet contracts? This part of the code?"

"What's going on?" Ms. Brooks asked.

I had weakened the camouflage over my face so that she could see me. The image must have looked rather odd, though she didn't comment on it. I relayed the news, and she told me to tell Beauregard that she had a plan. He crawled on hands and knees back to us and de-skinned his face. "Ma'am?"

"Since I can't get down there as fast as you can and I have no defense against those troops, I'll remain here. Once you get a ship airborne, hover over my way, drop the ramp, and I'll run onboard."

"Once we launch, we'll draw a whole lot of attention," Beauregard shot back. "The gunners onboard the carrier will open up and cut you down before you get near our ramp."

"Which is why I'll stay back with her," Pope said. "Draw their fire. See if I can turn that fire back on themselves."

"And if your conditioning doesn't work?" Halitov asked.

"Then I buy Ms. Brooks some time to get on board. See, Halitov, I'm ugly, but I'm not stupid. Her life's worth more than mine. More than yours."

"I appreciate that, Mr. Pope, but I'll be just fine by myself," Ms. Brooks answered sharply. "Right now, we need every conditioned person in our arsenal. Your life's worth a lot more than you think."

"Thank you, ma'am. But my mind's set."

"Sorry, Ms. Brooks. Your opinion in this argument is heavily biased; therefore, I'm stepping in to settle this," said Beauregard. "Pope, you stay back with her. Wait for us. They open up, you draw their fire. The rest of us are going down." He pursed his lips, gazed sympathetically at Ms. Brooks. "Just let us do this."

She cursed under her breath, then finally nodded.

"Our tacs can't penetrate the skin barrier, so there's no way to know how many we're up against or their positions," Beauregard said. "So—"

"The skin means nothing," I corrected. "Reach out through it, try to find the bonds between particles, skip along those bonds until you find a guard. Then do it again, and again, and again, and you'll find them all. It's what Yakata said. It's another sense we have, and we have to learn how to use it. I reached down there, and here's what I know: There are two squads. They're taking inventory. I'll mark their positions on my map and upload to yours. Count six near our transport, two posted at the bow, two at the stern.

There's another pair out near the wall. We take those two out first, follow up with the two near the ramp, and I think we can get inside."

"Don't fuck with me, St. Andrew. Are you sure?"

"I'm positive. The only problem I see is the hover to pick up Ms. Brooks. Someone has to fly the transport, even if it's just to issue voice commands to the autopilot. I'm not sure we have those commands. They don't come to me. Anyone else?"

Dina shook her head, as did Halitov and Pope.

"Maybe they'll be triggered once we're in the 'pit. Why would we have all the codes to access the ship and not have the skills to fly her?" asked Beauregard.

"The process was screwed up. Maybe that part got left out," Halitov argued. "We keep depending on something that just ain't there."

Beauregard grinned lopsidedly. "You'll get permission to bitch and moan after we break atmosphere."

"The colonel's boy has spoken," Halitov said darkly.

"I'll go in first. I can get down far enough to make the jump," I told Beauregard.

"Okay. So, you're point man again, which I wouldn't have bet on two weeks ago. I wish your brother could see this."

I turned away to hide the sudden sheen in my eyes. "I know. Let's hope the magic holds out. I'll keep the channel open. Soon as I hit the ground, I'll report."

Beauregard crawled back to his position, while Dina edged up to me. "That night outside the billet? I was right."

"About what?"

"That birthmark on your face. It *is* a blessing. *You're* a blessing." She resumed her place next to Beauregard.

Halitov de-skinned his face to show off his ugly grin.

"That kind of teasing you don't need. And do me a favor, if you die down there, do it saving my ass."

Tossing him a weak smirk, I looked away to Pope, who wore a distant expression. I imagined he was replaying that horrible day at the spaceport.

As was my wont, I bolted away, robbing myself of time to reconsider, then, instead of climbing down the ledges, I leaped from cliff to cliff, gauging my descent much more efficiently than my first drop. I came floating to a soundless landing behind one of the two guards posted out near the wall. I reported my position, then added, "Let me take him and the second one, then you come."

"On your mark," Beauregard answered.

Holding my breath, I crossed in front of the guard. If I touched him without tapping into the bond, our skins would rebound. I had used that move back in the admin building, but I sensed that wouldn't be enough.

Ixta is the fist, elbow, fist.

I de-skinned, wired myself to the quantum level, and struck. The Marine's head lolled back under my first blow, then I caught his chin with my elbow and flattened him with the second punch, delivered with the base of my fist. I chilled as a vivid memory of Yakata teaching me the move lit clearly in my mind's eye, then as quickly vanished. I pulled the guard's particle rifle out of his hands and hurled it away. Then I closed my eyes and dug my fingers into the seams where his tac met his wrist. The band came off, along with his hand. He shrieked as his combat skin withered. The whole attack lasted exactly one second.

The luxury of being able to incapacitate the enemy without killing was one I would not enjoy for long. I guess I was just weak, but my reasons for wanting to become an officer never included a thirst for blood. After killing Haltiwanger, I had vowed not to kill again. I believed I could still neutralize the enemy without robbing parents of their sons and daughters. I felt my own loss of Jarrett all too painfully. I felt fully justified and aided by my conditioning.

With the first guard gripping his bloody stump, I whirled to face the second, a husky woman whose ruddy cheeks shone clearly through her skin. She was older than the average private, about thirty, and had probably joined up to support her kids or find better work outside her colony. In the instant that I looked at her, I gave her an entire life. I knew all of her secrets. She was as real as they came—not just a soldier but a person who didn't deserve to die performing pathetic guard duty. It wasn't her fault that she was in the wrong place at the wrong time. And who the hell was I to dictate her fate?

I didn't know anything about war.

She opened fire, and the first accelerated round caught my skin even as the barrier activated. The next fourteen pounded my abdomen, sending horrific shudders through my bones and, for a moment, making me believe that I really was about to die. A few more rounds and the skin would give way.

Finding her bead in my mind, then coiling myself around the bonds between the particles that comprised it, I willed the incoming into a vertical line reaching up for the clouds. Before she could react to that impossibility, I slapped the rifle out of her grip, then went for her tac. Her wailing nearly made me stop, but I knew that much had to be done. She could easily get a new hand.

I should have killed her.

"Beauregard? Mark!"

As he, Dina, and Halitov came bounding down, leaping from cliff to cliff, I sprinted so quickly by the two guards posted near the transport's stern that they reacted only to the breeze of my passage. They had left the loading ramp down, so I pounded up and into the transport. In the cockpit, I realized someone had shut down my preflight, so I reactivated. That would cost us a few minutes. I also took up Beauregard's suggestion of trying to verbally trigger flying skills, but despite being in the cockpit, I sensed no tingle of new knowledge. If one of us didn't have an epiphany, we might have to leave Pope and Ms. Brooks behind—unless we could "borrow" one of the crab carrier's pilots. I considered the logistics of getting inside that ship and carrying off a pilot. I still didn't know if I could touch someone and make that individual share the experience of the bond. Once again, it seemed way too risky. I pondered the whole reason why we needed a pilot in the first place: to hover over Ms. Brooks's location. What if I could get her to the ship myself? I could run back up there, test my theory with the bond, and if she was able to drop into the gorge with me, then I could simply whisk her into the ship.

Of course, as I stood there, lost in my introspection, I failed to notice that the mnemosyne in my head had gone on strike. Not until I reached the back of the hold, drawn by a commotion outside, did I sense that the bond felt distant, unreachable.

Beauregard and Dina double-teamed one guard, bringing him down with a triplet of quitunutul moves that rendered their bodies jellylike and unnaturally flexible and the guard's body flat and unmoving.

Contrarily, Halitov engaged in a much more brutal and old-fashioned hand-to-hand technique. He had seized the second Marine's rifle and now swung it by the barrel, batting the soldier into unconsciousness with the stock. Incoming salvos tore up the gravel near his legs and sent him hightailing it up the ramp, along with Dina and Beauregard.

"Preflight's in progress," I called to Beauregard. "But I'm out. Conditioning's not working."

"You remember how to fly?" he asked.

"Nope."

"Let's see if I do." He shouldered past me, toward the cockpit, as Dina shut the ramp behind us.

"You see that guy's head?" Halitov asked me.

"You're a real hero," I muttered, then hurried to join Beauregard up front.

"Faith, my father says, can be a powerful weapon. Never knew what that meant until now." Beauregard grinned broadly as multiple Heads Up Displays curved around his pilot's chair.

"You remember how to fly?" I asked excitedly.

"No, you?"

I exchanged a baffled look with Dina.

"What're you smiling about, then?" she asked.

"The fact that I'm teaching myself right now. See that instruction manual flashing on the HUD? I take one look at the page, and I know it. Give me another thirty seconds. I'll fly us out of here."

Flicking my glance to the HUD, I realized that I, too, could glimpse a page and remember everything, despite the fact that I still could not tap into the bond. They had given us another skill, a different skill that harkened back to the old photographic memory. I remembered a word Yakata had used—*eidetic*, meaning an extraordinary and detailed recall of visual images. So we were supposed to vividly recall all that we had seen in our lives. While the process worked at the moment, I speculated that it, like the rest of our conditioning, would be subject to failure.

Beauregard gripped a narrow flight stick with several buttons set into its balled end. "Forrest? You're co-pilot. Halitov? Up to the cannon. If you don't remember how to operate it, learn. Now. St. Andrew? Get ready on the ramp. We're lifting off."

"Carrier's bringing guns to bear," Halitov said, pointing out past the canopy. "Guards are opening up."

"So go answer them," cried Beauregard.

Small arms fire pinged off the transport's belly, and in a second the much more potent thunder of particle cannons would strike the transport's protective energy skin, a shield much like our own skins, though less flexible because of its artificial energy source.

Halitov clambered up a ladder just behind the cockpit and squeezed into the gunner's chair. "Data's in my head. I can work this thing," he shouted.

I stood by on the ramp release and clung to a rung set into the bulkhead as the transport's big turbines bellowed to full power amid the boom and crackle of incoming cannon fire. The overhead rattled violently as Halitov cut loose a torrential bead of return fire accompanied by a string of hollered epithets to vent his fear.

The ship banked abruptly right, and through a boxy porthole I watched the canyon scroll by.

"We're almost there," announced Beauregard. "Okay, St. Andrew, lower the ramp!"

A quick tap, and the belly hatch dropped open. The wind howled in and knocked me against the bulkhead as the ramp began to extend.

We flew over the low-lying wall of rocks, and there was

Ms. Brooks, squinting against the thruster wash, a hand raised against the sun's glare. Pope stood beside her, his worried gaze focused on something I could not see until I edged a meter down the ramp, one hand on another rung, and leaned out.

An airjeep rose vertically from the gorge. I didn't recognize the pilot, though for a second he looked just like Jarrett. The woman in the co-pilot's seat was the same Marine whose hand I had severed. She brandished her rifle in her good hand and kept the stump of the other buried in an armpit.

With just fifteen meters to go until our ramp reached Ms. Brooks, the Marine in that airjeep squeezed her trigger.

Pope, already skinned, threw himself into the line of fire in a remarkable barrel roll that kept him two meters off the ground and sent rounds ricocheting off his spinning body. He held that roll for several seconds, then broke out, landed on his feet, and fell back to once more shield Ms. Brooks.

The ramp slammed into the ground. I yelled for Beauregard to hold his position. Ms. Brooks darted up toward me, while behind her, Pope illustrated to those two Marines that *chak* is the art of the turn. He darted a meter to the left, pivoted ninety degrees away from them, bolted back another meter, pivoted another ninety degrees, then bolted again as the Marine's incoming fire repeatedly tore through the air he had warmed.

I seized Ms. Brooks's wrist and dragged her the remaining few steps inside. She collapsed into the nearest seat, wide-eyed and breathless, then craned her head back to watch Pope start up the ramp.

"Come on!" I shouted, more to address my own nerves than his failure to haul ass.

In fact, Pope ran up the ramp with everything he had, but the Marine caught him squarely in the side of his head with a bead that locked on and held. He looked blankly at me for a second before the rounds chewed through his skin and blew him off the ramp. More incoming stitched across the gangway and forced me back into the hold.

"St. Andrew?" Beauregard called.

"Go! Go! Go!" I hollered over the din, then punched the ramp control.

Ms. Brooks turned and rose. "What about Pope?"

I lost my breath and felt stinging in the corners of my eyes. I just shook my head and ran toward the cockpit, a mental voice echoing over my footfalls: *I just knew that I wanted to be someone like him.* Pope had done exactly what he wanted to do and had lived out the reason why he had come to the academy.

"St. Andrew? Make sure they're strapped in back there and tell Pope to get on the other gun," Beauregard ordered.

"I'm on that gun."

He saw my expression. And knew. "Then just make sure Ms. Brooks is in tight. They've just scrambled four fighters. They'll catch us in the exosphere. We need nine more minutes for the computer to lay in the decoys and resolve the tawt to Rexi-Calhoon. I'm counting on you and Halitov."

With a terse nod, I turned and ran back into the hold, where Ms. Brooks had already buckled herself into her seat at the rear. I descended into the belly gunner's gelatinous dome and plopped into a gelseat suspended from above. Like my old rack back at the billet, the seat slithered up around my body. I slid on the gunner's glove, an alloy gauntlet that, according to my conditioning, turned your hand into a sensitive link between the targeting computer, the Heads

Up Viewer, and the big particle cannon itself. The weapon's big barrels jutted out from beneath my seat and could swivel and tilt to track any target breaking into my hemisphere. The viewer lit, feeding me sweeping scans of the darkening sky as we razored toward the void.

"Targets acquired," reported Halitov.

The corner of my HUV lit with four red blips. I balled my hand into a fist, then quickly extended the fingers, as though my hand were wet and I wanted to spray someone. That movement ordered the HUV to zoom in on the bandits, four hammerhead sharks with iridescent bubbles for bodies. Although they had been designated "atmoattack" jets, the name was old and deceiving. The fighters could operate in nearly every environment, save for those worlds whose atmospheres were comprised of certain corrosive acids. An initial scan indicated that their pilots had yet to arm nukes. No doubt they had been ordered to disable us.

From the corner of my eye I watched Exeter shrink away and yield to the great bands of 70 Virginis b, one of the most massive gas giants in colonized space. The planetary system's three inner moons, Triv, Azola, and Mylkic, shimmered faintly, their broken gray surfaces cooked and tortured by tidal forces and intense radiation.

Then, heralded by my proximity alarm, the fighters came in, grouped in a standard box formation and tearing a seam in that fantastic tableau. They streaked up behind us and peeled out of formation so precisely that I swore I was looking at the multiple reflections of a single craft. Two penetrated Halitov's field of fire, while the other pair swooped down into mine. I pointed my index finger, an act that armed the system and activated a targeting reticle in my viewer. My finger fell over one of the fighters as the one below it opened fire. I flicked my thumb. A stream of ball lightning belched from my barrels and cut over the other fighter's river of incoming. Dark blue veins of rappelled energy spidered over my dome and sapped away at skin strength.

"Gentlemen," Beauregard yelled in our headsets. "They're targeting the tawt. Still got three minutes on the resolve. Take . . . them . . . out!"

Beauregard had barely finished speaking when the fighter I had tracked burst into a fleeting conflagration.

A viewer to my left showed that Halitov had racked one up as well. But the remaining atmos employed their electronic countermeasures, and my HUV suddenly displayed multiple images of the fighter in my hemisphere, with no way to tell which was the real one—

Unless you had the ability to reach out into the void and search for the bonds between the particles of that fighter. Guided by instincts that had become strangely familiar, I began that search.

And failed.

Halitov's voice came thick and enraged through my headset. "What are you doing, St. Andrew? Fire!"

I waved my index finger wildly over the HUV and thumbed off beads at all those incorporeal ships. While my salvos shot toward their targets, I flexed my middle, ring, and pinky fingers, throwing up clouds of superheated metallic fragments in a rather uninspired attempt to draw fire away from the tawt drive, whose spherical housing bulged from the top of our stern.

The rest I can only report as I heard it from Halitov. The fighter I had been tracking broke through my incoming and punched an appreciable hole in the skin protecting the gunner's dome. The explosion activated the gelseat's auto anesthetization and safety lift feature, which hauled my suddenly unconscious self up and into a blast compartment that sealed as the dome was sheared away. Beauregard rolled one hundred and eighty degrees, bringing the fighter I had missed into Halitov's hemisphere. Then the cocky cadet "wove a web of fire so dense that no pilot could escape it." Not only did he blast my fighter into a memory, but its detonation took out his. Halitov: three. St. Andrew: one.

I remained in a cold, numb, drug-induced sleep for about an hour, and when I woke, Dina told me that we had already tawted to her home, Epsilon Indi, an eight-planet star system with an orange K5 sun sitting roughly sixty-six light-years from Exeter. We presently established a geostationary orbit of the fifth planet, Rexi-Calhoon, an Earth-like globe with a breathable atmosphere (perhaps thanks to Racinian influence) and multiple biomes similar to the North American continent.

Shuddering off the grogginess, I sat up, looked at her, and remembered. "They got Pope."

She glanced away. "I know."

"Funny. I really hated that bastard."

"Me, too."

We grinned through our tears.

As the others waited for clearance to break orbit and approach Columbia Colony, I brooded over my failure with the fighters and went through a half dozen scenarios in which I managed to save Pope's life. Halitov conveyed his heroics, then described the Seventeen System Guard Corps armada that hung in orbit around us: nine strike carriers, seven dreadnoughts, and thirteen destroyers sailing threateningly through space, guarding the new colonial government from Alliance strike forces that could, at any second, tawt in and attempt to seize the colonies. I'd had no idea that the corps had so many capital ships at its disposal. That would be only the first of many surprises promised by Beauregard and, later, by associates of his father.

Ms. Brooks, who still sat at the rear of the hold and had been speaking furiously via tablet to her aides in Columbia, called to me and Halitov. We headed back to her, and she told us to take seats. "I know both of you come from Gate-wood-Callista," she said gravely.

I lifted a hand. "I don't want to hear any more."

"Well, I do," said Halitov.

"There's an occupying force, but there are survivors. Believe me when I say we *will* respond. Communication with them is sporadic at best."

"If they're not dead yet, they will be," I muttered. "I'm sure the alliances are ready to make another statement."

"And we'll make ours."

"Ma'am, I think we'd both like to go home," said Halitov.

She nodded. "I'll send you there—with a regiment behind you."

"You can do that?" I asked, dumbfounded.

"I'm chair of the Security Council, and if I want you there, you'll be there."

"Ms. Brooks?" Beauregard said from the front of the hold. "Tower's just given us the go-ahead. All of you, buckle up for insertion."

I thought my life had changed quite a bit in the last few days. Those changes were nothing.

In the weeks that followed, I would slowly begin to mourn the loss of Private Scott St. Andrew, first year of Eighty-first Squad, gennyboy, and weakest link in the chain.

PART 3

The Fidelity of Dogs

12 › **The Exxo-Tally and** Inte-Micro Corporations, largely responsible for most of the colonial expansion in the prior century, had settled the planet of Rexi-Calhoon as a joint venture, and their influence was inescapable in the primary colonies of Columbia, Indicity (Dina's hometown), Tru Cali, Lincoln, Govina, and Rexicity. About nine hundred million resided on the planet, with twenty percent living in Columbia, a vast metropolis encompassing thousands of kilometers of mountainous terrain.

We set down in CESP—the Columbia Extrasolar Spaceport, located in Fortune Valley. As we descended the ramp, the strange smells and brown haze tinting the sky had all of us wincing. Ms. Brooks told us we would get used to the smog. I shook my head over the irony of polluting real fresh air. I guess it took someone like me, a person who had never breathed unrecycled air until I had gone to Exeter, to truly appreciate the damage we were doing. But the economy depended upon the manufacturing plants, which were, Ms. Brooks explained, now contributing to the war effort.

An airjeep carrying a first sergeant and a private came out to meet us on the tarmac. The sergeant introduced himself to Ms. Brooks, gave me, Halitov, Beauregard, and Dina a slightly terrified look, then helped us all into the back. We flew north for about thirty minutes, skimming the treetops. I got my first look at a real lake, whose waters appeared more murky than I had imagined. We swooped over a stand of trees, then braked into the forest and landed beside a wide security hatch set into the ground. The sergeant coded open the door, and we climbed into a small, open vehicle seated on a repulsor track. We whirred straight into the mountain, passing through six, maybe seven, security checkpoints until we reached a great chasm, a hub with perhaps twenty tunnels stretching away. Dozens of small personnel carts swept through the tunnels, and twenty meters to my left, a full platoon of forty stood in rigid formation, their duffels sitting before them as they waited to ship out.

"Welcome to Columbia Strike Base," Ms. Brooks said. "As far as we know, the alliances have no idea we exist. I have a debriefing to attend. I'll have the sergeant take you over to a billet to get cleaned up, then I'll call for you. I'm sure the generals would like a word."

My mouth fell open. So did Halitov's.

Ms. Brooks climbed out, then the sergeant took us on to a billet belonging to the Fourteenth Regiment, Rebel Company, Second Battalion, Thirteenth Platoon, Squads Thirty-seven through Thirty-nine. Beauregard and Dina commented on the claustrophobia associated with a subterranean barracks, but the arrangement seemed quite natural to tunnel dwellers like me and Halitov. Squad Sergeant Jama Chopra, an amiable, baby-faced, twenty-two-year-old whose forefathers had come from Bombay, introduced us to the supply sergeant, a nineteen-year-old black woman named Giossi who gave us fresh utilities free of charge. We took hot showers for as long as we liked, then Chopra took us over to the mess, where we grappled with plates of pasta and tanked down more water and juice than an entire squad. We had found some emergency rations on board the transport, but they had barely satisfied our appetites. During the meal, Chopra introduced us to Squad Sergeants Tamburro and

Stark, two fair-skinned, flaxen-haired women whom you would swear were sisters. They gazed at us like the airjeep sergeant had, their awe somewhat tempered by fear. Chopra explained that everyone at Columbia had heard something about the conditioning, but to the best of his knowledge none of the enlisted had ever met a conditioned soldier. With Ms. Brooks's arrival, the scuttlebutt had run rampant about the four cadets who had rescued her from Exeter, four *conditioned* cadets.

"Can you show us something?" Squad Staff Sergeant Holmes asked, his hazel eyes fully lit, his brow flexing up and down. "Some of us couldn't get into South Point."

"Yeah, but some of us don't wanna know what we missed," sniped First Sergeant Mai Lan from the end of the long table. The sergeant, though Asian, could very well have been Pope's sister. She had his rubbery skin stretched over knotty muscles, his persistent scowl, even his bad teeth. And I loved what she had done with her hair: your basic self-inflicted-butcher-knife-cut-while-drunk. She stared in my direction. "Some of us got fucked out of our opportunity because of testing biases and the encouragement of gennys to apply."

I opened my mouth. Beauregard squeezed my shoulder, then turned me toward the entrance, where our airjeep sergeant waited. "Ms. Brooks just called for us."

We were taken to a large conference room divided by a massive oak table littered with tablets, real paper reports, and drinks. Twenty or so people dressed in the black uniforms of the Seventeen System Guard Corps sat talking with each other or tapping on their tablets. Near the table's head, I spotted four generals, two men and two women, all graying and over fifty, all heavily decorated. I did not know who the rest of the people were or what they did. I recognized only their ranks. Perhaps they were aides or specialists of some kind. No one ever clarified it for us. I scanned the crowd for Commandant Marxi, but she wasn't there. One of the generals, Ms. Yllar Juvhixa, the woman who had declared the Corps's secession, rose and indicated that we should stand across from the table, out in an open area that led to a lounge with real leather furniture.

Ms. Brooks left her chair, smiled at all of us, then faced the group. "Ladies and gentlemen, these individuals represent the kind of training and conditioning we were doing at South Point before the attack. And if it weren't for them, especially Mr. Scott St. Andrew, I wouldn't be here to share the codes with you."

One man who identified himself as Colonel Felix Retorda of Intelligence asked Beauregard to relate the account of how we had commandeered the transport and escaped. Beauregard downplayed the event, but Halitov repeatedly stepped in to embellish and point out his contributions to Ms. Brooks's safe return. Dina answered a few questions regarding the occupying force's strength and a few inquiries that focused on our enhanced memories. I thought I could remain silent through most of it, since the others did such an articulate job.

"Mr. St. Andrew," called one of the generals, Joseph Strident, a white-haired Goliath who had probably been one hell of a combatant in his youth.

"Yes, sir?"

"You've been silent during most of this, but I listened to Ms. Brooks's account of how you pulled her out of her crashed transport, carried her to the Minsalo Caves, then defended her against two Marines and two cadets sympathetic to the alliances."

"That's right, sir."

"Son, I'll interpret your reticence as modesty. And since you're not enthusiastic about speaking, would you mind demonstrating a little of that power?"

I hesitated. "Sir, as Mr. Beauregard said, we can't always count on this process. Something went wrong, sir."

"Why not give it a try? I understand the conditioning enables you to harness the quantum bond between particles."

I felt more and more like a circus freak. I was getting flashbacks to my youth, to the days when I had to explain to the other eight-year-olds what this thing was on my face. But I knew that these people just wanted to see what the Corps's money had bought; the general's request had nothing to do with me personally. I also realized that if I made them happy, they might happily send me home.

I cleared my throat. "General, sir. I, uh, I believe I can honor your request."

And with that I leapt at him, gliding three meters through the air, over the shoulders of others seated at the table, then coming at him with my arms outstretched, my hands ready to lock on his throat.

But damn it, the bond didn't feel that strong. Would I actually choke him?

Even as his face twisted with shock, I suddenly dove, then rocketed myself boots-first toward the ceiling, where I landed with a slight impact, sighed with relief, then looked down on the stunned onlookers. Beauregard nodded to me. Dina winked. Halitov mouthed a curse, upset that he wasn't in the spotlight.

"There's no blood rushing to my head," I told the audience. "I can stay up here for as long as I like—or until the conditioning falters."

I bulleted across the ceiling, carefully avoiding the recessed lights. I reached the far wall and hustled right down it, hit the floor, then catapulted myself back toward the table in a *dirc*, the somersault and kick. I froze in midair, with the boot of my extended leg a hairsbreadth from the general's nose. The others groped for a reaction and finally broke into laughter, while a few blinked against the universe's magic made impossibly real before their eyes. I held that position a few seconds more, then barrel rolled up and over three others at the table, employing that variation of the *chak* I had seen Pope use on Exeter. I spun my way back toward Beauregard, then twisted into a reverse somersault and was about to land on my feet—

When the bond vanished. I crumpled onto my butt. "Sorry."

"No, that's quite all right," said the general. "Question. You didn't receive Accelerated Assimilation Training?"

"Sir, that's correct, sir." Beauregard helped me to my feet. "We had just started when the attack began. Our instructor was killed. We've been trying to figure this out on our own."

"I'll put in the request for an instructor, but I can't make any promises. Now, how 'bout a demonstration of your cerebro enhancement?"

"Sir, ask me a question about, say, a piece of equipment. We'll see if it works."

He queried me on the Alliance's atmoattack fighters, and I gave him the specs on four different models, the history of test flights, and even the latest innovations, which I suddenly realized were pouring directly into my brain from a wireless link to Rexi-Calhoon's satnet. The mnemosyne had the ability to access local data systems. I shared that with the general, who seemed far less surprised than I was. Beauregard chipped in to tell how he had learned on the spot to fly the transport, and Halitov pointed out how we had used verbal triggers in an attempt to recall some of our cerebroed data.

Once the meeting adjourned, Beauregard cornered the general and asked about his father. I cornered Ms. Brooks. "So what happens now?"

She gave me a funny look. "You don't know? I thought it was obvious. Maybe General Strident should let you know."

Ms. Brooks left me and interrupted Strident, who was in mid-conversation with a lieutenant colonel. The general excused himself, then approached, beaming.

"One hell of a demonstration there, St. Andrew. I understand you're a little uneasy about your future. Well, to be honest, son, we still own you for the next fourteen years. We made a commitment to each other. All the education you would have received at South Point is already in your head. Granted, you can't get to it so well. But I'm sure that'll improve over time. And you also have all the combat training you'll ever need. Once again, that's in there. We just have to help you find it. So, as far as we're concerned, while we'll continue to address the sporadic nature of your conditioning, you and the others are considered ready."

"Sir, ready for what, sir?"

"Mr. Scott St. Andrew, you are about to become a commissioned officer in the Seventeen System Guard Corps. You will hold the rank of second lieutenant and be assigned as a platoon leader. As a matter of fact, I've already got a unit in mind for you. They're an element of Strike Force Two-Four-Seven-A, the Gatewood-Callista campaign." He winked. "You wouldn't mind going there, would you?"

"Sir, no, sir. But do you really think I'm capable? I'm mean this conditioning, it's just—"

"Son, I'm putting colos with barely six weeks training out on the line. Trust me. You're ready. And you know what? The war won't wait for you; it won't wait for any of us. At eighteen hundred local we'll have a small ceremony where I'll present you with your lieutenant's star. Congratulations." He thrust out his hand.

"Thank you, sir."

We shook, then he slid an arm over Ms. Brooks's shoulders and pulled her away from me, whispering something about the ceremony. Someone shoved me hard in the arm.

"Fucking second lieutenants, you believe this?" Halitov asked. "Talk about the fast track."

"You overheard?"

"No, General Juvhixa just told us. So we each got a platoon. I heard we're shipping out in two days. Beauregard and Dina are going to Mars. Ms. Brooks worked it out. I'm going home with you, same battalion. We secure the colonies, we can go looking for our parents. I flat out told the general that's what I plan to do. She didn't have a problem with it."

I gazed across the room at Dina, who lingered near the door, speaking with a lovesick Beauregard. I caught her gaze, and her lips tightened.

Halitov looked at me, then her, then rolled his eyes. "Yeah, all right. I'll miss looking at her ass, but you? You don't need her. She's screwing you up. You should be glad she's leaving. And Beauregard? We can both live without him. Once he gets that commission, his superiority complex is gonna swell."

"Hey," I said with mock surprise. "Just like yours."

"In my case, it's not a complex," Halitov said, folding his arms over his sweeping chest. "It's a fact. But what pisses me off is that you're the one who should be flying this whole conditioning shit in our faces. You go from gennyboy to quitunutul master overnight. How does that *not* go to your head?"

"I guess I still don't believe it. It's all a dream. My brother's still alive. Haltiwanger. Clarion. Pope. None of this has really hit me yet."

Standing there with him, I didn't realize how right I was. Even the commissioning ceremony swept by like the cool current of some dream river. When I washed up on shore, I had a lieutenant's ten-point star pinned to my breast.

It was not until that night, when everyone else had drifted off, that I locked myself in the latrine and clutched that lieutenant's star so tightly that my palm bled.

They gave me the same platoon I had bunked with for the past two days, and I was less than ecstatic to have Mai Lan as my first sergeant. Chopra assured me that he would do everything in his power to establish a smooth transition of command.

During my first inspection of the three squads, I told them that after seven days of training we would ship out to Gatewood-Callista to take back the colony from an occupying force. I told them I was born and raised there. I told them I knew those tunnels as well as any native. I gave them a quick demonstration of the *dirc* and *chak* to establish a bit more credibility for myself—but that backfired when, during the *chak*, I lost the connection to the bond and fell.

Some first impression . . .

Most of my platoon had probably been trained by officers at least six to ten years older than me and with a lot more field experience. In fact, a few of the privates were in their late twenties, and I felt that gap all too painfully. They were stuck taking orders from a kid. I had to show them I was much more, even though I doubted that myself. One piece of advice that I found in my head, words of wisdom from Yakata himself, held that integrity, honesty, and a stalwart commitment to victory are a leader's best friends. If you show your people that you are only half committed, that integrity is but a word to you, and that honesty only works when it benefits you, then they will not follow. Your commitment to the ideals must be superhuman. I tried to explain that to Halitov, who told me after the first night that he was already having a morale problem with his platoon. The sergeants called him conceited and ill-prepared. I told him—as clichéd as it might sound—that he needed to model proper behavior, that he needed to explore his own training. The answers were there for the finding. He just snickered and walked away.

During the morning of our second training day, I was tested by the Corps's scientists. They hooked me up to another cerebro, one they said would help me to better recall my combat training. I did not feel any different when they were done, but I knew the operation of most major weapons, knew artillery procedures, knew how to react to EMP bombs, and that I had trained on all seventeen colonized worlds, pitting my platoon against varying numbers of Alliance troops. I had fought thousands of skirmishes, seen hundreds of faceless troops die, but all of it felt clinical, statistical, mechanical. I knew how to react to a multitude of combat scenarios, but none of them included watching a dear comrade, a man in your charge, spill his blood over your boots. If the experts had provided me with a psychological cushion against all the death I would encounter, I wasn't aware of it.

After testing us individually, those scientists brought Halitov, Dina, Beauregard, and myself together. They took us down into the lower tunnels, asked us to race and fight each other with the quitunutul arts. Although Yakata had said my conditioning was supposed to be three times more powerful than normal, I performed no better than the others, who struggled at trying to maintain a consistent use of the conditioning. One minute we could run at over a hundred kilometers an hour, the next we were out of breath and barely able to jog. The arts posed similar challenges. You'd launch yourself up for a kick, only to find that gravity had returned at exactly the wrong time. I began to think Yakata had lied to me—that was until the scientists asked us to begin projecting ourselves to places, to reach out and see things out of sight. The others had trouble with this, but I remembered how I had willed myself to Ms. Brooks's shuttle. I had ridden the bonds between particles, bonds that existed everywhere at once. With a thought, I had arrived. That kind of power scared me.

"Take yourself to the tunnel's end," one scientist asked me.

I closed my eyes, reached out, saw the tunnel, then forced myself there.

When I opened my eyes, I stood just behind the scientist.

"Did you see that?" Halitov asked. "One second he's right there, the next he's over there. That was weird."

"Yeah, but he never got to the end of the tunnel," Beauregard said. "You have something extra, St. Andrew. But so far it's not much."

I removed a plastic tablet pointer from my pocket. Then I remembered. A second scientist had gone to the end of the tunnel. He had handed me his pointer, and I had come back, although I hadn't planned on arriving behind the first scientist. The whole thing had happened in the blink of an eye, and my memory had just needed to catch up with my body.

"Shit, he *was* there," said Halitov. "Damn. How'd he get the pointer so fast?"

"All right," challenged Beauregard. "St. Andrew, go to Earth. Bring me back a hot dog."

"Stop messing around," Dina said.

"No. That's—" I broke off. The bond was gone. And suddenly, I felt very tired, so tired that I actually fell onto the scientist.

"What's the matter with him?" Dina asked.

"We're not sure," answered the scientist.

They helped me up.

"I need to sleep. That's all. Just sleep."

The subterranean rifle range allowed my troops to experience a decent simulation of urban combat via preprogrammed holographic opponents. Still weary from my tests with the scientists the day before, I went to the range's computer and programmed a no-win situation. I was curious to see how Mai Lan and my staff sergeants would handle defeat.

We entered a city that could easily be mistaken for a colony on Gatewood-Callista, though most of the buildings were facades. One squad of fifteen guardsmen skinned up and fanned out to the left, another to the right, and the third ran straight up the middle of a wide boulevard.

I had programmed three hundred holographic snipers to fire at us from the windows, rooftops, and ground vehicles. Although they fired only laser light that would automatically deactivate our skins, their weapons sounded real.

The place erupted.

I ran across the street and kept close to a wall. A gauntlet of light beams clogged the street. Six people from the Three-eight bought it right away. Another four from Chopra's squad dropped to their knees. Stark's people got massacred; only three privates were left.

"Platoon, fall back," I ordered. "Fall back!"

When I glanced over my shoulder, I saw Mai Lan standing in the middle of the street, screaming at two privates: James Kim and Michelle Maz. The only experience I had had with those two was shaking their hands and saying hello. Both were about my age and seemed as serious as they were scared. They flinched as Lan continued to swear at them.

"Computer? Stop the sim," I ordered, then de-skinned.

Gunfire died. The lights grew brighter. I jogged out toward Mai Lan and the privates. "Sergeant? Report."

Mai Lan gave me a look before snapping to. I wasn't sure if she had smirked, so I dismissed it. "Sir, these two privates disgraced the platoon by failing to obey your order, sir."

I leveled my gaze on Kim. "Is that correct, Private?"

"Sir, yes, sir."

"Why did you fail to obey?"

"Sir, I can't say, sir."

"You can't say?"

"Sir, I'll tell you, sir," said Michelle Maz. She gave Lan a dirty look.

"Sir, the privates became confused," the sergeant quickly interjected. "At the moment you ordered them to fall back, I was on the tactical frequency and had ordered them to advance. They hesitated, and subsequently both were shot."

"I see. Private Kim, why did you hesitate?"

"Sir, I'm not sure, sir."

"And Maz?"

"Sir, I guess I was just confused, sir. Sorry, sir."

"All right. Let's form up and try this again. And let's make sure that when my order comes in, you obey it."

"Sir, yes, sir," they replied in unison.

I went back to the computer, added on another fifty snipers, but this time I had them changing their positions much more rapidly.

We walked into another ambush. I allowed myself to get killed right away, then watched and listened as Mai Lan directed the platoon.

"We gotta fall back," screamed Staff Sergeant Douglas. "C'mon, Lan! Get us out of here."

"And I just lost two more," yelled Staff Sergeant Pariseau.

"I'm down to four," Staff Sergeant Holmes frantically reported. "Three. Aw, shit! I'm dead."

"Tamburro, you're in," Lan ordered. "Enter that brick building on the corner. You're on that nest on the roof. Chopra? I see Douglas is out. You take the rest over to the right side and—"

Lan got shot.

I stopped the sim and went around the corner to her position, passing by a dozen privates looking pissed and lying on the street. Lan sat on the curb, glancing up at the rooftops. She heard my approach and stood at attention.

"What happened, Sergeant?"

"Sir, we got our asses kicked, sir. I was surprised you died so soon, sir."

"Sergeant, what made you think you could take on this force?"

"Sir, I thought that was our job, sir."

"We won't win every battle."

"Sir, aren't we supposed to die trying to win them, sir? I didn't think we were allowed to pick our fights."

"Think again. I have no intention of taking this platoon into a no-win situation—which is what this is. Suicide missions are a last resort for desperate moments. When we get to Callista, if we're heavily outnumbered, I *will* order this platoon to fall back. You think that's an act of cowardice, Sergeant?"

"Sir, some might think so, sir."

"I asked if *you* think it's an act of cowardice."

"Sir, I think it is, sir."

"And you'd rather sacrifice the entire platoon to avoid being called a coward."

"Sir, I didn't join the Guard Corps to *fall back*, sir. I'm here to fight."

"And I need fighters, but you're no good to me dead. If I say fall back, you fall back. That is not an order that is open to interpretation. Understood?"

"Sir, yes, sir."

"Get the squads together. Let's do it again."

"Sir, aye-aye, sir."

That night in the billet, my platoon divided into the cliques I had noticed my first day with them. Lan spent most of her free time with Douglas, Holmes, and Pariseau. Supply Sergeant Giossi joined their card games. Chopra liked to work on the exercise machines with Kim, Maz, Phrawphraikul, and Squad Corporal Van Buren—whom I had seen more than once clutch his heart after an hour on the treadmill. Van Buren was nearly thirty, and I heard him tell Chopra that he was, in fact, getting too old for this shit.

Tamburro and Stark, the sisterlike staff sergeants, had formed a singing group with Corporals Cintia and Du Ponte. I had never heard four females sing a better harmony. I told them I'd be amazed if they didn't get a recording contract after they were discharged. They just smiled.

I kept circulating around the billet, trying to get to know my people a little better, trying to draw privates like Joyce Jozayt and Mark Durrance and Laura Koris out of their shells. Most of them seemed intimidated, and even when I softened my tone, they kept theirs military terse. The only real friend I had was Chopra. And that had been his choice from the start. I guess most of them needed to trust me before they would open up. Training exercises wouldn't earn me much.

The night before we would ship out, I took a magnificently long shower. I was about to leave my stall when Chopra and Lan came into the latrine. I leaned over to open the door and realized that they hadn't noticed me.

"So what do you think, Jama?" Lan asked.

"I think we'll be all right."

"I don't know. It's gonna be tough with a rookie spear-heading us. Blind leading a whole lot of the blind."

"I thought he did pretty well on the range this week. He didn't get nervous or screw up. He gave the orders, and a couple of times we beat the sim. I like him. He's a good guy. Just give him a chance."

"Oh, I'll give him plenty of rope. He hangs himself with it, that's up to him. You know, he's a conditioned cadet, but he's only showed us his power a couple of times. You saw him fall that day. He's afraid to use it. Know what? This whole conditioning is a bunch of bullshit. Just an experiment that went wrong. And now we got the fucking monster leading us."

"I think we're lucky to have him. I think he's just holding back because he doesn't want to scare us."

"Oh, he's scared me, all right."

"Don't be such a pessimist."

The showers clicked on. I shrank in my stall and stayed there until they finished, dried off, and left.

I hated Lan. I didn't need her to help me feel insecure. I was already an expert.

A few hours before we were all scheduled to board the transports, I caught up with Dina in the mess. She and Beauregard had also been assigned to the same battalion and were headed straight for Alba Patera on Mars.

"Are you scared?" she asked.

"No, not at all."

She punched my shoulder. "Me, too." She sighed, stared off into a thought. "I should have called my parents."

"You didn't?"

"I thought it would be too hard."

"You should have called."

"You know," she began suddenly, "I feel like we've known each other for so long."

"Yeah, we're like brother and sister," I said grimly.

"I love Paul."

"Where did that come from?"

"Every time I look at you, it hurts. So maybe now it's good that I go."

"No, it's not."

She looked away for a moment, then grabbed my head, pulled me forward, and kissed me long and hard. Trouble was, I was caught so off guard that I hardly enjoyed it. The whole time I should have been thinking, *Wow, this is great. Maybe it's only a good-bye kiss, but it's one hell of a good one.* Instead, I kept thinking, *Oh, my god, she's kissing me.*

Slowly, as though the effort pained her, she pulled away,

still cupping my head in her hands. I had never seen her eyes so close. I had never shuddered so hard.

"I love Paul," she repeated. "Because he needs me. There's a lot of pressure on him. He'd fall apart. I know that. But you . . . you're okay, Scott. You'll always be okay." On that note, Second Lieutenant Dina Anne Forrest hurried toward the mess hall's exit.

"You love him because he needs you?" I called after her. "What do *you* need?"

I was hoping she would pause at the door, glance back longingly, and explain. But she strode on with no indication that she had even heard me.

"Okay, sir?" Chopra asked, suddenly at my side and still munching on a nut bar.

It took a moment to realize that the *sir* he had mentioned was, in fact, me. "Yeah," I muttered.

"The Three-seven is ready to depart. The Three-eight and Three-nine are on the line."

"Very well. Answer me a question, Sergeant. Why have you been my liaison and not First Sergeant Lan? You have your own squad to manage. You're violating the chain of command."

"Not exactly, sir. First Sergeant Lan ordered me to serve as liaison, sir."

"That's her job."

"Yes, sir." Chopra's face paled.

"What's going on, Sergeant?"

"Sir, nothing, sir."

I scrutinized him a moment more, saw that his lips were held behind an order from Lan, then decided I would question the first sergeant herself. It was no secret that Lan didn't like me and probably wanted to do all she could to avoid direct contact. But I would not tolerate her pawning off her job to an already heavily burdened squad sergeant. "All right, Mr. Chopra. Let's get ready to load up."

Our assault ship, the SSGC *Triumph*, stood on her multifingered skids below a pentagonal launch tube that had been bored through the mountain. The Rexi-class troop transport more closely resembled a blocky, unmarked freighter than a military attack ship. Her appearance was intentionally deceiving. Stubby wings could be extended for atmosphere operations, and her missiles were mounted to retractable hardpoints and concealed behind dull, black blast plates. Her sizable crew of two pilots and four gunners (most transports were operated by half as many personnel) made me feel a tad more comfortable as I took a seat in the hold with the rest of my platoon. While the *Triumph* was capable of hauling an entire company, the Corps took no chances in packing that many soldiers into a single ship. We were told to expect heavy resistance once we made planetfall.

My tac flashed an alert for incoming message from Paul Beauregard, so I skinned and took the call. "St. Andrew here."

"We didn't get a chance to say good-bye. Just wanted to wish you luck, Lieutenant."

"Uh, and you, too," I answered, surprised that he had even bothered.

"I heard they got a full regiment in Ro, another one in Vosk. We'll match their numbers there, but those Alliance troops have a lot more experience. I'm you, I bleed everything I can out of my conditioning."

"I'll try."

"This is it, Scott. This is what we wanted. We have to be ready for it. Stay in touch if you can."

"You, too." As I de-skinned, I began groping for subtle

reasons why he had called me. Perhaps Dina had mentioned my name; maybe after all we had been through together, she had persuaded Beauregard to say good-bye, which was the least he could do.

No, that wasn't it at all. Dina wasn't thinking about me, and he just wanted to do the right thing to make himself feel better.

Chopra had taken a seat to my right, and I noticed that the seat to my left remained empty. I craned my head to spot First Sergeant Mai Lan seated in the back of the hold, behind all three squads. We still had a few more minutes until launch, so I rose and walked down the center aisle, provoking stares from more than a few privates.

"Lieutenant," Mai Lan acknowledged, shooting to attention.

"Have a seat. Let's talk." I slid past her and took the chair to her left. "You've been avoiding me."

"Sir, I've been extremely busy coordinating with the squad sergeants. As you know, not a single troop has ever seen real combat. And most of us sergeants have only been through the live fire trials, most of them except me. I've fought drones and gunners on ten different colos."

"You're changing the subject, Sergeant. We're about to ship out, and I need to know what's going on here." My hands had already balled into fists.

She stared at me, her gaze as steady as any Pope had shot my way. "Sir, I don't understand, sir."

"You ordered Sergeant Chopra to serve as platoon leader liaison. That's your job."

"Sir, as I indicated, sir, I've been extremely busy."

"Do you and I have a problem, Sergeant? Because if we do, we need to settle it here and now."

"Sir, there's no problem, sir. Equipment's checked out. Our people are ready. Sir."

"Fine. But I want you to relieve Sergeant Chopra of his liaison duties. I want you to report directly to me, as indicated in the OPM, section forty-one, paragraph twenty-two. Would you like me to recite it for you, Sergeant?"

"No, sir. I understand, sir. Sergeant Chopra will be relieved of that duty, sir."

"Now, why don't you come up front and sit next to me. These privates need to see that. And remember, they gave me this platoon. I didn't pick it. Lieutenant Callis was transferred to Mars, and there's nothing we can do about that. I know you two were close. Anyway, I've been trying to make the best of it. I expect you to do the same."

"Sir, yes, sir."

She followed me to the front and sat, her expression unreadable but her gaze darting from me to the cockpit hatch. Chopra gave me a worried look that I shrugged off.

The pilot finally issued the warning cue, and we strapped up and braced for launch. Acceleration dampeners kicked in, but not before our bodies were plastered down into our seats under a shoulder-slumping, four-G blastoff. I closed my eyes and waited out the six minutes until we cleared the planet's atmosphere.

After a curt announcement to that effect, the pilot shut down the thrusters, and as we glided through space via inertia, he told us to stand by. I did not realize anything had gone wrong until a second after the tawt drive had been engaged. Mai Lan turned to me, her jaw falling slack, her eyes bugging before they lifted to the overhead.

13 ❯ **The tawt had** come on so quickly that if my stomach had sunk or my vision had narrowed, I didn't notice. We materialized about seven hundred million kilometers from Lalande 21185, a dim red dwarf star 8.1 light-years from Earth. What gained my attention and Lan's were the multiple missile strikes from an Eastern Alliance destroyer that had targeted us from a range of two hundred and ten thousand kilometers. Our co-pilot went on to say that we had made orbit of planet Gatewood-Callista but that a carrier group had been waiting for us with a pair of destroyers spearheading the formation. For the time being, the only evidence of that harsh reality was the awful drumming on the hull, but that would change quickly.

"Skin up!" I ordered in preparation for a hull breach. "Set for squad frequencies. Remember to report directly to your corporals." I winced over that last order; it was more than a little obvious.

"We're still under fire. Insertion locked in," cried the pilot. "They've set up a few SAM sites. Countermeasures away!"

A horrific bellow from the stern drowned out the pilot's last word, and I felt the wind of escaping atmosphere jerk my head despite the skin's protection. A gaping seam had been torn in the overhead. Beyond the hole lay a smoky tunnel of darkness whose sides lightened and swirled as the pilot plunged into Gatewood-Callista's deep cloud layers, stained blue by an abundance of methane. Not unlike Exeter,

Callista orbited a gas giant, in this case Lalande 21185 b, whose mass was similar to Jupiter's and whose planetary rings extended several million kilometers from the planet.

"Skin damage to stern," reported the pilot. "Hull breach. I still have control."

"All right," the co-pilot said. "Here comes the SAM fire."

For a second, I was paralyzed, imagining the *Triumph* rolling, climbing, and diving to avoid the incoming missiles, their warheads designed to eat through the ship's reinforced skin and alloy hull. Then I wondered if I could take my thoughts into the mesosphere and recognize the bonds of those missiles. What if I could sever those bonds?

Buffeted violently by the pilot's evasive maneuvers, I closed my eyes and called upon that strange new sense.

"First missile prematurely detonating," hollered the co-pilot. "Same for the second. And the third."

"Fourth missile locked on," said the pilot. "It's going to—"

I guess the missile was quicker than me, or the conditioning had failed. The missile struck the troopship head-on, shucking off the last of her skin and blasting apart the cockpit. Past the toothy, sparking remnants of the bow, a grayish brown plain blanketed in frozen methane shone through the moon's perpetual twilight and hurtled toward us. I estimated our altitude at five hundred meters and decreasing fast.

"On your feet!" ordered Sergeant Lan.

"What are you doing?" I asked.

"Sir, preparing for a crash-landing, sir! Platoon, reach for the ceiling."

Then I understood. Our crash would actually involve three impacts: the ship hitting the ground, our bodies hitting whatever was around us, and our organs slamming against our insides. We would first strike the surface with a force that would probably snap our straps and pull our seats from

the deck. While we were skinned, we could sustain that
force, though we would need to transfer the kinetic energy
by bouncing up and down between the deck and ceiling.
That would help ease the third and often fatal impact. I
remembered Pope telling us about those cadets who had
jumped from Whore Face, only to bounce themselves into
IDOs. Lan had chosen a controlled version of the same. It
might work.

We slammed into the surface at a fifty-two-degree angle,
then the entire fuselage unexpectedly flipped over, tossing
us toward the ceiling. Our skins registered the blow with a
sharp rebound that sent us caroming haphazardly toward our
seats. I figured Lan had hand-and-boot rebounds in mind
when she suggested that we reach out, but as I spun back in
midair, having just smashed into my seat shoulder-first, I
gazed across a sea of tangled limbs.

A rock the size of my head shot through the hold, missing
me by less than a quarter of a meter but colliding with a private in the rear. While his skin deadened most of the impact,
the rock still drove him back into his comrades. Six privates
in all tumbled toward the breach in the stern.

The inverted fuselage finally hit the surface, though it
skated on via inertia. The bulkheads shook and thundered.
More debris filtered in from the tear, and by the time the ship
finally stopped, there was so much dust in the cabin that I
ordered everyone to infrared. Too busy to worry about lead-
ership issues, I monitored the squad frequencies as privates
sounded off to their corporals and reported injuries.

My biggest concern was getting my people out of that
wreck. We were a ripe target for Alliance atmoattack fighters, whose pilots might very well zero in on and finish us. As
the corporals began issuing their reports to Lan, I put all
three staff sergeants on evacuation detail—Douglas at the

breach in the stern, Pariseau at what was left of the bow, and Holmes at the standard side hatch, which a private had managed to key open.

"Go! Go! Go!" I roared. "Fall back to the ridgeline west of us. Make sure your tacs are set for autoenvironment."

I hoped that everyone heeded that last admonishment. If there was one thing I knew, it was the change of Gatewood-Callista's surface. Methane melts at a temperature of $-182.5°C$, and our skins needed to account for that fact to provide us with traction and keep us warm in Gatewood-Callista's balmy mid-day temperature of $-199.6°C$. Free of the limitations of a conventional suit, our skins would adjust to meet other demands, like the .899 gravity and an atmosphere so thin that it exerted a pressure on the surface one hundred thousand times weaker than Earth's atmospheric pressure at sea level.

As I hustled through the bow breach, nearly tripping over a torn conduit, I realized that I had larger worries than skin settings. We had crash-landed in a rocky vale, and Global Positioning System reports in my HUV indicated that we were two kilometers south of our designated drop zone. We had landed just a quarter kilometer northeast of Ro's main spaceport, two kilometers of tarmac with a cluster of six heavily shielded control spheres rotating atop a five-hundred-meter-tall arbor. The rest of the mining colony lay below, safe from micrometeorite bombardment. We were supposed to come in from behind the port, blast our way into a maintenance tunnel, pass through several airlocks, then fan out to engage in close-quarters urban combat against a force that had already staked out prime defensive positions. Satellite surveillance piped directly into my viewer indicated that one of the two battalions occupying Ro had been left at the spaceport.

"Lieutenant St. Andrew? Report?" That from my company commander, Captain Elizabeth Bentley-Jones, whose signal originated from the designated drop zone.

"We're on the ground, ma'am. Crash-landed." A platoon report spilled across my display, uploaded to me by Lan, who realized I was linked to the captain and would need that information. I couldn't fault the first sergeant's efficiency. "Two CFs," I told the captain. "Both from the Three-seven." I hesitated as I read a familiar name: Van Buren, Juzza. He had been Chopra's squad corporal. Audis Phrawphraikul, a descendant of Taiwanese ancestors and probably the most earnest and intense corpsman in my platoon, was the other combat fatality. We lost him when the hull had been breached; his seat straps had not been properly fastened. Damned stupid way to go. Van Buren, it turned out, had suffered a heart attack during insertion, and his skin had grown too weak to maintain an atmosphere.

"Ship's crew?" the captain inquired.

"Pilots assumed dead, as are the gunners."

"All right, Lieutenant. I want you to take that ridge and follow it north to grid one-nine, where you'll meet Lieutenant Halitov's platoon. I want both of you conditioned boys in first. Halitov's DBT is already getting to work. He should be ready for you by the time you get there. You got two hours."

"Ma'am, I concur, ma'am. ETA: two hours. We're moving out." I switched to Lan's private channel. I could just make her out through the dim, crimson light. She hunkered near the ship, directing the last pair of privates toward the line. "Sergeant?"

"Sir, yes, sir?"

"We'll regroup at the ride, then we're going north."

"Sir, I know, sir. I monitored the channel. Staff sergeants are already getting the squads moved out."

"Very well. I'll meet you up there."

A moment prior I had admired Lan's efficiency, but her eavesdropping and jumping ahead of me, well, I wondered how long I would let that go. She wasn't doing anything I would not have done, but she seemed a little too comfortable giving orders that should have come from me. I gritted my teeth, found the bond, and bolted ahead of my rifle-toting troops, reaching the ridgeline minutes before them. Had any privates actually been paying attention to me, they would have seen a smear in their infrared displays, a smear that congealed into a human-shaped silhouette.

"Nice trick," Lan said, once she joined me on the ridge. She gave me a dirty look as she tossed me my rifle, which I had forgotten to unclip from beneath my seat.

We looked down on the vale, about two hundred meters below. As a child, I had flown over that very landscape during one of my infrequent trips to the surface. Tunnel traffic was often so severe that people traveling from city to city would hire a surface taxi that would zip them to their destination in a matter of hours instead of days. But that luxury would cost you nearly ten times what you would spend traveling in a ground car through the tunnels. The trains ran regularly, but unless you were a soldier or armed, you would do best to avoid them. I doubted the trains were running now. I doubted anything was functioning normally.

The artillery fire began about twenty minutes into our hike. Conventional shells exploded west of us, releasing "smart schrap," your garden variety sharp-edged, self-propelled projectiles that homed in on skin emissions, struck their targets, rebounded, then homed in again. Kind of like throwing a handful of needles at someone, needles that would repeatedly stick you until you fell.

Lan, Douglas, Holmes, and Pariseau ran near me at the head of the platoon. I detached myself as Chopra, Tamburro, and Stark waved on their squads. I thought I could find the source of that artillery and render the battery useless by cutting the bonds of its targeting computer.

But even as I closed my eyes, a shell went off twenty meters ahead. When I opened my eyes, I saw ten, maybe fifteen of my people floundering on the ground and shrieking as the smart schrap scintillated and poked their combat skins at a rate of one hundred thrusts per second. I watched one, two, three, four skins dwindle. Thankfully, the schrap killed those privates much faster than the hypoxia or low surface pressure would have.

More skins darkened. A half dozen privates ahead charged back to get a look for themselves. In fact, a small crowd of grimacing combatants gathered around the dead and dying.

And that's when the inexperience of my troops really hit me. Didn't they realize the enemy troops manning that battery had locked our location and would now fire for effect? I reached for the bond, came up empty.

I can't recall what I screamed at my people, but my words did nothing. Another round struck about fifteen meters below us, burrowed into the mountain wall, and heaved a great fountain of debris that rained down and booted the loiterers back on course.

Every corporal and two privates in each squad were field medic certified, as was I, though I wouldn't discover that until hours later. We didn't need medical help for those fifteen. Assessing their injuries took three seconds: penetrating trauma to every major organ. We left the bodies behind, but their names burned brilliantly in my viewer: Barker, Borkman, Chastain, Currie, Dehart, Dzoba, Gonzalez, Hyatt, Koris, Shionoi, Silberberg, Ubanhe, Vardikos, Wong, and Yilmaz.

Half my platoon gone. And one of them, Silberberg, looked a lot like Jarrett.

I had spent a week training with them and had reviewed each of their records and registered much more than the mathematics of their loss. I imagined their parents receiving the news and became even more determined to find my own father—if he was still alive.

By the time we reached grid one-nine, I had lost two more troops to artillery fire: Privates Romer and Hussain of the Three-nine, who had been pulling up the rear when the shell struck. My gorge had risen as I watched their deaths.

The grid itself turned out to be a ravine into which Halitov's Drill and Blast Team had burrowed a four-meter-wide hole by employing a trio of extremely powerful particle borers. I stood next to my fellow Callistan as he showed me the hole.

"Anchors are set," he said. "We go about fifty meters down to the tunnel overhead. Beautiful call. We're right in the middle of an airlock. Alloy's the standard five-twenty. My drill team's burning through now. I called for air support to take out that battery. They're en route." He sighed deeply and turned away. "Some fuckin' insertion, huh? That carrier group screwed us. We didn't crash like you guys, but we took a couple hits. Landed here, off the DZ. Hey, you all right?"

Had he noticed my trembling or the tears welling in my eyes? Maybe both. I studied what was left of my platoon. On my order they had strung themselves out along the west side of the ravine, sweeping the zone with their QQ90s. Six left in the Three-seven. Eight in the Three-eight. Six in the Three-nine. And then there was me and First Sergeant Lan. I told myself there was nothing I could have done. We crashed. I moved them out. The artillery struck. But if I had considered taking out the battery sooner, those people might still be alive, and Lan would have had less reason to do what she did.

"St. Andrew?" Halitov called again.

"Yeah, I'm fine. Just lost half my platoon. What could possibly be wrong with me?"

He just shook his head. "The captain wants me and you to drop in first. We'll secure the lock so the rest can rappel down."

"It's good to be home," I mumbled.

"Fuck yeah, it is. Vosk team's already penetrated the alliances' perimeter. We're kicking some ass over there, and no one in that regiment is conditioned. Of course, they're betting a lot on our unreliable skills. Still, I think we'll be all right. And you know what? My platoon doesn't need yours. These people are committed. Better people than we had at South Point—whether they hate me or not. Hey, there's my call. They're finished burning. You ready?"

I nodded.

A private suddenly flew out of the hole, having set his skin's gravity to one quarter. Two more followed him, and all three had riflelike drills balanced in the crooks of their arms. While still falling, they adjusted their tacs' gravity to Earth standard and dropped heavily onto the ice. One hustled over to Halitov, saluted, and said. "Ready to blast, sir. Plates hanging on by threads."

"Drop the bombs," ordered Halitov. "Here that, everybody? We're dropping. Fall back! Fall back!"

While he evacuated with his DBT to the east side of the ravine, where his people had found good purchase and cover within icy grooves, I rejoined my group, crouching beside Chopra. "Talk to me about morale, Sergeant."

"Sir, funny you should ask, sir. I've been wanting to talk to you about that myself."

"I know they're scared. I know you are. Hey, so am I. But it's not like we can change our minds."

"Sir, Lan's been telling us that those people died on the ridge because of you."

"What?"

"She said you ordered us to take that course. She said that was a mistake. She wanted to follow a course along the base, where we'd be better shielded from the artillery. I think she's already won over the staff sergeants."

"What do you mean by 'won over'?"

The ground quaked and splintered as the Electromagnetic Pulse (EMP) bombs detonated below. All electronic equipment, including particle rifles and a long list of other ordnance within a .789-kilometer radius, would be rendered useless. Our skins, powered by our own life forces, were immune to the effect. Research into equipment powered by our life forces had already yielded short-duration links for pilots who could tap into their engines and fly through EMP zones. Weapons powered by our own bodies were still in development, though they would become available before the war's end.

"St. Andrew?" Halitov beckoned. "Let's go!"

I slung off my rifle, hit the manual release on my bayonet. The long, narrow blade shot out. Two-handing the weapon, I jogged toward the hole and met Halitov. "I go first," he said.

"How do you feel?" I asked, questioning his link to the bond.

"I'm good. You're going to see some stuff that'll make Yakata look like an amateur."

"Just jump."

He took in a long breath and stepped into the darkness.

I waited another second before I took the leap and watched Halitov's infrared-enhanced and skinned form drop away from me. He timed his descent well, slowing as he passed through the plate torn away by the EMP bombs, and alighted with surprising grace on the airlock's deck. I landed about a meter to his left, though I stumbled a little, having misjudged my velocity.

The airlock was one of many linking a complex lattice-work of square freight tunnels through which trains hauled ore to pressurized and unpressurized zones for storage. Though the airlock breach would register on Alliance scans, we hoped that the battalion commander would dispatch no more than a squad to check it out. After all, that officer had only about seven hundred troops to keep order among a population of two million spread through several hundred kilometers of chasms and tunnels. The only thing the commander could rely on was the fact that projectile weapons were forbidden on colos. Sure, they would probably encounter a few rebels with illegal arms, maybe even a few with illegal tacs, but for the most part they were dealing with sheep.

Until our arrival.

As we turned toward a pair of transparent permaglass doors about ten meters away and standing twenty meters tall, forty wide, the doors rumbled open about two meters and froze. I exchanged a worried glance with Halitov, then we split up, he darting to the left wall, me the right.

An Alliance Marine, bayonet sticking from his rifle, skin glowing in a camouflage pattern of gray and brown, hustled through the gap, followed by another, who edged furtively along the door until he reached the corner. No doubt more Marines lay behind the doors, probably stretched out on their bellies.

Halitov stole his way along the lock, running on the wall, then leaping down in front of the stunned Marine. He slammed the Marine's rifle out of the way with his own, then, exploiting the bond to circumvent the rebound of skins, he gutted the man with an angry cry that drowned out his victim's shrieking.

I frowned at him for a second before realizing that the other Marine was mine. I charged up on the soldier, who blinked and opened her mouth as I materialized improbably before her. I shook with the notion that I had to kill her, that I should ignore her beautiful blue eyes, high cheekbones, and the fact that somewhere out there was a mother and father. I had seen Halitov kill with impunity. This was my job. My duty. And my failure in the past had resulted in Pope's death. I should have killed that guard—the way I would kill this Marine.

I lowered my rifle, then brought it up, sensing the bond and pushing the bayonet through the Marine's skin and into her heart. One of her ribs scraped along my blade as I drove it deeper and watched blood gurgle up and leak past her lips. She shed her dimming skin and dropped to her knees, one hand wrapped around the barrel of my rifle. I jabbed her again, and her head slumped. She fell onto her side, freeing my blade.

I took one more look at her, then lowered to my knees and puked over my utilities.

Halitov shouted something.

An unfamiliar voice resounded behind me. "Halt!"

There, a meter back to my right, stood another Marine, a tall Hispanic young man with a thin mustache. The tip of his bayonet barely touched the skin over my neck as Halitov arrived in a blur behind him, then punched his back with his blade. I pulled away as the Marine collapsed.

"What the fuck you doing?" Halitov shouted, saliva bubbling around his lips. "There's more behind the lock. Come on, motherfucker!"

I saw what he had—a potent, primordial rage that tainted his blood and set his temples throbbing—and at that moment I needed it. Or maybe I just needed to detach myself from the killing and function like the conditioned machine they wanted me to be. I found a scintilla of reconciliation in thinking about dead troops above. This was for them. I tossed down my rifle, pulled a K-bar from my right hip sheath, another from my left. I razored past Halitov, through the gap, and whirled to find eight more Marines lying behind the door. My entrance brought them quickly to their feet.

It's difficult to describe the rest without portraying myself as a coldhearted and ruthless killer. I have no desire to glorify or condone what I did, or to paint myself as some war hero who deserves medals for, in the end, tearing apart families. I did not want to kill them. But I knew what would happen if I failed. I knew my duty. Truth was, they just worked for the wrong side. If I had met them in a bar, I would have bought them a drink. They would be my friends because, like me, they were soldiers.

Three Marines stood to my right along the airlock doors, with the other five behind me. I lunged for the first one ahead, with blades sticking from the ends of my fists. I slammed my right blade into the first one's heart, then spun left and past him in a *chak* that pulled my right blade from him and drove it into the second. With my back facing that Marine, I caught the third with my left blade, listened to the revelatory hum of dying skins, then gaped at the five now in front of me.

Were it not for the EMP bombs, those Marines would have opened up with so much particle fire that I doubt I could have evaded it. But all they had now were their bayonets, their fists, and their desires to stay alive.

All five charged me.

I leapt above them, pivoted in a one-eighty, then came behind two, driving my blades down so hard that they penetrated the tops of their skulls and dug into their brains. They clanged heads and fell forward as I yanked free my K-bars.

Then, as the remaining three spun to face me, I dashed to their left, kicked up into a *shoru,* then slid by, arms and legs outstretched as I severed each of their jugulars. They dominoed to the deck, skins flickering as they clutched their necks and blood spurted between their fingers.

"Holy fuck," said Halitov from somewhere behind me.

"Alert your staff sergeants," I said evenly, not bothering to look at him. "The lock is secure."

Rumors of how I and Halitov had "easily" taken out an entire squad spread through both platoons. I guess we should have policed up those bodies before allowing our people to pass through the lock. Then again, that kind of carnage did inspire fear. I reasoned I could use a little of that given Lan's recent conspiring.

We humped for about fifteen hours through more of the freight tunnels, encountering only a few drifters who cheered at our entrance, then we finally reached the city limits of Metra, Ro's main municipality, now a ghost town held under martial law, with citizens cowering in their apartments. The downtown district closely resembled big cities on an Earth of centuries past and had been built within a magnificent, circular chasm, two kilometers wide and about a kilometer high. Lights built into the rock helped to simulate daytime, as did a holographic sky operated by members of the artists' guild, who created "weather" as they would a tableau on canvas. Presently, the holo shown a brilliant night sky that, after seeing the real vacuum, seemed exceedingly artificial to me. We kept close to the walls of buildings, darting forward in intervals, with Lan having volunteered to walk point. I had not spoken a word to her about what Chopra had told me. A right time had yet to present itself.

As we hustled across the intersection of L6 and G5 streets, I spotted the dilapidated old building where I had gone to elementary school. I remembered riding the train in from my family's apartment in the narrow tunnels of suburbia. A new school had been constructed three streets down, the old one converted into miners' low-income housing and obviously all but abandoned by the landlord. Even the Colonial Church of Christ's diocese office next door had fallen into squalor.

"St. Andrew?" Halitov called on my private channel. His platoon continued its sweep several streets down to our east.

"Here."

"Something's wrong. Damn, I wish we had those EMPs. I'd drop one right now and not feel bad about it."

"You send out a pulse wave, and there goes the life support system. Anyone without an e-suit is dead—and that's most of the city and 'burbs, including my father. You do that, and trust me—I won't be happy."

"We're gonna get ambushed. I know it. They got our tacs jammed up good. We're just walking into a killing zone."

"Yeah, maybe," I said. "Only they'll do the dying. You good?"

"Still on, though I don't have enough magic to take out eight Marines. You're a fuckin' butcher, you bastard."

I grimaced. "Just keep going. We're only twenty blocks from the rest of the regiment."

He started to say something, but a triplet of particle fire erupted on my chest. I rolled out of the next salvo to see an Alliance Marine leaning out of a fourth-story window across the street. "We're taking fire," I yelled to Halitov.

Perhaps twenty or thirty more Marines rolled to brace elbows on windowsills. So many beads shaved our paths that I ordered everyone into the office building behind us.

"Belay that order," screamed Lan. "Douglas? Pariseau? String out along the avenue ahead. Holmes? Take your people down L-Eight. I'll meet you there. We'll see if we can catch them from behind."

"Belay *that* order!" I shouted. "Everyone into the building. Now! Sergeant Lan? You're relieved of duty. Fall back inside and wait for me."

Her reply came in a whisper: "Fuck you."

And as I retreated to the door behind me, Lan sprinted across the street and met up with Holmes's people. They vanished behind the corner.

More particle fire chewed into the building around me as I swung open the door and ducked into a dark lobby to find

Chopra and two other privates, Kim and Maz, with their backs pressed against the wall to my left.

"What's she doing out there?" I asked the sergeant.

Chopra's lip twisted. "Sir, it's called mutiny, sir."

14 ❯ "**St. Andrew? Where are** you, man? Can't pick you up. I got two squads coming in on the fire zone from flanking positions."

After a few heartbeats, Halitov's words registered; I was still reeling from the fact that First Sergeant Mai Lan had organized and executed a mutiny right before my eyes. Grumbling was one thing—but mutiny? Did she have any idea what her punishment would be? Did she really think she could get away with it? Her foolishness stunned me as much as the act itself.

"Damn it, St. Andrew, are you there?"

"Rooslin," I gasped. And he must have known something was wrong because I rarely used his first name. "I'm in trouble. We're on G-Five. The V-Tah Office Building. But most of my platoon is on Biza Avenue, with another squad on L-Eight."

"We're coming to reinforce."

"Lan's taken over my platoon."

"Say again?"

"My first sergeant has organized a mutiny."

"A mutiny. Holy shit. Know what? You go out there and take out that fuckin' bitch—or I will!"

"I'm thinking we got at least three squads out here posted in sniper positions. I'll work on them first. Then I'll go for her." I craned my head to Chopra and the two privates. "Stay here until I call."

"Sir, aye-aye, sir," answered Chopra. "We'll be ready."

I swore under my breath as I headed outside. Only three people had remained loyal to me.

You'll always be a gennyboy first, an officer second. The only way you'll get respect is by earning it through what you do—and even then they'll talk behind your back. I'm telling you this because you're my brother. You have to hear it.

With my pulse raging in my head, I vowed to kill every Marine posted in the apartment buildings, not because it was my job or because they worked for the wrong side, but because I wanted to show Lan how lethal I could be. I ran into the middle of the street, set down my rifle, closed my eyes, and jumped straight up. I rose about four stories, then wrenched back into a reverse somersault to call even more attention to myself. I didn't know if anyone had ever tried what I was about to do, but it was the only thing I could think of that had a chance of working.

Judging from the report of particle rifles, at least ten beads came my way. I felt each hit, realizing that the number stood even higher at twenty-one. The Marines posted in the buildings were so eager for a target that my appearance probably had them salivating. I stretched the bonds between particles, creating a subatomic wall around myself. As each bead struck that wall, it curved back toward the Marine who had unleashed it.

As I finished my revolution and dropped toward the street, all twenty-one Marines fell away from their windows. Once I hit the street, I scooped up my rifle, ran across the street, then bounded up the apartment building. At three stories high, I veered right, moving across the disorienting field of stone overlaid by a grid of permaglass windows. A Marine stuck out his head from a window off to my right. I swung my rifle, opened fire. The sparking stream caught him squarely in the back of the head. He fell forward onto the sill, writhing violently until the fire penetrated his skin and tore away half his head. Singed hair and flaming tissue plummeted to the street.

Spotting two more Marines posted in the second-story windows of another apartment building ahead, I sprinted all out, reached the edge of my building, then fired myself across the intersection. Spectators on the ground would have seen a soldier flying sideways through the air and landing with bent knees between the tenement's second and third stories.

The two Marines cocked their heads at my impact, and no, they weren't expecting an attack from someone walking on the side of the building.

But I wasn't expecting the third Marine, who had popped up from a window behind me. As I fired at the two in front, that third one cut loose a thick stream that jackhammered into the small of my back. I leaned toward the Marine behind me, continuing to fire at those in front, with one about to fall. I crouched a little, then sprang in a *gozt*, the bullet thrust, picturing myself as a missile spewing particle fire from its tail. I balanced the rifle between my legs, not missing a beat with my stream as I collided head-on with the third Marine. The rebound sent her tumbling toward the street and me blasting boots-first toward the remaining soldier ahead. The rifle slipped from my grip, spun away. The Marine turned his weapon on me, was about to fire, when I plowed into his head, dragging him over the sill, one leg dangling free. My momentum forced me past him, and he let out a scream as he finally dropped to the street, where he would join his comrade and probably bounce until his skin weakened and he broke bones.

I snagged a window frame, came to a muscle-pulling halt,

then shot to my feet and hurried to the end of the building. Hunks of stone and shattered glass pinged off my skin as Marines posted in the building across the street homed in. Eleven muzzle flashes gave up their locations, and I unceremoniously manipulated the bond and turned their fire against them. Nine killed themselves. Two others managed to stumble back into the building and cease fire. "Chopra? Move out. Take the building on the northeast corner of L-Eight. Got at least two Marines in there."

"Sir, aye-aye, sir!"

Thundering footfalls erupted from below. One of Halitov's squads charged along the sidewalk. Three more Marines popped up on the roof of the next building. I charged them, cutting forty-five degrees across and leaping over window after window until I reached the corner of my building and dove across the alley and toward them. They traded fire with Halitov's squad as I tumbled into my landing and withdrew K-bars. All three Marines lay on their bellies, firing furtively over the edge. I came up behind them, a phosphorescent reaper in camouflage. I slashed the first one's throat. The second saw me, began to turn, and I was on him. One, two, three stabs. He fell onto his back, belching blood. The third one got off a few rounds before I leapt on her, released one of my blades, and used my free hand to choke her.

"Don't kill me. *Please.*"

She was my age. Dark hair. Big brown eyes. Someone's daughter.

I used to wonder what I looked like as I hovered over that young woman, her life balanced in my grip. Did I show compassion? Was I absolutely stoic? Did I know my duty?

It took me a long time to realize that at that moment I had become Halitov: rigid, flushed, possessed.

"Please, don't do it. . . ."

Grunting loudly, I slid my blade into her heart, turned it, yanked it out, stabbed again, turned the blade, yanked it out. Stabbed her again. Turned. Yanked. Stabbed. Stabbed. Stabbed. Stabbed until her chest and face were drenched in blood.

"St. Andrew? My squads are in," announced Halitov. "Where are you?"

The K-bar fell out of my hand. I rolled onto my back and, panting, stared at the simulated heavens.

They say it can take years for the guilt to finally hit you. Mine comes in and out like the tide. There are good days and bad. I didn't forget my sense of duty. And I'll never forget the faces.

A thought shuddered me back. Lan still commanded my people. I gathered the blades and took off, monitoring the general frequency.

With a near-blinding rush of adrenaline, I came down the side of a building and found my dear first sergeant hunkered in a doorway, firing on a wide, single-story warehouse atop which a line of Marines had found excellent cover behind an alloy walkway so thick that even our accelerated rounds could not penetrate it. Meanwhile, Halitov had ordered his third squad behind the warehouse, while Lan and the others busied those behind the walkway.

I dropped behind Lan. She held her fire, craned her head, then jammed the rifle into my chest, our buzzing skins driving both of us into opposite walls.

She fired. The round ricocheted off my shoulder as I knocked the rifle up with my forearm, then kept coming, using the bond to neutralize our skins and bring my arm across her throat. Once I had her pinned, I found her tac. Her scream sent shivers through me as I tore off her hand, along with the band. Her skin faded. She gaped at the blood jetting from her stump, at the hand lying on the stone with the tac beside it, then at me.

"You're relieved of command," I said, then remembered my corpsman training. "We'll stop that bleeding with GCX, then we have to rinse that hand in normal saline, bag it up, and get it back to the regiment."

"You fuckin' bastard. Look what you did!"

I de-skinned and leaned toward her, face to face, nothing between us, particle fire still gnawing at the walls outside. "You're done."

"St. Andrew?"

As I cocked my head toward Halitov, who had abruptly ducked into the doorway, I felt a punch to my abdomen, followed immediately by a cold, stinging sensation, like icicles slicing through my innards. My gaze averted.

First Sergeant Mai Lan's K-bar stuck from the center of my chest. I assumed I was about to die and wished I been killed by someone I did not know, someone who did not hate me with those bloodshot eyes, someone who was merely following orders and I happened to be in the wrong place at the wrong time, someone who might, months, years, or decades later, feel a modicum of guilt over taking my life. But dying at the hand of the woman who had destroyed my first command seemed far too unfair and, for the time being, ruined my faith in the universe. I shrank into Halitov's arms.

They patched me up pretty well at Metra Regional Medical Center. Fortunately for me, I had "chosen" to be stabbed just ten blocks from a major civilian hospital with some of the most advanced life-saving equipment on the moon.

Within seven standard days, we took back Ro from the alliances. No major surprise there. Our numbers had been nearly even, but Halitov and I had tipped the scales a little our way. Still, the real push came in the form of civilian rebels, some armed only with clubs, who tipped off our squads and occasionally took on Alliance Marines themselves. Several of the mining gangs even joined forces with a middle-class citizenry they had once terrorized. Our stratified community had finally discovered common ground. If only all of humanity could do the same . . .

Chopra, Kim, Maz, and Lan were the only members of my platoon not arrested and shipped off for court-martial. Even then, jabchatter had it that the mutineers would not be imprisoned but sentenced to serve manual labor jobs that supported the war effort. The colos needed every able-bodied person, malcontent or otherwise. Chopra, Kim, and Maz would be reassigned to another squad. Lan's fate had already been decided. It seems that someone had shoved her out of the doorway and directly into the Marines' line of fire. All sixteen pieces of her had been hauled away in a body bag.

The remainder of my platoon shuttled off, sans dramatic departure. They had no opportunity to spit on me and swear revenge, nor was I granted an opportunity to question them. I was interviewed once by a Guard Corps lawyer, as were Halitov and everyone else. And that was that. No time or money for a lengthy inquest.

They let me leave the hospital after two weeks and gave me a day's leave, after which I was to report back to my regiment for reassignment. Halitov had been granted the same and had already gone off to Vosk, which we had also won back, to search for his parents. Back at the academy, he had rarely spoken of his family, and I learned only when he was leaving Ro that he had a sister a year older than us who was thinking about joining the Western Alliance Navy at about the time he had shipped out to South Point. He might now have a sister fighting for the other side.

I risked a train ride back to my old apartment building, a modest, two-story affair lined up with a thousand others within an oval-shaped tunnel. The hydroponic lights had been shattered by particle fire, most of the grass had turned yellow, and the shrubs stooped in leafless decay. Despite the occasional pedestrian or ground car, the place appeared deserted and forlorn of all hope.

The steps to my second-story front door produced a squeaking that gave me pause. I walked up and down those steps several times, listening to my youth.

"Who's out there?" came a familiar voice from behind the door.

"Dad?"

The door cracked open to reveal a tired-looking eye that abruptly grew wide. "Scott . . ."

My father rushed from behind the door and nearly knocked me off the landing with his embrace. "It was . . . I thought I'd never . . ."

"Take it easy, Dad. Let's go inside." I led him into the apartment, stunned as I got a better look at him: beard untrimmed, white hair thick and matted, tunic and slacks so wrinkled that he must have slept in them.

We crossed into the living room, now a murky, open space with furniture piled against the windows. I gagged over a nasty order emanating from the kitchen, and once there, I stared in horror at the piles of garbage stacked near the back door, at the dirty dishes towering up from the sink, at the food caked all over the stove. My father had always been anal retentive about keeping our home neat.

"They wouldn't let us take out the trash. Turned off the water until just yesterday. It'll take a while for the smell to get out of the bathrooms. Sorry you have to see it this way."

He reached out, touched my lieutenant's star, and recoiled as though he had contaminated his finger. "You're already commissioned? And Jarrett, too?"

I wasn't ready to tell him about Jarrett. Maybe I should have. Waiting did not make a difference for either of us.

He let out a long sigh and massaged his eyes. "So what're you doing here? What happened at South Point?"

We sat, and I gave him the abridged version, omitting the conditioning and finishing up with the crash-landing, my stabbing, and the fact that I would now spend three precious days with him before heading back to the war. My failure to include Jarrett in the summary should have raised questions, but I think he had already discerned the truth and had reasoned that if I did not voice it, it would not be real.

"My office has been closed since the attack. Nothing to do but read. Only thing on the screen is the military channel. Bunch of threats and brainwashing, and I've seen every movie in our collection at least twice. God, I heard about the Seventeen coming here. I wouldn't have imagined that you'd be with them. It's a miracle."

"Well, Ms. Brooks worked that out for me and this other lieutenant, guy named Halitov. He comes from Vosk."

"I see. You know, I'm looking at you now, and I can't believe I endorsed this." He tugged at the sleeve of my black utilities. "I don't want to sound negative, but you'll go out there and die. And for what? Loyalty to the colonies?" He rose and retrieved a pamphlet from the countertop. "Someone shoved this under my door. It's propaganda from a rebel group. Look at the quote there."

I read the words: "Histories are more full of examples of the fidelity of dogs than of friends. Alexander Pope."

"In all their rhetoric, that's the only thing that makes sense."

"Dad, these rebels helped us take back the city."

He snickered. "You ever wonder why?"

"Yeah, because this is their home. It's our home."

"So that makes them loyal to the colos?"

"Yeah."

"Scott, they're loyal to their own desires. That's it. And that's our damned curse. We're a greedy, selfish bunch. And we're poised to kill ourselves."

My father, the mineralogist, the pragmatic scientist who had little use for philosophy and had spent the better part of his life staring at magnified core samples, had voiced one of his rarely heard opinions about something beyond our colony. The Alliance occupation of Gatewood-Callista had robbed him of much more than decent living conditions. He had always had a comfortable cushion of research on which he would lay his head at night and sleep, dreaming of his minerals and venturing no farther than Ro and its environs. The science that had always reassured him had been stripped away. He had finally realized after all these years that there was a magnificently large galaxy out there, a galaxy that encompassed our moon and affected it for the better and for the worse. He could no longer deny that.

After a meal of canned meat and vegetables that actually made military food seem appealing, we spent several hours walking around the old neighborhood. My father pointed out damage caused by the Marines and swore over their actions. We visited Katka and Vivian, two of my father's scientist friends. The elderly couple asked me to describe my war experiences and probed me until the details became too painful. The two women gazed at me with admiration, the kind I had expected from my father, but I realized that they could offer their support and remain fully exempt from losing a son. They asked about my brother. Before I could answer, my father suggested that we go.

Programmed twilight befell the suburb as we returned to the apartment. My father switched on the screen, and one wall of our living room lit with a news report. Members of my battalion stood at posts on every corner of the city. Citizens had emerged from their apartments in droves to applaud the Guard Corps's actions. One exuberant group hoisted a private into the air and carried him down H10 Street, while a female reporter narrated the action. My father called down the volume and stared grimly at me. "How long you think this'll last?"

"I don't know."

"The Seventeen can't keep troops here indefinitely. Maybe they'll leave a small force, but we'll be attacked again. Maybe the next time there won't be any survivors."

Though I had already prepared my retort, I held it back. My father's depression was speaking for him. He had lost a wife, a son, and another would soon tawt off. At the moment, he could find nothing positive in his life, and all I could do was try to understand.

He cooked me another meal, apologizing for his meager culinary skills, then produced a bottle of real Kentucky bourbon and poured us glasses. Though my father and I had shared drinks before, we both coughed against the burns with an air of reverence.

Pleasantly numb, I headed off to the room I had shared with Jarrett for most of my life. Our gelracks slid out of the wall, and I pulled out Jarrett's and climbed into it, sweet traces of his cologne still clinging to his pillow. I spent maybe an hour just staring through the shadows at our Guard Corps paraphernalia, at the posters of bikini-clad women that adorned our walls, at Jarrett's collection of colonial flags, at my collection of rare minerals given to me by my father, at the conventional photographs of our family on vacation last year in the winter resort at Isyil. That vacation was the last time we had all been together.

Muffled footsteps resounded near the door. I pretended to be asleep but kept one eye open to a slit. My father paused in the doorway. He stared at me sleeping in my brother's bed, covered his face with a hand, then turned away, weeping softly.

I barely slept, despite the reassuring familiarity of my old room. I could not decide whether my visit was a happy homecoming or the somber return for a funeral. Back at South Point, I would lie in my rack and address my homesickness by pretending I was back in my old bed and chatting with Jarrett. But now I wanted nothing more than to be in my old rack at South Point, lulled to sleep by the *shraxi* and triplets and shouted awake by Pope.

In the morning, my father and I ate in silence. Afterward, I told him I had to get back.

He shrugged. "Tired of being depressed by your old man, huh?"

"No."

"Well, it's okay."

"Dad, I should tell you about Jarrett."

He went to the kitchen window, eyes growing vague. "Just tell me how."

I described our rushed conditioning and about how Sysvillian had notified me of Jarrett's death.

"They didn't tell us everything about that conditioning," my father rasped when I finished. "They never said it was experimental, let alone Racinian."

"We learned more about it when we got there. I guess it was all classified. They wouldn't let me see his body."

"And they haven't contacted me. This is bullshit. Once the comm's up again, you can bet I'll be contacting them. I'll demand to see those remains. I'll hire an attorney if I have to. I don't care if there's a war on or not."

"I have to go."

He slapped palms on my shoulders, gazed hard at me, soaking up as much as he could, then locked me in a final hug. "I love you, Scott. Please come home."

I hurried outside but lingered on the bottom step. Then I turned back and saw my father staring at me from the kitchen window. He gave a ragged salute, which I returned.

Martial law had been lifted, and people jammed the train back to Metra. I swore over having not changed into civilian clothes. My uniform had me answering so many questions that I eventually retired to a rear car, found a seat in the back, and asked not to be bothered. I thought about my father, alone in that little apartment, and I began feeling sorry for him, for me, for our family. Things had happened quickly, and more often than not, I could find no reason in them. I wondered what would happen if I got off the train and took a taxi back. Could my father hide me from the Guard Corps? Would he? Did he even deserve to be placed in that position? I wanted to blame someone for what had happened. I wanted a name. But the enemy had become amorphous and out of reach, its will carried out by the unsuspecting.

The train doors finally opened at my stop. I got off and trudged my way to Battalion Command, which had been established on the first floor of a bank building, while the Quonset huts of a more permanent post were being constructed across the street, in an open lot. I found Captain Elizabeth Bentley-Jones's desk. The company commander narrowed blue eyes on me as deep grooves branched her cheeks. She had probably grown up on a warm world, its sun having weathered her face. Or, perhaps, she wore the burdens of command a little too heavily. "Your folks live here, don't they, St. Andrew?"

"Yes, ma'am. I saw my father, ma'am."

"That's good."

"I'm ready for reassignment."

"Conditioning makes you gung ho, too?"

"Ma'am, I'm not sure, ma'am."

She eyed the chair beside her desk. "Sit, Lieutenant."

As I complied, she rooted around in her breast pocket, came up with something, and held it tight in her palm.

"We haven't confirmed the number yet, but we think you and Halitov killed as many as sixty enemy troops. Those may very well stand as the highest kill ratios of single combatants engaging in hand-to-hand."

"Other people were conditioned before us. I'm sure given the same circumstances, they would've done better than us. I'm still not even sure how this all works—or even why it does."

"Don't be modest, Lieutenant. You're arguably the most powerful conditioned officer ever produced. And the Seventeen has every intention of rewarding you for your efforts, though I wish we had the resources to put together something more formal." She held up a first lieutenant's star between her thumb and forefinger. The star matched the one already pinned to my breast, save for the princess-cut sapphire in its center. "Approval just came in this morning. Congratulations."

I accepted the star. "Thank you, ma'am."

"It took me ten years to become a captain, young man. Maybe it'll take you another ten weeks, if that." She eyed my birthmark. "The underdog gets his revenge. I was the outcast in my family. But I've made out better than any of my brothers and sisters. I've been in all seventeen systems, seen things they'll never see. I don't regret anything. Neither will you."

"Yes, ma'am."

"Now, as for your reassignment, well, they've asked me to loan you out to the Thirty-first Regiment, Quasar Company, First Battalion, First Platoon. They're on Mars. Thaumasia region."

Mars. Dina and Beauregard were there. Was it sheer coincidence that I was bound for their sector? Not at all. For a time, though, I thought my transfer was solely orchestrated by the Guard Corps.

"Battalion commanders are putting together some kind of black op. I don't know much, but they're teaming up a bunch of conditioned officers. Halitov's going with you. As a matter of fact, he cut his R&R real short, too. Got in last night. We're bivved at the hotel down the street. You'll find a rack over there. You still have forty hours until your transport arrives, so I suggest you head over and relax. Could be your last break for a long time."

"Yes, ma'am. I'll do that, ma'am. And one more thing. At the hospital they said I don't need a shrink because all of my defense mechanisms are built into my cerebroed data. But a lot of that stuff I still can't get to."

"You want to talk to somebody?"

"I don't know. Maybe. Got a minute?"

"Lieutenant, I wish I did. Besides, I don't think I'd be

much help. This might come as a surprise, but while a lot of people recently died under my command, I have never taken a life myself. Were I you? I'd go talk to my buddy, Halitov. He might be the only one who really understands."

Because Halitov would not open his locked door, I enlisted the aid of two privates, who summarily smashed it in.

We found the newly promoted first lieutenant lying naked in his hotel room bed. He had slashed open his wrists and had cut a series of curving lines across his pectorals, like the gills on a fish. He had smeared blood all over his face and neck, and now it cracked and flaked off. He held his first lieutenant's star between his gritted teeth.

The two privates turned back and retched. I stood frozen a moment until I realized that the son of a bitch had not killed himself. His gaze seemed vacant and focused on the ceiling, but his chest did, in fact, rise and fall.

"Rooslin?"

He spit out the star. "Get the fuck out."

"He ain't dead," said one of the privates.

I turned to him, a soldier about my age. "Leave."

Actually, the two could not wait to get out of there. I closed the broken door after them, then approached Halitov. "The captain told me that I should talk to you. She said you might understand."

"Oh, I do," he snapped. "I understand everything. I see through it all. You can pile five million kilometers of bullshit in front of me, and I'm lookin' right through it like it's a fuckin' window and I'm seeing my mother and stepfather lying there in their apartment, both fuckin' shot in the head and fuckin' flies are buzzing around 'em. And nobody's even gone in to fuckin' check on them. They've been lying there for weeks, and nobody's gone in to check on them.

Nobody's gone in to check on them. NOBODY'S GONE IN TO FUCKIN' CHECK ON THEM!"

"I'm sorry."

"Bullshit! What the fuck do you care? Not your parents. Ain't your sister who joined the Alliance Navy. Have you ever smelled a body after it's been dead for two weeks? How would you like to carry one out of your apartment? How would you like to carry your dead mother's corpse out of your apartment? Do you know how that locks you in? How that seals you up? How they laugh at you? They're not gonna let you out until you're fuckin' dead—just like her." He sprang from the bed, stood in front of me, a ghastly, wounded being, then raised his fists, howled at the ceiling, and passed out.

I skinned up and got on the general frequency, requesting a corpsman to come up and help me get Halitov to the hospital, where we would spend our remaining time before shipping out. I thought for certain they would issue Halitov some form of medical discharge or time away to grieve. They pumped him with drugs and sent him on his way.

As we boarded the transport to tawt out to Mars, I realized that the captain had been right. Halitov was the only one who really knew how I felt. Trouble was, neither of us really knew how to listen.

PART 4

The Walking Wounded

15 ❯ **Our transport pilots** initiated a tawt drop to Mars. We arrived in geostatic orbit, our computer calculated known threats, then it tawted us to evasion inclinations as needed. Nine separate tawts later, our stomachs felt as though they had been removed and tied around our ankles. Speckled curtains of darkness obscured our peripheral vision and would not fade for several hours, according to one of the gunners.

While our original orders called for a drop into the Thaumasia region, we received an addendum as we broke into the atmosphere. We headed southeast of the original coordinates and eventually landed on a makeshift tarmac approximately one kilometer northeast of Darwin Crater in Mars's southern hemisphere. We skinned and stumbled out of the hold, along with about twenty other officers we had picked up at Kennedy-Centauri.

Halitov's cuts were nearly healed, and the sleeves of his utilities hid most of the powdery residue of synthskin. I knew his happy pills were beginning to wear off when he paused on the ramp, turned to me, and muttered on my private channel, "They killed my fuckin' parents. They're all gonna die."

"I'm sure they will. Let's go."

Most of the others had been to Mars before and glanced perfunctorily at heavily cratered uplands. Scott St. Andrew the tourist ventured a few meters from the ramp, raised his hand to the small orb of Sol, haloed in blue by atmospheric distortion, and marveled at the rust-colored terrain that terraformers centuries earlier had sworn would soon support vegetation. They might have pulled it off, were it not for the lack of funding. Instead, Mars continued on in slow decay, as it had for millions of years. We slapped mining complexes on the planet, and over the past two centuries depleted nearly seventy-five percent of its resources. When we were finished, we would simply abandon it in favor of more lucrative sites.

"Lieutenant St. Andrew?"

A stocky corporal whose skin had been set to crimson camouflage turned his face transparent and cocked a bushy brow as he crossed in front of me.

"Yes?"

"I'm here to escort you and Lieutenant Halitov below."

The corporal led us along the tarmac, toward a hemispherical bunker entrance that had risen from the regolith. We walked down a long flight of portable steps, then trudged along a freshly burrowed tunnel with permafrost laced through its heavily grooved walls. We reached an airlock, passed through, and came into one of ten or twenty interconnecting hallways that divided a series of twenty or thirty small compartments. The corporal suggested that we deskin, then he read our expressions as we stared at the unadorned metal. He explained that the entire command center had been set up in a matter of hours. The walls, floors, and ceilings folded in on themselves, as did the halls. You simply burrowed a chasm large enough, inserted your alloy sections, and hydraulics mounted to the exterior plates did the rest. The corporal compared the setup to pulling the cord on an inflatable life raft. He was approximately one second into his explanation when the cerebroed data regarding temporary command post operations flashed in my head, with images lifted directly from training holos. I feigned my interest and nodded politely.

At the end of the hall, he keyed open a door. We sighed at the basic briefing room. Lightweight folding chairs formed a semicircle around a rather beat-up-looking table where about fifteen or so cerebros had been haphazardly stowed.

Two officers whose blue utilities IDed them as pilots sat in the front row and glanced back at our entrance. One rose, a dusky-skinned man whose gaze targeted my cheek. I suddenly realized he was a captain and snapped to. "Sir."

"Stow that, Lieutenant." He proffered a hand. "I'm Andropolus, Andrew A. I'll be your G-Twenty-one pilot. And this is my right, Lieutenant Caylyn Goosavatic—but don't let her name scare you. She's really a nasty bitch once you get to know her."

Goosavatic f-ed him off under her breath, then lit a generous smile. "Gentlemen, we've heard a lot about you. Jabchatter, of course, but some of it has to be true, right? Especially the part about how amorous you are."

Halitov gazed quizzically at me. I guess he didn't know the word, and I was not about to explain it to him. "Any idea what the op is?" I asked Goosavatic.

She shrugged. "Demo job, probably. We've been runnin' a lot of them. Alliances have remote sensors all over the place. We take 'em out; they drop new ones back in. With those sensors in place, we can't make a move without them knowing about it. Still, I got a feeling this one's a lot hotter than that."

"For once, she's right," said Andropolus.

The door opened, and in stepped seven more guardsmen. It took nearly ten minutes to complete introductions. I met Second Lieutenant Richard Ramsey, a graduate of South

Point two years prior; Second Lieutenant Linda Paris, a South Point alumna—class of 2098; Sergeants Pitar Zhai, Mana Ochoa, and Casey Stark, three young, raven-haired women who boasted of being the only noncommissioned officers ever conditioned; Corporal Regina Hooker, an angel-faced blonde who had absolutely no idea why she was present; and Second Lieutenant Joseph Lee, a nervous-looking giant of a man and a graduate of ROTC at the University of Kennedy-Centauri. As we dispersed and took seats, the door opened once more. Paul Beauregard paraded into the room, in mid-conversation with Dina, who suddenly shifted her gaze away and scanned the group until she found me. Beauregard gritted his teeth as she hurried over, hunkered next to my chair, and rubbed my hair, which had been coming in nicely since the shaving at South Point. "First Lieutenant?" she asked, spying my star.

"It's just a pin."

"Now you and Paul outrank me."

"And so do I," Halitov said, leaning over and tapping his own first lieutenant's star.

"I heard about Callista," she said. "Then I heard you were coming here. I couldn't believe it was so fast. I mean, are you all right?"

"Ten-hut!" Beauregard shouted.

Quasar Company commander Captain David Doyle hustled into the room, ordered us as we were, and began distributing cerebros. Another five minutes passed, and two more corporals joined us, the dour-looking Jenta Heloise and the bored Toma Ric, both temporarily transferred from the Third Platoon. In all, sixteen of us had crowded into the small room. Dina wound up in a seat next to Beauregard, but twice I caught her stealing looks at me.

Halitov raised his hand, just as Doyle was about to begin.

"Yes, Lieutenant?"

"Sir, I'm not sure if you're aware of this fact, but Forrest, Beauregard, St. Andrew, and myself still haven't completed our Accelerated Assimilation Training. And I know that at least St. Andrew and I have been thrown into combat without that training. We heard we might get it. Any idea when? I'm hoping before this next op."

Halitov impressed me. He sounded somewhat rational and less like the psychotic I had carried out of that hotel room.

"Sorry, Lieutenant, but I haven't received any information regarding your AAT. I was told we could borrow you, and I assumed you were fully trained. That's not the case?"

Beauregard stood. "Sir, while we haven't received extensive AAT, there's no reason to believe that we're not fit for duty, sir. I think Mr. Halitov is just being a little modest, sir. We're all well aware of the numbers he and Mr. St. Andrew racked up on Gatewood-Callista."

"Very well, then. Mr. Halitov? Your request is duly noted and will be forwarded to Regimental Command. In the meantime, you all have a briefing to download. When everyone's finished, we'll discuss your concerns. Begin."

I slid the cerebro behind my head, then rolled my wrist to read my tac. The filename Doyle wanted us to download scrolled up on my small screen. I tapped to accept.

A warm feeling spread through me, as though I were very cold and had just downed eight ounces of brandy. I could not explain the sensation; perhaps it was in realization that I miraculously knew every detail of the upcoming mission: Classified Black Op 2111X, Mars Campaign, Thaumasia Region. Or maybe the mnemosyne in my head were up to something.

Halitov ripped off his cerebro. "Fuckin' suicide," he mumbled.

"Excuse me, Lieutenant?" asked Captain Doyle.

"Nothing, sir," Halitov replied, shifting in his seat. "I've finished the download, sir."

I raised my hand.

"Lieutenant St. Andrew?"

"Sir, I'm a little confused. We're supposed drop in on the west side of Argyre Planitia and take out some comm dishes and a subterranean intelligence headquarters that coordinates data from their remote sensors."

"That's right, Lieutenant. We've tried taking out the sensors, but they keep replacing them. Now it's time to go to the source. We knock out that headquarters, we blind them for ten or as many as fifteen hours. Then we move in with our offensive in Valles Marineris. Where's the confusion?"

"Well, sir, I understand that SAM sites or EMP prohibit getting atmoattacks in close enough for an air strike, and I also understand that artillery fire from our end might take out the dishes but won't penetrate to the depths we need it to. I also realize that the alliances can use personnel via their tacs to temporarily power the facility, so EMPs are no good. I guess I'm wondering why we're blowing it up at all. Seems to me that they can set up another intelligence headquarters as fast as we set up this command post, sir."

"Lieutenant, you're absolutely right. I wish I had an answer for you. But our orders come down from Battalion Command. We must assume that they've considered your reservations. In any event, we're not here to debate the orders. Our job is to carry them out. Understood?"

"Yes, sir." I tried my best to hide my disgust. Halitov's whispered epithets hardly helped.

"Sir, as op commander, I'd like to, with your permission, make a few adjustments to our assignments," said Beauregard.

Doyle frowned. "Such as?"

"Well, first I'd like to switch Halitov and St. Andrew. I want Halitov to lead the reconnaissance team, and I want St. Andrew with me as op executive officer."

"I'll approve that."

I knew exactly what Beauregard was doing. I had originally been assigned to lead the recon team—with Dina and Lee. Beauregard wanted to keep me away from Dina, and what better way than to promote me to Op XO?

What Beauregard had not counted on was Halitov's protest. "Sir, if the op commander intends to replace me with Lieutenant St. Andrew, then I'd appreciate hearing some justification for my removal, considering that Mr. Beauregard just went on about the numbers I generated on Callista."

Doyle hoisted his brows at Beauregard.

"Sir, it's a matter of temperament. Halitov's more visceral, St. Andrew more cerebral. I want a thinker as XO. I'd rather spearhead us with a killer."

"That's biased and subjective," Halitov argued. "Where's your evidence?"

Beauregard drew in a long breath, closed his eyes a moment, then nodded. "I got a hospital report that says you tried to kill yourself. I got an obituary of your parents. I got an Alliance Navy assignment sheet with the name Victoria Halitov on it. Do you want me to go on? I got stuff from when you were a kid. Stuff that almost ruled you out of getting into South Point. Psychological reports from a primary school in Vosk. Major aggression problems after a particular incident wherein you were—"

"That's enough," hollered Doyle. "Mr. Halitov, you will accept your position as recon commander. Are we clear?"

Halitov's sneer would not falter. "Yes, sir."

I guess Beauregard had counted on Halitov's protests and had thoroughly researched his life, if not all of our lives, which I realized was within his right as an officer. We had signed away our right to privacy when we had signed up with the Corps.

Regina Hooker spoke up. "I have a question, sir. I guess I'm on the DX team because of that last job we did. I'm happy to be here, and I know if we can get in there, we'll set up a nice bang. But intell indicates that there's a garrison of about sixty, and they're dug in really well. No doubt, there's at least a squad or two within the headquarters itself, plus techs and administrative, who are probably armed." She gestured flagrantly to the group around her. "What's wrong with this equation?"

"Corporal, I understand you haven't had much experience with conditioned personnel," Doyle replied. "If all goes well, those numbers won't present a problem."

"Sir, has anyone mentioned to you that our conditioning tends to randomly shut down?" asked Halitov.

"I'm well aware of that, Lieutenant. Not all of you have that problem, and it doesn't happen to all of you at the same time. It's a risk we have to take."

"So we can blow up an intelligence headquarters that they'll replace in a week," someone muttered behind me.

I tossed a look over my shoulder. Sergeant Casey Stark shook her head.

"Now, in deference to Lieutenants Halitov and St. Andrew, who've just come down from a rough tawt, we won't launch for another two hours. Until then, I suggest you gear up, eat, pray, do whatever it is you do. Any other questions? Negative? Then you're dismissed."

Dina cut me off before I reached the door. "There's a little mess hall. Want to go?"

I lifted my chin toward Beauregard, who conversed heatedly with Doyle. "I don't want to cause trouble."

She smiled her perfect smile. "You won't."

"You figure it out?"

"What?"

"If you love him."

She grabbed my arm and pulled me outside. "Hey, you know we were up near Alba Patera. I'll tell you one thing, you won't believe what you can do with the quitunutul arts here. Variations in point-three-nine G. Wild stuff. You don't even have to try for it. It's just there."

"Wait a minute. I want Halitov to come."

She recoiled. "Really? Wasn't it yesterday that he paid someone to cut your rope?"

"I don't want him to be alone."

Back in the briefing room, I found Halitov glued to his chair, hands clasped behind his head.

"We're going to eat," I said, cocking a thumb over my shoulder.

"You want a fuckin' captain's star?"

"No. Just wondering if you want to come."

He huffed, slapped palms on his hips, and stood. "Tell you one thing, if they're going to send me out to risk my life, they'd better be servin' up some fuckin' gourmet food."

Dina sat opposite Halitov and me, stabbing her tofu burger and talking so fast we could barely keep up. She told us about a battle her platoon had fought about a kilometer east of Olympus Mons. Western Alliance crab carriers had dropped in just before the EMP bombs had gone off. About three thousand troops on each side had clashed in a scene cut and pasted from a medieval warfare file. She and Beauregard had been assigned to platoons in the rear guard, and only when the battle had begun to look bleak did Doyle cut them loose. I don't know what happened next. She refused to go on, narrowing her eyes against tears. She did add that they had pushed the line forward several kilometers but that the next day a score of carriers had dropped in. Alliance troops had easily won back ground that nearly two thousand guardsmen had given their lives to claim.

"Remember that day in the billet when we chose sides?" Halitov asked out of nowhere.

Dina and I nodded.

"Boy, did we fuck up."

I looked at Dina, pursing my lips and asking her with my eyes to excuse his behavior.

Halitov rose and kicked away his chair. "I heard somebody say we can shower." His gaze favored Dina. "Where's it at?"

"End of the hall. Make a right, then a left. There's a sign."

Sans thank-you or good-bye, he left. I thought of going after him, but he was just going to take a shower. He'd be all right.

"I have to take orders from that?" asked Dina.

"Just watch him for me."

"He tried to kill you."

"And he saved my life." I leaned toward her, wanting to discuss more important matters. "So, you figure it out yet?"

She leaned back, folded her arms over her chest. "Nothing to figure out."

"Your mind's set?"

"Yeah. I'm just so worried about telling him. I feel like I led him on. I just feel terrible."

Admittedly, when it comes to relationship matters, I am dense. I had no idea what she was talking about for the first few seconds, and my face bannered that fact.

"Why are you looking at me like that?"

"Like what?"

"Don't you understand? I want to be with you, Scott."

"With me?" I made a silly grin. "Are you sure? Paul has connections to keep you together. And he really loves you."

Her face grew flush. She squirmed. "I just wish there was an easy way to tell him. I don't know what he's going to do. . . . But I don't want to think about that now. We have some time. This place is small. We can hide."

I was three seconds away from darting out with her and ripping off my clothes when Halitov pounded back into the room. "I can't find the fuckin' shower. I can't find it! I can't find it!" He smote a fist on the wall and began to cry.

"It's all right," I said. "I'll help you find it. Come on." I looked to Dina. She understood.

The G21 Endosector Armored Troop Carrier waited on the landing pad like a quad-winged predator aching to thunder off on a hunt. I spotted Andropolus and Goosavatic atop the ATC's beaklike bow and behind the seamless, seed-shaped canopy. As we drew closer, the wind whipped up Mars's powdery sand, and a pair of dust devils tangoed in the distance.

"How're you feeling?" I asked Halitov.

"You referring to my connection to the bond or my fucked-up mental state?"

"Got my answer."

"Don't worry about me. Just watch your step out there. There's gonna be bodies all over the place. I wouldn't want you to trip."

"You know what they say about revenge," I began.

"Yeah. Get some."

"It won't make you feel better."

"We'll see."

Captain Doyle saw us off from the foot of the ATC's gangway, and I saluted him as I entered the hold. Jumpseats equipped with old-fashioned safety bars you pulled down over your shoulders ran along the bulkheads. I scrambled to find a seat away from Dina, so as not to make her feel uncomfortable. I assumed she hadn't told Beauregard yet, but maybe she had. I had been with Halitov for the rest of our two hours before shipping out and hadn't been able to speak privately with Dina. I chanced a look down the row, glad that she had chosen to sit away from the colonel's son.

We clicked the stocks of our QQ90s into their deck mounts between our legs, lowered our bars into place, then waited for Beauregard to acknowledge our vitals and the status of our equipment. The check-in went off smoothly, and he signaled to Andropolus. Turbines wailed, and their vibration eeled up into our seats. I shook off a chill; for a moment I thought I had never been on a ship so small yet so powerful. Then the cerebroed training crashed in and reminded me that I had traveled on ATCs hundreds of times. I felt accustomed to the angles forced on me by the jumpseat.

In an effort to evade the Alliance's sensors, Andropolus kept us within three meters of the surface. To awe and distract us, he activated a holo readout captured by the ATC's nose camera. The center of the hold radiated with images of the rock-strewn landscape rolling by at a dizzying pace. He abruptly banked hard west, slipping stealthily into the mountainous terrain encircling Argyre Planitia, an impact basin whose broad, rugged rim extended from three hundred kilometers to eight hundred kilometers from its center.

"Two minutes," cried Beauregard over the general frequency.

Second Lieutenant Lee, who sat to my right, closed his eyes and whispered something unintelligible, a prayer perhaps. I liked Lee. His fresh face invited conversation, and I had watched him spar with Sergeant Stark, who sat to my right. She had droned on and on about what a waste the whole mission was, and when she had finally finished, Lee conceded to several of her assertions while making an eloquent and fully supported claim in favor of the Valles Marineris offensive and our small contribution.

Yes, I liked Lee. I liked all of them. But I was glad that we were little more than acquaintances.

"All right! Here it comes," said Beauregard. "Recon's out first. There'll be a pass off to your right. Take it. Remember, we're about a quarter klick east of the target. Security team follows. DX team? You fall back with me and the XO."

XO. I had to remember that was me.

"Ten seconds to TD," reported Andropolus. "Ramp engaged."

A band of light woke across the top of the stern, then widened as the ramp rumbled down.

"Careful out there," said Goosavatic. "Gale force winds. Visibility's down to a hundred meters and falling fast."

"Okay. Ready on the line," ordered Beauregard.

Halitov slammed up his safety bar, unclipped his rifle, then charged to the rear of the hold and paused at the red line painted along the ramp's edge. Dina stomped up behind him, and I spied for her glance; none came. Lee unloosed himself and fell in behind them, as did the security team: Paris, Stark and Ochoa. I waited for Ramsey, Zhai, and Hooker of the DX crew to shoulder their bulky packs and form up, then I stood, freed my own rifle, and joined Beauregard at the end of the line. Corpsmen Heloise and Toma would remain on the ship and establish a prehospital emergency surgical unit while Andropolus hid the ship between mountains. When he came back for us, Heloise and Toma would be more than ready to care for the injured.

"Hey, Rooslin," I called on his private channel. "You need help, you call."

No response.

"Squad? Are you ready?" cried Beauregard.

"Sir, we're ready, sir!" they shouted.

"Very well. Go! Go! Go!"

As Halitov faded into the swirling wind, followed closely by Dina, I looked to Beauregard, who had sounded so much like Pope that I wondered if he realized it.

"Déjà vu?" he asked.

"Yeah."

"Wish he was with us. And Scott, keep an eye on my Dina for me, will you?"

Guilt stricken, I nodded, bounded down the ramp, and sprinted right. A string of hillocks carried me up a half dozen meters, and I caught a glimpse of the security team through draperies of dust. The three had already readjusted their G settings and stomped on as though in Earth-normal gravity. I kept my setting to Mars-normal, taking three- and four-meter strides.

Once Beauregard and I found a position up top, we would send out the security people to establish a perimeter. Halitov, Dina, and Lee would journey on to the HQ to gather as much intell as they could. Cannon emplacements and garrison numbers had probably changed since the recordings we had downloaded at the briefing.

Beauregard, his G setting also Mars-normal, sailed by me, then floated down into a gully and wasted no time ascending the next hill. The hillocks heaved into a significant ridgeline bearing an uncanny resemblance to the one back on Gatewood-Callista. I wanted to tell Beauregard that we should not follow that line, but I doubted he would listen to my superstition.

"Recon team? Report?" cried Beauregard.

"We're moving in," answered Halitov. "One hundred meters from their wire. Looks like standard concertina shield. Only way that's coming down is if we kill the people generating it."

Standard concertina shield provided a ten-meter-high energy barrier around the headquarters, and it, like the rest of the place, was powered by the life forces of individuals inside. The fence did not present a significant problem for conditioned combatants, but bringing down that shield would afford us a faster extraction in case our conditioning failed. I voiced that concern once I met up with Beauregard, who agreed that once we got inside, we would target the personnel generators as the DX people planted their charges.

"Looks like we got the same three big dishes," Halitov went on. "Standard hemispherical bunker top. Count four cannon emplacements at cardinal points relative to the bunker. I'm picking up some sniper nests in the foothills. Holy shit. How the fuck?"

"Halitov?" shouted Beauregard.

"Fall back!" he screamed. "Lee? Forrest? Fall back!"

"Halitov? Report!" demanded Beauregard. "Halitov?"

No reply. And none from Dina or Lee, either, though the blue dots representing them continued beaming on my viewer, their vitals elevated but strong.

Beauregard's voice broke as he belched out orders. "Security team? Move in on recon's position. DX? Bring me up on your HUVs. Maintain a hundred-meter gap east. Move out!" He threw an urgent look my way. "Get over there. Find out what's wrong."

16 **>** **Halitov, Dina, and** Lee had ascended dangerously close to the HQ, so close that I assumed
their skin emissions had been detected. Fortunately, I was
wrong. But what Halitov had seen made me wish they had
been spotted.

Darting across the ridge, my pace hinging on the bond, I
overshot their location, descended the mountainside facing
away from the HQ's colossal dishes, and picked up all three
of them in my HUV as they hustled back toward Beauregard's position, with our security team still headed toward
them.

"Halitov? I'm behind you. Report."

"Just fall back," he told me.

I ducked behind a wide boulder and paused to survey the
area. No movement, heat sources, skin emissions. Empty
zone. What the hell was he talking about? I climbed about
twenty meters to the summit, dropped to my stomach, and
peered over the edge. About thirteen Marines moved slowly
along the opaque shield barrier's exterior side. They divided
and began checking for integrity with scanning wands, their
skins blending in so thoroughly with the shield's crimson
camouflage that I could only pick them out via minute traces
of skin emissions. They shifted causally, their rifles held
loosely in their free hands.

"Commander," I said on Beauregard's private channel.
"I'm monitoring the target at a range of three-two-two-

point-four meters. Got a squad outside the fence. Standard perimeter sweep. I have no idea why Halitov called for retreat."

"Better get back," he answered. "I do."

I shifted around the boulder—

And faced a Western Alliance Marine, his gray-and-azure utilities suddenly hidden by his skin's camouflage of burnt sienna washing into a deep clay red that then mirrored the landscape, rendering him invisible to the naked eye. Via my HUV I saw that he stood a half-head taller than me, his tan, angular face growing visible a second—*Jarrett, is that you?*—before he slapped my rifle away with a blow so strong that I gasped. He reached for my neck, oblivious to the rebound of our skins. But his skinned hands passed through my shield and locked onto my throat. I saw his face again. He was *not* my brother.

My K-bar slid easily from its hip sheath. I plunged the blade into what should have been the Marine's chest. I had stabbed air. In the millisecond it had taken for me to pull out the blade, he had released my neck to somersault two meters back. He withdrew his own K-bar, bent his knees, and muttered a report to his CO. We had just lost the element of surprise.

Three dust clouds rose behind the Marine, neared him, then gathered into the forms of Beauregard, Lee, and Halitov, their rifles trained on the guard.

"He's conditioned," I said. "Don't fire."

But they ignored me. Three lightning-licked beads converged on the Marine, then curled back and targeted my comrades. But those diverted beads struck three more walls that bent them back toward the Marine. Within a few seconds, an extraordinary gauntlet of rebounding rounds clogged the air between them.

At once I realized what Beauregard and the others were

doing. With the Marine's attention focused on them, I lunged at his back with my blade, drove it down across his neck, ripped it across his spine, then withdrew and severed his jugular.

"Hold your fire," Beauregard cried.

The Marine dropped. Once-ricocheting beads unfurled and dug long tracks across the ridge. Then the cacophony fell off into the droning wind.

"I think the whole garrison's conditioned," said Halitov. "We watched those perimeter guards jump the fence. Low G or not, you don't do that without a little alien help."

"But how?" I asked. "Exeter's the only conditioning site, and the alliances didn't learn of its existence until the attack. They're already producing conditioned Marines? What about the accident? The machines are back on-line? Maybe these are just former guardsmen who chose the alliances."

"Or maybe the alliances have discovered another conditioning site," said Beauregard. "In which case, we've already lost this war."

I heaved a sigh. "We can speculate later. They already know we're here. I say we withdraw. Maybe Doyle can reinforce us."

Beauregard shook his head. "Squad? Are you ready?"

"We're ready, sir!" came a shout from all but me.

"It's suicide," I shouted.

"What I've been saying," added Halitov.

"Our mission is to take that HQ," Beauregard fired back. "And we're taking it. Everybody check your HUVs. I've noted your positions. Get in place. On my mark you will launch from the foothills and descend onto the HQ grounds. Security team takes the entrance. Recon and DX will supply diversion. DX? You'll drop the bombs as we go in. Expect heavy fire. Find the bonds. Use the arts. You know what to do. Move out!"

"Find the bonds. Use the arts. What a crock of shit," Halitov said over my private channel as he charged off. "He's fuckin' us because he doesn't wanna disappoint his fuckin' daddy."

"Scott?" Dina called. "If they're all conditioned, then we'll really need you."

I didn't know what to say. "Yeah. Okay."

With my designated position flashing in my HUV, I stared a moment more at Beauregard, then swung around and shot off, paralleling a jagged fissure that twisted down into the foothills. Beauregard gave the signal two seconds before I reached the crest of my hill. As I ran straight off the edge, the others plunged toward the HQ: Paris, Stark, and Ochoa from the north; Ramsey, Zhai, and Hooker from the south; Halitov, Dina, and Lee from the east; and Beauregard, whose foothill formed a sharp, ruddy peak about thirty meters from mine in the west.

Before any of us hit the ground, the Marines outside the fence were already airborne, intent on hurtling the shield barrier to take us on. All four cannons began booming so loudly that my skin's external audio barely compensated in time.

I can only guess how Paris and Stark died. Maybe cannon fire had caught them before they could utilize the bond. Maybe their conditioning had failed them. Maybe they had just grown too afraid to think clearly. I hit the ground, rolled out of my cannon's stream of particle fire, came up on my hands and knees, and stole a look to my left. Paris lay on her back, skin growing faint. Stark's legs lay a few meters from Paris, her torso a few meters from them. Sergeant Mana Ochoa, the only survivor of our security team, hollered,

"Lost Paris! Lost Stark!" as she threw herself forward in a *biza*, the head drive. Cannon fire pinged off an invisible, cone-shaped barrier she had formed over her head. She glided over the cannon emplacement and toward the bunker entrance's grimy gray dome.

"St. Andrew?" called Beauregard. "Get with Ochoa on that hatch! DX? Where the hell's our pulse wave?"

I crawled up to the dome, rose, then circled toward the lone sergeant. Particle fire chewed up my path, dented the bunker beside me, and sparkled through my HUV. Unlike the soldiers I've seen in old films who continually faced enemies with extremely poor aim, rounds steadily hammered and weakened my skin, so many coming in so fast that I stopped worrying about them and focused all of my attention on Ochoa and that hatch. I rounded the corner and ducked into a triangular doorway. The sergeant had blasted in the four-centimeter-thick hatch with the sheer force of her momentum. She lay on top of the alloy plate, blood pooling around the remains of her head.

My gaze lifted to meet the muzzle of a QQ90. I contemplated the weapon and the dark-uniformed Marine who held it long enough to mutter a curse. She jammed back her trigger.

Warnings flashed in my HUV. Skin strength down to twenty-one percent. I had never allowed it to become so weak, and it could take ten or more hours to rebuild. I reached for the rifle, but a quartet of explosions resounded behind me. The ground quaked as the EMPs' concussion and electromagnetic pulse wave passed through us, shorting out the processors in the cannons and rifles.

The Marine's bayonet telescoped out from her rifle. She never got the blade near me. As I ran her through with the

K-bar I had pulled while the EMPs had gone off, I realized she was not conditioned. And as she fell, sloughing off her skin, I fell against the side wall in utter astonishment. She wore the black utilities of the Seventeen System Guard Corps. Since we were running a black op, we wore tan, non-descript jumpsuits that in no way identified us as guardsmen. Even our tacs would not give up our identities, having been encrypted. The Marines outside wore standard Western Alliance uniforms. Was she on our side?

"St. Andrew? Report."

"We're in," I answered Beauregard, then dragged the woman's body into the empty dome and toward a pair of lift doors beside which stood a stairwell entrance.

Ramsey and Zhai staggered breathlessly into the room, brandishing bloody K-bars. Halitov arrived a second after Dina, they, too, with blades jutting from their fists.

"Who's that?" asked Halitov, gaping at the guardsmen at my feet. "And what's she doing in our utilities?"

Beauregard arrived, panting and bug-eyed. "Lower this fucking bunker! Now!"

Zhai was already jacking into the panel, her dark eyes going distant for a moment. The dome vibrated, threw us up a few centimeters, then lowered itself.

"How many left outside?" I asked Beauregard.

"Three Marines. Two cannon operators. I'm guessing that at least the Marines are conditioned. And we just lost Hooker and Lee. Hey, what the . . ." He trailed off as he scrutinized the woman's black uniform. "Who is she?"

"Don't know," I answered. "She fired at me as I entered."

"Ramsey? Scan her tac."

The dark-skinned lieutenant with raccoon's eyes drew a pen scanner from his demo pack, aimed it at the woman's tac, waited a few seconds for his reading, then directed the pen at an open space in front of us.

A holo of the woman bloomed to life. She stood in full dress uniform in front of the admin building at the Guard Corps enlistment facility on Drummer-Fire, a colony world in the UV Ceti star system. "Private Taberi, Nosa. Seventeen System Guard Corps. Identification: q-one-five-b-three-four-x-nine-one." She nodded at the camera, then the image trickled toward the floor.

"Maybe she was a POW trying to escape," said Ramsey. "She didn't recognize the XO's uniform and fired at him."

"Could be," said Beauregard. "Let's get down and lay our charges. Need a code for the lift? We'll take the stairs."

Zhai planted two small charges on the stairwell doors and summarily blew them off their tracks. We descended smartly, with Halitov on point, a blade in each hand. I placed myself in front of Dina.

We reached the first of four levels: comm and intell systems, administrative, billet, and maintenance and power. Zhai blew the door's lock with a microcharge, then she and Ramsey slinked off to set up charges within the five separate stations where sensor reports were received, analyzed, and conveyed back to the alliances' regimental commanders. I asked Beauregard if he wanted me to go with them. No doubt that even the system operators were armed and prepared for attack.

"Negative. You're with us down to maintenance and power. Even if they fail, we can still cut the power."

Once we reached that level, Halitov leaned against the hatch and closed his eyes. "Where the hell's the rest of the garrison? Supposed to be like sixty. We get all the way down

here without a single Marine to challenge us? And did anyone else but me realize that we didn't take any sniper fire
from all of those nests?"

"Maybe they moved a lot of people out of here. Maybe
they heard about our offensive," suggested Dina.

"Commander?" Ramsey called on the general frequency.

"Go," responded Beauregard.

"Sir, we've encountered no resistance. Picking up FY-
Ninety charge emissions, and they ain't coming from our
packs. Power's going down all over the place, sir."

"Shit. Meet us up top. Get the dome ready to move!"
Beauregard's cheeks were ashen. "Must've seen us coming,
got out another way, and rigged the place to blow."

"That's nice," said Halitov. "They did the job for us. Of
course, we die."

"Maybe tomorrow," said Beauregard, his gaze burning on
Halitov. "I'll be up top in two seconds." He grabbed Dina's
wrist, and together they blurred up the stairs as overhead
lights winked out.

Funny how it all came to me at that moment, with only
about thirty seconds until the entire intelligence headquarters would explode and bury itself under tons of icy rock and
permafrost.

I sifted through my memories as though they were pages
on a tablet. I reviewed everything Captain Doyle had said
about the operation. Why was the mission a black op? Why
conceal our identities? And what was a woman wearing a
Guard Corps uniform doing inside—

Unless the facility actually belonged to the Seventeen,
and surface patrols had concealed their identities by dress-
ing in Western Alliance uniforms. What if Doyle were actually working for the alliances? What if he had brought us in

to take out one of our own installations? What if we had just lost five good people while helping the wrong side?

My theory would have to wait. Halitov and I opted for fastest route up the stairwell: the walls. We made it into the dome in a respectable four seconds.

Ramsey and Zhai arrived just behind us, their skins splattered by a sizzling black goo I recognized as acipalm-three, a recently developed incendiary substance controlled by nanotech drones and programmed with the nasty talent of robbing gluons which mediate the strong interaction between subatomic particles like quarks. With the bonds between those quarks beginning to shatter, Ramsey's and Zhai's skins would soon succumb. The acipalm would then orchestrate the same theft of gluons from their bodies.

"Booby trap," explained Ramsey, his face pale with terror as he stared at his chest.

Zhai began screaming and running around the dome, up the walls, and across the ceiling.

We could only watch and keep out of range.

Ramsey flailed his arms as the acipalm finally broke through. His shoulder melted, as though a ghostly carnivore had placed white-hot lips on his flesh.

With a shrill cry, Zhai dropped to the floor and writhed violently as the dome gave a slight groan and began to rise. She lay still by the time we reached the surface.

Beauregard had already called Andropolus, so as we climbed over the fallen hatch and emerged outside, the ATC's downdraft blasted dust and pebbles out of our path. The ship descended about thirty meters ahead. The shield barrier had dropped. No sign of the remaining Marines and cannon operators in my viewer.

In order to escape the residual effects of the EMP bombs, co-pilot Goosavatic had tied her tac directly into the ATC's fusion generator, so when the ship suddenly dropped forty meters like a rock, I figured she had grown too weak to continue or that something had gone wrong with her link. We dove onto our bellies as the ATC struck a horrific blow, sending shock waves through the regolith.

As those waves died, the dull, volcanic rumble of the erupting HQ took over. My legs felt wobbly as I joined Halitov, Beauregard, and Dina in a retreat for the ATC, whose landing skids had been crushed but whose fuselage and cockpit had remained intact.

Behind us, the ground splintered open, with some clefts growing as wide as several dozen meters to swallow the comm dishes amid blustering wind and sand.

Two figures bolted away from the fallen ATC, and my HUV immediately IDed them as corpsmen Heloise and Toma. A long-range radar report alerted me to a pair of incoming atmoattack jets in the north, while another pair of Guard Corps ATCs streaked in from the east—all ships powered by their pilots' life forces and impervious to the pulse wave. ETA on the atmos: four minutes, with three on the ATCs. I assumed the corpsmen were in retreat because of those incoming aircraft, but when we reached our ATC and found Andropolus and Goosavatic slumped in their seats, point-blank particle fire having bored through their skins to penetrate the backs of their heads, I concluded that the corpsmen had shot them. Both Heloise and Toma were conditioned, and I doubted their ranks and identities.

Halitov, never one to keep questions to himself, hollered, "What the fuck is going on?"

"I think this installation was ours," I yelled. "Doyle or someone else sent us in to kill our own people. Heloise and Toma probably have orders to make sure we don't come back."

"I think you're right," said Beauregard. "Check your HUVs. Major Alliance troop movements in Valles Marineris. It's their offensive. Not ours. Fuck!"

The skin crawled on my neck. I whipped around. There, on the overhead just behind an unsuspecting Dina, hung one of the conditioned Marines, a woman who was on our side but did not realize who we were. Comfortably inverted like a bat, she punched one K-bar into Dina's back, dragged the other across her throat.

Dina's eyes ignited. Blood splayed across the front of her uniform as she fell to her knees, gave me a pleading look, then tipped onto her side. The Marine sprang off the overhead, rolled, and landed on her boots, then accosted me with both blades. I stood there, rooted in agony, my heart triphammering. Should I go to Dina or take on the Marine?

A screaming Beauregard threw me against the bulkhead as he drew a K-bar and took on the Marine himself.

In the interim, two more Marines bounded up the gangway and into the hold.

It's hard to convey with any certainty exactly what I did. The memory is fused with so much emotion that the details defy even my conditioned memory. I know this much: I cried fiercely as I killed both of those Marines, tore off their tacs in my preferred method. Their skins died. They decompressed.

Meanwhile, Halitov had hauled Dina with surprising gentleness to the front of the hold. Her skin flickered.

I found Beauregard just outside the ATC, on his knees and driving his K-bar into the Marine who had attacked Dina. The woman lay supine and had, of course, died after the first two strikes to her heart. Later on, reports would indicate that Beauregard had actually stabbed her thirty-seven times before I tore the K-bar out of his hand and shoved him back into the ATC. Once in the hold, he took one look at Dina, saw that she still clung to life, and his mindless rage tightened into something much more deliberate and controlled. "Seal the hold," he ordered me. "Try to pressurize."

The ramp came up, but the crash had damaged the pressurization controls. I fiddled with them for a few seconds more, then made my report as Beauregard pulled Andropolus out of the pilot's seat.

"Fuck it, then," he said. "Her skin's failing. One of you tie in. I'm using mine to power the ship."

I checked my skin reading. Fifty-one percent. Still really low. Not enough to loan out to Dina without killing myself. I told Halitov, who eyed me blankly, then slowly shook his head. I called up his skin's reading in my HUV: ninety-two percent. "You got enough," I cried. "Hurry up."

He visibly trembled. "I can't. Nobody else can come in here. It's me. All by myself. No one else is allowed."

With hands guided by the bond, I penetrated his skin and choked him. "She's gonna die."

"I know. I know. But she can't come in here." He ripped my hands off his neck. "She can't hear them laugh."

Dina's body suddenly stiffened, as though she had been shocked. Her skin dissolved. I looked away, sparing myself her decompression.

Maybe a minute later, I glowered at Halitov, whose expression lay on the brink of tears or rage, then I stumbled my way toward the cockpit. "Dina's dead."

"For now," Beauregard qualified as he pulled back on the control yoke, taking us into a hard climb. "This ship's tawt-capable."

"So what? We have to get back. We have to tell them what happened. We're the only ones who know."

"Dina's not going to die. I'm taking her to the Minsalo Caves. And that's fuckin' that." A holograph to his right displayed the galactic tawt projection: a gleaming blue line extending from Mars and out some seventy-five light-years to Exeter. Thousands of calculations scrolled below the image.

Part of me thought, *Screw the war. All that matters is her. We need to take her to the caves. There might be a chance.*

But the voice that had convinced me to become a soldier, the one that always reminded me of my duty, argued against trying to save her. Jarrett had died. Joey Haltiwanger. Pope. So many more. And now Dina. We all had to accept that. Somehow. We had to think of the Corps first—no matter how god-awful that felt. "Paul, the alliances still control Exeter. We won't even get near the moon, let alone the caves."

He tightened his lips.

"We'll be going AWOL," I added.

His expression turned incredulous. "Like I give a fuck after what they did to us?"

My knees felt weak. "We should turn back. If there's a traitor, we have to let them know. If we don't, a lot of people will die because of us. We might even lose the war."

"Thanks for your opinion, Mr. St. Andrew. You and Halitov take seats. Soon as we break atmosphere, we're tawting."

"No."

"What?"

"I said no. You're not going to do this. You're commander of this op, but I don't have to obey an order I find unconscionable."

He fixed his gaze on his instruments, the canopy banded by the mauve Martian sky. "Unconscionable? You fuckin' idiot. You don't think she's worth it? You of all people? You don't think I know how you feel about her? Go sit down!"

My K-bar flashed from its sheath and hung balanced over his neck. "Land."

"Scott, I'm not gonna let her die. So you'd better cut me right now!"

"She's already dead. What if the caves can't bring her back?"

"Then at least we die trying."

"So you make that decision for me and Halitov?"

"All right. I understand." He thumbed a pair of buttons to activate maneuvering thrusters, then banked hard and descended so quickly that I nearly fell against the canopy.

"What are you doing?"

"Coming up on the command center," he said. "Blow the belly hatch. You guys can jump."

"No."

"Then you'd better use that fuckin' blade, because I love that woman back there and nothing else matters. I'm taking her to Exeter."

"What if she doesn't love you?"

"I know she doesn't." He shot a glance to a navigation display. "If you're getting off, do it now."

My hand tensed. Biting back a curse, I pulled the K-bar away from his neck, then rushed out of the cockpit and to a control panel on the bulkhead to my left.

The belly hatch, a two-meter-by-two-meter pocket plate positioned in the center of the hold, slid open.

Halitov, who knelt over Dina's body, glanced at the hatch, then cocked a brow.

"He's taking her to the caves," I explained. "We get off here."

"Let's go with him."

"Stay if you want." I couldn't have cared less if he came

or not. In truth, I didn't blame him for Dina's death, only for failing to help her. But my scowl and tone said otherwise. I neared the open hatch, stole a look at the surface sweeping by about twenty meters below, then leaped out.

A few seconds later, Halitov followed. I smiled blackly as we came to gentle landings on the command center's tarmac. During the entire mission, our conditioning had not once failed us, yet the events could not have unfolded more miserably.

Beauregard coaxed the ATC into a seventy-degree climb until the ship became a dark dot against the sky, a speck, the barest pinprick, gone.

Three broad shadows passed over us, accompanied by a distinctive booming that my cerebroed memories said was produced by CFRT military cargo ships. One of them lumbered into view, its long, pentagonal fuselage heavily shielded, its wedge-shaped bow dipping slightly as it turned on final approach and sprouted multijointed landing skids.

Just ahead, the entire subterranean command center had folded back in on itself, creating a massive sinkhole and ringing the bunker entrance with piles of stone and regolith. Four Guard Corps engineers manipulated a hydraulic crane that resembled a mechanized fire ant, with the crane apparatus angling up from its back. Behind the crane awaited ten more engineers near another cargo ship that had already landed and had opened its massive bay doors to accept the center.

Two sergeants supervising the loading jogged over, both drawing sidearms. "Who are you people?" the taller man asked.

I raised my palms. "I'm First Lieutenant Scott St. Andrew, and this is First Lieutenant Rooslin Halitov. We need to see the regimental commander. It's an emergency."

The sergeant grinned. "Emergency? More like a war."

"Where's the RC?" I demanded.

"Probably with everyone else—up in Valles Marineris. If you're guardsmen, what are you doing here?"

"We don't owe you a fuckin' explanation," snapped Halitov. "We gotta get to the RC—now!"

"Sergeant, can you get us up there?" I asked, a tad more civilly than my esteemed colleague.

"Tell you what," the sergeant began, scrutinizing our weary expressions and bloodstained uniforms. "I'll get you on a ship, but until we confirm your IDs, you're both under arrest."

17 ❯ We never made it to Vallis Marineris. The pilots of the light cargo ship on which Halitov and I had hitched a ride were ordered away from the rolling plains of the battlefield. We wound up landing at another temporary command center a thousand kilometers east, near Samara Vallis.

There, our tacs were decrypted to confirm our ID, then, under the dubious gazes of two company captains from the Thirty-second Regiment, we sat in a debriefing room and told our story. I informed one captain that I would submit to a cerebral scan so that he could literally see what I had seen. He took me up on the offer. Within the hour, he was a believer. Within another hour, the evac order came in. The Corps was pulling all troops off the planet in a "temporary withdrawal," but I knew better. Mars was one of the original Sol colonies, and the alliances had so thoroughly imbued the planet's citizens with a patriotic spirit that I doubted our presence had ever been welcomed. In fact, many of the locals acted as informants, contributing to our loss of over seventy-one thousand troops there. I held no animosity toward Mars's people; those who sided with the colos would sacrifice their careers, their pensions, perhaps even their lives. The Seventeen had come to support the Inte-Micro Corporation, whose execs had refused to allow Alliance inspectors inside the Olympus Mons Mine. Alliance troops had invaded the mines. I guess what bothered me most was that we had come to Mars to liberate a corporation, not a neighborhood.

Instead of returning to our old regiment, Halitov and I were ordered back to Rexi-Calhoon, where we met with General Strident, the ivory-haired Odysseus who had given me my first star. I had never seen an office more harried, with aides bustling about, calls coming in on multiple monitors, and dozens of other high-ranking brass pouring over holograms. Strident guided us to two chairs facing his desk. "I've read your reports and reviewed your scans," he said wearily, then dropped into his own chair. "Some news. An ATC penetrated the alliances' no-fly zone over Exeter. The ship landed. No sign of Beauregard or Forrest."

In deference to the general, I staved off my reaction. He would not appreciate my grinning over a first lieutenant who had gone AWOL. Still, the news did not mean that Beauregard had been successful in getting Dina to the caves. And while those caves had healed wounds, we had never seen them restore life.

"We tawted word to Colonel Beauregard," the general went on. "It'll take another sixteen hours before he knows." Strident leaned forward, widening his eyes. "Gentlemen, what you did . . . it was in the best interests of the Corps. Maybe you'll hate yourselves for it later, but consider this: If Lieutenant Beauregard survives, he'll be court-martialed— and conditioning or not, he'll be sentenced to manual labor. A waste of a talented young man."

As Strident spoke, I felt more and more like I had betrayed Dina. Beauregard was the one who had made the right decision. The talented young man wasting his life was me.

A call came in over the general's tablet. He spoke quietly, delayed a meeting by ten minutes, then faced us, his expression grim.

"Sir? Can't Beauregard's father do something to help?" asked Halitov.

"No."

"He was trying to save a fellow guardsman's life," I said, just shy of a whisper.

"Lieutenant, save your testimony for the court-martial. In the meantime, thanks to you we've cleaned up the Thirty-first Regiment. Our investigation indicates that Captain Doyle had nothing to do with that attack on our own intelligence headquarters. He believed the center was operated by the alliances."

"Was it the battalion commanders?" I asked, figuring I would work my way up from Doyle.

He nodded. "Lieutenant Colonels Pell and McTear, both South Point graduates. Pell had ten years with us, McTear sixteen. You were right about Heloise and Toma. They were Eastern Alliance Marines, second lieutenants with false transfer orders from Third Platoon. We picked them up, but Pell and McTear shuttled to Vallis Marineris and defected long before we could reach them. What's worse is that they handpicked your team from some of the best people in the regiment. They figured your group would either do a very efficient job of DXing our own command center or die. Either way, they would gain something."

"Sir, I can't believe that Captain Doyle didn't suspect anything," said Halitov.

"I can't fault Doyle. He's responsible for over one hundred and fifty people. No one in his position would have realized that Heloise and Toma were never members of Third Platoon. Trust me. There are just too many names, too many faces. Which brings me to the second reason why I asked you here." A dangerous gleam lit in Strident's eyes, a gleam I had seen before. Another call came in. He rolled those gleaming eyes, took it, put off another meeting, then gathered his thoughts. "The Fourteenth Regiment has been assigned to escort the *Eri Flower* on Epsilon Eri Three, but I've decided that neither of you will be returning to that regiment. I'm transferring you both to the Ninth. That regiment is assigned to the Assault Carrier *Auspex*, which just happens to be in orbit. Her skipper's waiting for you."

"Sir, where are we headed, sir?" I asked.

"Kennedy-Centauri. We've already lost Ortorado and Zedong. You, Captain St. Andrew, will be leading your company into Plymouth Colony, while you, Captain Halitov, will be taking yours into Rockwa. Of course, you'll have full battalion support." He held up two pins, gold octagons, each bearing a diamond at its center. We knew them as "captain's gons."

I stared at the pins but did not dare reach for one. "Sir, may I speak candidly, sir?"

"You may. But be brief."

"Sir, I'm eighteen years old. If it weren't for this war, I'd be a first year at South Point. I've only commanded one platoon, which, sir, mutinied. I realize that I'm needed, but I don't believe I'm ready for that much command responsibility, sir."

"And sir?" Halitov interjected. "I feel the same. I, well, I'm not sure how to say this, I have . . ."

Strident waved a hand, then his gaze went distant. He seemed preoccupied by something, and it took another moment for him to return to us. "Mr. Halitov, believe me, we know all about your emotional challenges. We've found counselors specializing in your kinds of issues, and I've finally located an AAT instructor. You'll meet her on the *Auspex*."

Halitov closed his eyes. "Sir, I'm grateful for the promotion to captain, but I have no desire to lead my own company, at least not now. I realize I'm not supposed to have a choice in this, but I'd deeply appreciate it if you would assign me to Captain St. Andrew's company. I'd be honored to serve as his XO."

It had been a while since Halitov had surprised me. We had barely spoken since his refusal to help Dina, and when we did exchange words, I was curt, my tone all business. He could not meet my gaze for more than a few seconds, and his guilt had already drawn lines on his face and around his eyes.

"The problem with your request, Mr. Halitov, is that we're making every effort to evenly distribute conditioned personnel, who, by the way, represent just nine percent of our fighting force. Two conditioned captains in one company will be viewed as a waste of resources. How do you propose I justify that to my colleagues?"

"Sir, I'm not sure, sir."

The general lifted his chin at me. "What's your take on this flood of humility, Mr. St. Andrew?"

I glanced at Halitov. "Sir, while I'm not sure I understand why Mr. Halitov has made this request, I'd feel much more confident taking on the responsibility of company commander if he were my XO. It's a weak reason, but I think as a team we would be much more effective."

An aide burst into the room, a young woman who looked pale, waved a tablet, and said something to the general with her eyes. He nodded. She left. Strident's gaze then alternated between me and Halitov. He leaned back, thought a moment more, then grudgingly nodded. "Very well, then. We can make this work. You'll report to the *Auspex* ASAP. I'll have your new assignments uploaded to your tablets. Any other questions or concerns?"

"Sir, no, sir," I replied, then Halitov echoed. We rose, saluted, then spun on our heels and started for the door.

"Gentlemen, I regret that the urgency of war has forced us to abandon the pomp and circumstance attached to promotion. However, you should take these." He held up the pins between his thumb and forefinger.

Halitov and I flushed as we turned back and accepted our captain's gons.

The general's expression grew earnest and, surprisingly, his voice cracked. "God bless you both."

We left the office and shuttled up to our assault carrier, unaware that as our ship pulled out of orbit, Strident lifted a pistol to his temple and proved his superior marksmanship. His blood splattered over the casualty report he had been reading. A few drops also caught a picture of his daughter, whom he had just learned had been murdered by Alliance Marines.

Tawting to Kennedy-Centauri would be anything but an uncomplicated affair. We needed to stop off in six other systems to take on or drop off personnel. We were told that the entire trip would last an uncharacteristic two days. I had barely settled into my three-meter-by-five-meter quarters when my hatchcomm beeped. "Captain St. Andrew? It's Captain Kristi Breckinridge, your AAT instructor."

"Thought we weren't scheduled until nineteen hundred," I answered, tripping over my duffel as I headed to the hatch in boxers and T-shirt.

"We're not."

The hatch cycled open. Breckinridge stood a few centimeters taller than me, and in spite of her utilities, I could tell she was in excellent physical condition, breasts small and firm, muscles not too large. Her dark hair was razored short, over the ears, cropped close to her neck, and she had gelled it back, away from her narrow face. She cocked a brow and widened her pale blue eyes. "May I come in?"

I tipped my head and shifted aside.

She crossed directly to my tiny desk, whose top folded up into the bulkhead, and took a seat. "Captain, General Strident recruited me from the Colonial Wardens to help you and Captain Halitov complete your assimilation. Unfortunately, that'll be impossible."

"Why?"

"I'll explain. But first I come bearing an offer from my CO, Colonel Beauregard, who's setting up a meeting for you on Kennedy-Centauri."

"What's this about?"

"We'd like you to join the Colonial Wardens."

I threw my head back and laughed. "My last platoon mutinied on me—and what happens? I'm selected for an elite black op mission, we kill some of our own people by mistake, and I end up promoted to captain. Now I get an offer to join the most powerful special forces group in the Corps. Maybe I should go fight for the alliances. I can become a general!" I shook my head. "Do any of you people realize who you're dealing with? I'm a colo. I grew up in a tunnel. Look at my cheek."

"Which is exactly why you're so valuable. On Kennedy-Centauri you'll meet a woman who's just like you: epineuropathic residuum and extraordinary capabilities. Only difference is, her conditioning is flawless and her assimilation is complete. She's your future."

"But you just said I can't complete my assimilation, and I bet that's because my conditioning is screwed up. How is this woman my future?"

"We'll recondition you."

"I thought Exeter was held by the alliances."

"It is. And the conditioning machines there are not functioning properly. About eight months ago, the Wardens found another facility on Aire-Wu. We've kept its existence to ourselves because, Mr. St. Andrew, we have our own plan for winning the war, a plan that doesn't include the new colonial government, a plan that'll show you what those blue lights were and reveal the truth about your brother."

"What are talking about? My brother's dead."

"They won't allow me to tell you any more."

"So you're baiting me with lies and false hopes to join your coup," I said, disgusted that she had wasted my time. "Why don't you just make it easy on yourselves and defect to the alliances?"

"Because we believe in colonial freedom. We just have a better plan to obtain it. This new government supported by the Seventeen will fall. You were on Mars, one of the first colonies. The alliances didn't beat us with hardware. Propaganda helped win over seventy-five percent of the population. Kind of hard to defend people as they're stabbing you in the back."

I rubbed my stubble-laden cheeks in frustration. "And it's kind of hard to fight in a Corps when you realize that its special forces are doing the same." I wondered if it had occurred to the Wardens that the colonial congress and Security Council might have learned about their secret. I remembered how Ms. Brooks had been so emphatic about delivering those tawting codes. Maybe those codes led to Aire-Wu and the second conditioning facility . . .

"Captain, I didn't mean to dump all of this on you. And you're right; I could be lying. I could be a plant to test your loyalty, but I'm not. You're in a position to help a lot of people. We're not asking you to do anything but your duty."

"You're asking me to betray the new colonial government."

"We won't take over the government. We're just going to give it a nudge in the right direction."

"And you need me to help do that."

"Exactly."

I glared at her. "I'm a tool. Use me."

"You don't think you're being used right now?" She snorted. "Joining us is the logical choice. We can guarantee your transfer."

"I don't know . . ."

"At least attend the meeting. You owe it to yourself. And were I you, I'd take a long, hard look in the mirror."

I shook my head as she left. Something about her tone finally drove me to my latrine, to the mirror above my sink. I assumed that I was supposed to examine the man beneath the skin, but I could not get past the skin itself. A fresh hint of crow's-feet spread out from my eyes and vanished into my cheeks. Halitov's face bore the same lines, though I had attributed his to guilt. A few gray hairs had sprouted at my temples. I came within a few centimeters of the mirror. *Ohmygod.*

About an hour later, Halitov arrived with a bottle of Tau Ceti vodka, which, he explained, he had just received from one of the platoon leaders as a welcome gift.

I lay in my rack, trembling, hardly listening, imagining that I felt myself dying by the second. When Halitov urged me to get up and share a quick drink with him, I shook my head. "Remember that woman in the Minsalo Caves? The one I told you about?"

He insisted on pouring me a glass, brought it over. "We're

aging prematurely. I know all about it. I first noticed it back on Mars. I didn't want to say anything. We're burnin' twice as bright. Should we have expected anything less of the military? Maybe that's why they keep promoting us; they know we're gonna drop soon. Anyway, we got just what we wanted—our ticket out. 'Course, we bought it on credit. Have a drink."

I took the glass, sniffed the vodka, then raised my glass.

He turned away. "There's nothing to toast. Just drink."

"Yeah." I winced over the burn.

"They couldn't find me for three days," he said quickly, keeping his back to me. "I was only eight. Those little fuckin' punks were waiting for me at the train stop. Locked me in a cargo container. Hid it in the basement of a restaurant, in the compressor room. They spent a few hours each day laughing at me. I remember the voice of this old man who had found me. He must have been a Terran from England. Real soft voice. He used a few words I didn't understand. I remember he started crying as he carried me out of there. I couldn't see anything that first day. I spent a couple years with a shrink, who eventually told my parents that I had learned to cope with the experience. Fuckin' jerk. I don't know. It's just when it comes on me, the memories, they're . . . I can't help myself. Sometimes, I don't remember what I've said. It's like I go back there and can't even see where I am. That night I had you in your rack? I wasn't even there. I should've told you this sooner. I should've told you when I noticed the aging, but I guess it doesn't bother me. I got nobody left. Nobody will miss me."

"What about your sister?"

"Haven't heard anything. She could already be dead."

I finished my vodka, coughed, then crawled to the edge of my rack.

Halitov shielded his face with a hand and wiped away tears as quickly as they fell. "Scott, you don't know how sorry I am about what happened with Dina. You don't know how bad I wanted to help. I wish I could make you understand. Fuck!"

I understood, but I wasn't sure that telling him would make a difference. *He* was the one who needed to understand. "Listen to me, Rooslin. There might be a way around the aging."

"How?"

"I met our AAT instructor. What I'm about to tell you is as classified as it gets . . ."

Halitov had assembled my company in bay thirty-nine, a spectacular hangar berthing about sixty insertion vehicles whose holds bore dozens of tac-powered hovercraft we would need on Kennedy-Centauri. The planet had a breathable atmosphere, and life-support systems were not a consideration, so localized EMP bombs would be dropped in Plymouth. Each of the one hundred and sixty-two people in my company knew very well that once we made planetfall, all of the high-tech weaponry in all of the colonies could not help them. Bayonets. K-bars. Rocks. Sticks. Fists. Iron wills. Those would be our weapons. That is, until researchers finally developed those sidearms and rifles powered by our life forces. Of course, other researchers would develop weapons to render those weapons harmless. We would return to the intimacy of our hands.

I was supposed to give my people the proverbial welcome message in which I introduced myself as the new company commander, detailed my philosophy of command, and shared my expectations. I paced before the long, rigid rows of personnel at parade rest, eyeing soldiers who were, for the most part, older than me but just as worn-looking. I finally reached the small dais that Halitov had rolled up, and ascended to look out across the group, praying that they had not seen me shudder. "Ladies and gentlemen, my name is Captain Scott St. Andrew. I'm your company commander. This is where I give you the pep talk and make all those threats about how I'll be booting you in the ass if you're not keeping up with me."

That drew a few mild grins.

"Truth is, I never wanted to be here. I went to South Point so I could get off Gatewood-Callista. In the beginning, it wasn't about freedom or anything as remotely noble. I just didn't want to be a second-class citizen, a gennyboy with no future. I figured service with the Seventeen was the next best thing to being a Terran myself. I'd become an officer. I'd be respected, even with this birthmark on my face. Then, when I got to the academy, I started thinking about what a soldier really is. I started thinking about that life, and I realized that I couldn't wear the uniform just to get off my colony. I needed a better reason, otherwise I wouldn't make it. Ladies and gentlemen, we're fighting for what United States President Abraham Lincoln called 'a just and lasting peace,' for the honor and dignity of calling ourselves free people. That is the good fight. That is why we wear the uniform. Of course, this means you might have to stare some young woman in the eye. She's so close you can smell her breath and count the freckles on her nose. You give her an entire life. You know all of her secrets. She's as real as they come—not just a soldier but a person who doesn't deserve to die. It's not her fault she's in the wrong place at the wrong time. Who the hell are you to dictate her fate? So just this once, you'll show some mercy. You let her go. You feel good about yourself. The military hasn't turned you into a mindless killer. You can still get the job done without tearing up families. Then a few minutes later you watch that same woman kill your squad sergeant with the fortitude that you lacked."

Of course, they saw right through me, and that was exactly what I wanted.

"Our job—our *duty*—is to kill the enemy, and we will kill. We will show no mercy. But we will always be conscious of our actions. Most of all, we will never, ever forget. Ladies and gentlemen? What's the best company?"

"Sir, Zodiac Company, sir!"

"Who will own Plymouth Colony?"

"Sir, Zodiac Company, sir!"

I stood before my cheering people, and it might have been pride I felt, I was too nervous to tell. I did know that I had never believed in anything as deeply as what I had told them. I knew that from that point on I would take nothing for granted, savor every moment, and—for the first time— really live.

APPENDICES

Appendix A
Chronology of Important Events in Galactic Expansion

SEARCH PARAMETERS:
   2062–2301
   Twenty-first Century Multinational Efforts
   Twenty-second and Twenty-third Century Alliance and Corporate Expeditions

2062
Lunar subterranean research facilities are established ($23 trillion over budget). Industrial ring station at Lagrange Point 5 engages in zero-G production of purer metals and more perfect/larger crystal growth.

2068
First Martian outpost is founded, paving way for colonization via corporate sponsorship. The rich, the politically affluent, and the scientific community flock to Mars. Construction begins on orbital living environments.

2071

Europa deep-core drilling operation draws 150,000 workers and becomes largest offworld settlement to date. Efforts yield discovery of microorganisms living beneath ice crust. Concurrent experiments in molecular nanotechnology give rise to first generation of new high-strength, low-weight materials for computers and launch vehicles.

2077

Titan moon mine goes on-line. During first month of operation, 1,902 miners killed in worst offworld disaster. Terraforming experiments with blue-green algae begin on Venus.

2085

Oberon mountain mines yield $500 trillion in resources during first six months of operation. Profits dubbed by media as "Shakespeare's Blessing," since moon was named after character in A Midsummer Night's Dream. Need for skilled workers creates job rush among lower and middle classes, who leave Terra in droves. Physically challenged persons seek freedom of zero-G living environments.

2099

During construction of way station on Neptune's moon Nereid, ruins of ancient alien race are discovered. Humanity has proof that we are not alone. Unable to decipher the aliens' name, scientists simply call them "The Race." Corporations and licensors make fortunes on everything from alien T-shirts to nose rings.

2101

Rim stations are constructed in orbit of Pluto and moon Charon. Experiments with faster-than-light travel via Telic drive result in serious loss of equipment and personnel. Exploratory ship Godspeed estimated to lie six trillion years in future.

During next four decades, upper-class residents of many offworld colonies begin to return home. Living offworld, though initially glamorous, is ultimately rough and miserable. Real estate prices on Terra soar. Middle and lower classes are slowly driven off Terra for "better opportunities" offworld.

2144

Alien engine dubbed the Tecnocabalistic Drive System (TDS) yields development of second-generation Telic drive: the Trans Advanced Wave Theory (TAWT) drive. First craft equipped with TAWT drive reaches star Rigil Kent A with forty thousand volunteers. Some colonists have terminal diseases or genetic defects from offworld living and seek a sanctuary to die or live without persecution. Colony established on planet Kennedy-Centauri. Despite deaths, population is projected to quadruple within twenty years.

2158

Rogolov-Barnard is discovered in the Barnard's Star solar system. First extrasolar mining operation established in primary colony of Lhasa. Population reaches four million within two standard years.

2179

Multinational exploratory ship *Driftmadien* finally completed in Rogolov-Barnard orbit. Ship leaves for Wolf 359 solar system and returns within a year with news that the second planet from sun is suitable for colonization, though conditions are not much better than on planet Kennedy-Centauri. Citizens of Rogolov-Barnard are lured to this new colony with promises of triple pay by multinational conglomerates who seek to exploit this new world's natural resources. Nearly one million leave to settle on Wolf Bane II.

2180

Driftmadien is scheduled to leave during February 2180 for Lalande 21185 solar system, 1.5 light-years away, but the ship is held back because of political turmoil on Terra.

During the next forty years, bloody conventional and biological wars lead to the establishment of the Eastern and Western Alliances, which "unite" people of Terra in two great superpowers reminiscent of the twentieth-century balance of power. Alliances' first act: declare Earth a "protected planet" because ecological catastrophe looms on horizon. Colonists are only allowed to return to Earth via new passports approved by the government. Processing time: five to ten years. Criminals with sentences of five or more years are deported to the newly established Uruk Sulcus Penitentiary on the Jovian moon Ganymede.

2220

Expansion resumes in earnest, while Terra barely escapes ecocatastrophe. Satellite Gatewood-Callista is discovered in the Lalande 21185 system, orbiting Saturn-like gas giant 21185 b. This moon is a harsh, inhospitable world rich in ore deposits. Within four years, subterranean colonies and accompanying mining facilities serve as home to nearly ninety million. Gatewood-Callista becomes the most profitable colony in existence and boasts most complex orbiting launch and research platform to date.

2233

Colonial expansion resumes after a second lag due to market crash. Inte-Micro Corporation violates Colonial Prudence Order and "tawts out" 11.2 light-years. Ursula-Gates is discovered in orbit of star 61 Cygni A. In a series of brilliant legal maneuvers, lawyers from Inte-Micro Corporation claim squatters' rights for this new world and establish a precedent for independent exploration (the Colonization Ordinance of 2233 is written and approved by the alliances). Inte-Micro will own the colony but pay heavy taxes for the right to sell goods and services to other Alliance-held colonies. Extraterrestrial artifacts found on the planet are the exclusive property of the alliances.

2234

Riding on the heels of Inte-Micro's victory, Exxo-Tally Corporation launches a colonization effort to planet Drummer-Fire in the UV Ceti binary star system. Among the colonizing team are the astronomers who discovered the planet: Michele Drummer and her husband, Paul Fire. The planet is quickly dubbed a sister world of Mars since its atmosphere and surface are similar. The first attempt at colonization fails, as nearly ten thousand are lost in one sandstorm that lasts several months. By year's end, a second attempt is launched, Quonset City is founded (population 21,000), and in March 2236 miners uncover vast archaeological ruins of "The Race," now known as the Racinians. Nearly one million researchers pour into Drummer-Fire, turning the colony into a Shangri-La for scientists and a lucrative venture for Exxo-Tally Corporation.

2237

Sirius (B I) is founded by Eastern Alliance explorers. Large deposits of oil and natural gas are discovered at planet's poles as well as on ocean floor. With help of Exxo-Tally Corporation, alliances build first offworld deep-sea oil rigs and, utilizing Racinian tecnocabalistic methods, draw more oil from the planet in one year than was drawn from Earth during the entire twentieth and twenty-first centuries.

2242

Inte-Micro Corporation explorers venture to the Luyten 789-6 solar system and discover the first relatively warm planet in orbit around a red dwarf star. In its warmest regions, Lorellus's surface temperature reaches −20°C. The corporation begins building mobile manufacturing plants to produce electronic components from semiconductor materials. Executives envision a global industrial park that can operate sans environmental regulations.

2255

Planet Aire-Wu,· colonized by the Inte-Micro Corporation, becomes the first known world with a breathable atmosphere. Planet is remarkably similar to Earth, though oceans make up only fourteen percent of its surface. More Racinian ruins are discovered, and scientists speculate that alien technology created the breathable atmosphere. Aire-Wu becomes the chief exporter of grain, raw timber, asbestos, and gypsum. Nearly seventy-one percent of its surface is forestland. Both Inte-Micro and Exxo-Tally establish corporate headquarters on Aire-Wu's lone moon, Theta-Marcus.

2266

Mining of bauxite begins on the fifth planet in the Ross 248 solar system. Inte-Micro Corporation CEO Tamer Yatanaya names planet Allah-Trope and declares it a retreat for Muslims being persecuted by Eastern Alliance powers. Allah-Trope becomes the first offworld colony with one predominant religion.

By year's end, floating research operations are dropped onto planet Epsilon Eri III—a world entirely covered by warm oceans whose salt content is only slightly higher than that of Terra's oceans. Thousands of new microorganisms are discovered. Aquacultural experiments yield new food sources for a human population that now numbers twenty billion, with six billion living in Sol system colonies and nearly five billion in extrasolar settlements.

2268

During a miscalculation of his ship's TAWT drive, Aire-Wuian freighter pilot Nicholas Popkin accidentally reaches a moon of gas giant 70 Virginis b in a star system seventy-eight light-years from Earth. Popkin becomes farthest human from home. (Data speculative. No other information available.)

2271

Unhappy with present costs and security conditions provided by Eastern and Western Alliance military, Inte-Micro and Exxo-Tally propose the formation of Twelve System Guard Corps, a military force operated and funded by the corporations. Alliances oppose formation unless the Guard Corps becomes a branch of alliance military. Corporate execs reluctantly agree. The Twelve System Guard Corps is formally created on April 8, 2271, by act of the East-West Assembly.

2273

World of Nau Dane is found in Ross 128 system and claimed by Exxo-Tally Corporation, though the right to colonize this new planet remains under dispute for nine years. Eastern Alliance explorers arrive on the dark side during the same month, claim the world for their own, and name it Zheng He. Exxo-Tally representatives square off with Twelve System Guard Corps troops. No shots are fired, but the incident marks the beginning of a cold war between colonial corporations and alliances.

2284

First convention of business and political leaders from all extrasolar and solar colonies is held in Columbia Colony, on planet Rexi-Calhoon. An informal assembly is created. Negotiations begin to establish a new Colonial Alliance. Two high-ranking officials from the Twelve System Guard Corps attend this convention to listen to arguments about why they should break from the alliances and become a new colonial military force.

By midyear, nearly one million Exxo-Tally employees have been killed on the frigid world of Icillica, in the Procyon Binary star system. Akin to the old Russian Arctic and yielding similar deposits of nickel, iron ore, and apatite, Icillica is predicted to become the next Gatewood-Callista and geologic cash cow for colonies. Life support systems in forty-seven of fifty-one mining facilities go offline, as do all three redundancy systems. Corporate investigators declare the malfunctions an act of sabotage but cannot gather enough evidence to formally indict alliance military.

2285

Construction begins on the agricultural domes of Tau Ceti XI. No other planet has soil more fertile and adaptable to Terran-based crops. With grain production on Aire-Wu cut in half by an unknown disease, Tau Ceti XI becomes the leading producer of grain, forage, fruit, nut, vegetable, and nonfood crops, as well as the leader in development of new chemicals from organic raw materials. Inte-Micro and Exxo-Tally begin formal and covert negotiations with Twelve System Guard Corps representatives who favor colonial secession. Construction begins on the first colonial military base within Tau Ceti's agricultural domes.

2299

Kapteyn Beta, a small, geologically active world in Kapteyn's Star system, becomes the last formal colony (as of this access date), with a mere 10,000 geologists and volcanologists living on an orbital ring station in gravitationally stable Lagrange point. A second, nonscientific, station is completed by the end of the year for "industrial use." Researchers contact colonial officials to report that the second station is an alliance military outpost.

2300

The Twelve System Guard Corps is renamed the Seventeen System Guard Corps. Representatives from all offworld systems make formal announcement of the formation of the new Colonial Alliance. East and West Alliances fail to recognize new government.

2301

Expansion halts.

Appendix B
The Seventeen Systems

SEARCH PARAMETERS:
  Seventeen System Guard Corps Operational Zone

SYSTEMS FOUND:

Barnard's Star	61 Cygni A/B
Epsilon Eridani	Epsilon Indi
Kapteyn's Star	Lalande 21185
Luyten 726-8A	Procyon A/B
Rigil Kent A	Ross 128
Ross 154	Ross 248
Sirius A/B	Sol
Tau Ceti	UV Ceti A
Wolf 359	

COMPILER'S NOTE: This search result accounts for major extrasolar colonies established during initial Terran Alliance, Inte-Micro, and Exxo-Tally efforts. At least twenty-two other settlements exist throughout recorded territory. For a complete list, search "settlements, all, Seventeen Systems."

Appendix C
Extrasolar Colonized Worlds as of Terran Year 2301

Planet/ Satellite	System and Position	Sun Spectral Type	Distance from Terra	Surface Gravity (Earth = 1)	Atmosphere
ALLAH-TROPE (terrestrial planet) Wit-Su Colonial Tolerance Index Rating: 4.3	Ross 248 5 of 7	M5 (red)	10.3 ly	0.967	Primarily hydrogen and helium, with traces of methane and ammonia
AIRE-WU (terrestrial planet) Wit-Su Colonial Tolerance Index Rating: 10	Ross 154 2 of 3	M5 (red)	9.4 ly	0.981	Oxygen and nitrogen (breathable) Possible Racinian terraforming intervention
DRUMMER-FIRE (terrestrial planet) Wit-Su Colonial Tolerance Index Rating: 3.4	UV Ceti A/B 1 of 1 in orbit of B	M6 (red)	8.4 ly	0.799	Carbon dioxide nitrogen pressure 1.01 of Terra (sea level)
EPSILON ERI III (terrestrial planet) Wit-Su Colonial Tolerance Index Rating: 9.8	Epsilon Eridani 3 of 6	K2 (orange)	10.7 ly	1.002	Oxygen and nitrogen (breathable) Possible Racinian terraforming intervention

Principle Terrain	Colo Date	Sponsor(s)	Pop. (millions)	Primary Colonies	Chief Exports
Craters, large basins akin to Luna or Mars	2266	Inte-Micro Corporation	100.4	Bannah Nasser Mubarak al-Bukarhi	Bauxite Acetylene gas (indicates planet once had warmer climate)
71% forest biome 14% oceans	2255	Inte-Micro Corporation Exxo-Tally Corporation	897.9	Cynday New Sky Orokean Butanee Zhou	Grain Timber Asbestos Gypsum
Impact basins, desert biomes	2234	Exxo-Tally Corporation	120.9	Quonset Sandhuk L-Town Y-Town	Crude 57A (lubricant) Antimony Beryllium
Ocean (100%)	2267	Inte-Micro Corporation Exxo-Tally Corporation	221.2	AQ-Tower Jones-Rigi Plat *Eri Flower* (vessel)	Magnesium Bromine Zeolites Halite Fish crops New biologics

Planet/ Satellite	System and Position	Sun Spectral Type	Distance from Terra	Surface Gravity (Earth = 1)	Atmosphere
GATEWOOD-CALLISTA (satellite) Wit-Su Colonial Tolerance Index Rating: 5.0	Lalande 21185 Sole moon of 21185 b	M2 (red)	8.1 ly	0.899	Hydrogen, helium, ammonia, deep cloud layers
ICILLICA (satellite) Wit-Su Colonial Tolerance Index Rating: 4.8	Procyon A/B Sole moon Pro. C	White dwarf	11.4 ly	0.787	Hydrogen, with traces of oxygen and nitrogen
KAPTEYN BETA (terrestrial planet) Wit-Su Colonial Tolerance Index Rating: 10	Kapteyn's Star 1 of 2 orbital research platform	M0 (red)	12.7 ly	0.322	none
KENNEDY-CENTAURI (terrestrial planet) Wit-Su Colonial Tolerance Index Rating 4.6	Rigil Kent A 3 of 3	G2 (yellow)	4.3 ly	0.994	Carbon dioxide, methane, nitrogen
LORELLUS (terrestrial planet) Wit-Su Colonial Tolerance Index Rating 4.4	Luyten 726-8A 3 of 4	M5 (red)	8.9 ly	0.692	Hydrogen, nitrogen, methane (thin cloud layers)
NAU DANE (terrestrial planet) Wit-Su Colonial Tolerance Index Rating: 4.5	Ross 128 1 of 1	M5 (red)	10.8 ly	0.821	Hydrogen, argon, nitrogen, with 2% oxygen

Principle Terrain	Colo Date	Sponsor(s)	Pop. (millions)	Primary Colonies	Chief Exports
Rocky crust covered by frozen methane	2220	Inte-Micro Corporation	200.1	Ro Sung-Hy Vosk Isyil Ubango Little Brooklyn	Steel Aluminum Magnesium Titanium Gold/Silver Glass Quartz
Craters covered by frozen water and methane	2283	Exxo-Tally Corporation	200.5	Regal Victory Augusta Wintadia Colyad (mines)	Nickel Iron ore Apatite
Volcanic (active)	2299	Exxo-Tally Corporation	.01	(1) Kapteyn Beta Research Platform	Data
Cratered uplands, polar ice caps, multiple surface types	2144	NASA Coca-Cola Inte-Micro Corporation People's Republic of China	150.3	Rockwa Plymouth Peking II Zedong Ortorado	Iron Ore Copper Feldspar Heavy tourist trade
Semi-cratered lowlands, massive faults; seismic activity	2242	Inte-Micro Corporation	330.3	ComCo Mystock Telstock Popkin Vil Tuary	Rare and ferromagnetic minerals Semi-conductor materials
Rolling uplands; strangely devoid of impact craters	2273	Inte-Micro Corporation Eastern Alliance	470.4	Nuevo-Seoul Shangzo Ki-ti-Ka Jutland Holberg	Chromite Aluminum Molybdenite

Planet/ Satellite	System and Position	Sun Spectral Type	Distance from Terra	Surface Gravity (Earth = 1)	Atmosphere
REXI-CALHOON (terrestrial planet) Wit-Su Colonial Tolerance Index Rating: 10	Epsilon Indi 5 of 8	K5 (orange)	11.2 ly	1.012	Oxygen and nitrogen (breathable) Possible Racinian intervention
ROGOLOV-BARNARD (planetoid) Wit-Su Colonial Tolerance Index Rating: 1.4	Barnard's Star 1 of 1	M5 (red)	5.9 ly	0.899	None
SIRIUS B I (terrestrial planet) Wit-Su Colonial Tolerance Index Rating: 5.1	Sirius A/B 1 of 1	White dwarf	8.6 ly	0.877	Nitrogen (27%), oxygen (22%), ten other trace elements
TAU CETI XI (terrestrial planet) Wit-Su Colonial Tolerance Index Rating: 9.1	Tau Ceti 11 of 13	G8 (yellow)	11.9 ly	0.904	Nitrogen (88%), oxygen (11%), still unbreathable
THETA MARCUS (satellite) Wit-Su Colonial Tolerance Index Rating: 3.4	Ross 154 Sole moon of planet Aire-Wu	M5 (red)	9.4 ly	0.386	Carbon dioxide, argon, nitrogen
URSULA-GATES (terrestrial planet) Wit-Su Colonial Tolerance Index Rating: 7.7	61 Cygni A/B	K5 (orange)	11.2	0.888	Nitrogen (41%), oxygen (16%), and other elements

Principle Terrain	Colo Date	Sponsor(s)	Pop. (millions)	Primary Colonies	Chief Exports
Multiple biomes similar to North American continent	2282	Inte-Micro Corporation Exxo-Tally Corporation	898.7	Columbia Indicity Tru Cali Lincoln Govina Rexicity	Grain Timber Ore Varied nonfood crops
Heavily scored and cratered (Mercury-like scarps)	2158	NASA Coca-Cola Exxon Dell People's Republic of China	110.1	Jennaton Austinia Lhasa Ymen Kunming	Iron Ore Cobalt Copper Quartz
Oceans, two major land masses, varied terrain	2237	Exxo-Tally Corporation East and West Alliances	290.7	Rig 91 Rig 21 Rig 41	Crude Oil
Four major land masses; fertile valleys; oceans	2285	Inte-Micro Corporation Exxo-Tally Corporation	771.7	Domcity Outba Cammil Tau Ze Shefas Lylah	Grain, forage, fruit, nut, vegetable, and nonfood crops Organic chemicals
Volcanic plains, basins	2255	Inte-Micro Corporation Exxo-Tally Corporation	10.4	IM and ET head-quarters	None
Multiple biomes, liquid water	2233	Inte-Micro Corporation	500.2	Intville Goame Setti Halis Tylyd	Iron ore Platinum

Planet/ Satellite	System and Position	Sun Spectral Type	Distance from Terra	Surface Gravity (Earth = 1)	Atmosphere
WOLF BANE II (terrestrial planet)	Wolf 359	M6 (red)	7.6 ly	0.578	None
Wit-Su Colonial Tolerance Index Rating: 6.1	1 of 1				

Principle Terrain	Colo Date	Sponsor(s)	Pop. (millions)	Primary Colonies	Chief Exports
Scarps, craters, mountain ranges, plains	2180	Multi-national	40.9	Shang Ledroit Vosu Reegor	Multiple mineral exports

Appendix D
Chain of Command, South Point Academy,
70 Virginis Star System, Planet Exeter
(established September 1, 2278)

The South Point Academy Corps of Cadets is an elite, covert, carefully selected group of individuals who constitute an officer's training regiment in the Seventeen System Guard Corps. The regiment is commanded by a cadet colonel and staff, with the direct supervision and advice of the commandant and the tactical officers. Under the cadet colonel's control are the Regimental Band and the four battalion commanders and their staffs, each of whom is commander of one of the four barracks in which cadets are billeted. Each battalion consists of four companies, each commanded by a cadet captain, with the exception of Seventeen Company (support), commanded by the commandant. The company is the basic administrative unit to which all cadets will be assigned. Each company is further divided into three platoons, each under the supervision of a cadet second lieutenant. The platoons are separated into three squads, each headed by a cadet sergeant.

SOUTH POINT REGIMENT, as of 2301

Commandant: Marxi, Julia J., GEN.
Regimental Commander: C/COL. Bryant, M. J.
Regimental XO: C/LT. COL. Butler, D.

1st Battalion	2nd Battalion	3rd Battalion	4th Battalion
LT. COL. Huntington	LT. COL. Bayshore	LT. COL. Nesconset	LT. COL. Derazi
XO: MAJ Showr	XO: MAJ Yakata	XO: MAJ Sui	XO: MAJ Ahiaz
Co. 1–4	Co. 5–8	Co. 9–12	Co. 13–16
Alpha	*Echo*	*India*	*Nova*
CPT Bojotovic	CPT Rigetta	CPT Kavacha	CPT Coen
XO: 1LT Boas	XO: 1LT Palladino	XO: 1LT Bauer	XO: 1LT Wajaha
Bravo	*Foxtrot*	*Kilo*	*Oscar*
CPT Eisentov	CPT Farra	CPT Goven	CPT Silver
XO: 1LT Diouje	XO: 1LT Williams	XO: 1LT Humpfire	XO: 1LT McNab
Comet	*Galaxy*	*Lima*	*Romeo*
CPT Arpaio	CPT Tondini	CPT Eubanks	CPT Abdulhalek
XO: 1LT Sasaki	XO: 1LT Lovel	XO: 1LT Tayyarb	XO: 1LT Smith
Delta	*Hotel*	*Meteor*	*Tango*
CPT Kennedy	CPT Revernick	CPT Locwood	CPT Viers
XO: 1LT Jalaty	XO: 1LT Knarr	XO: 1LT Messervay	XO: 1LT Karoza
Platoons 1–12	Platoons 13–24	Platoons 25–36	Platoons 37–48
Squads 1–36	Squads 37–72	Squads 73–108	Squads 109–144

SOUTH POINT REGIMENT, 3rd BATTALION, KILO COMPANY, 27th PLATOON, as of 2301

Platoon Leader: 2LT Sysvillian, Amber C.
Platoon Sergeant: 1SG Haddad
Supply Sergeant: SFC Owendove

Platoon SSG: Panwa   Platoon SSG: Cue   Platoon SSG: Rodriguez

79th Squad	**80th Squad**	**81st Squad**
Squad SGT:Cutler	Squad SGT: Superack	Squad SGT: Pope
Squad CPL:Yosemite	Squad CPL: Rocola	Squad CPL: Gorbatova
PVT Anson	PVT Ague	PVT Beauregard
PVT Cotto	PVT Carstaris	PVT Clarion
PVT Enlai	PVT Fayvette	PVT Forrest
PVT Guy	PVT Garrison	PVT Halitov
PVT Jones	PVT Ji	PVT Haltiwanger
PVT Kahn	PVT Kalvin	PVT Narendra
PVT Omans	PVT Rousseau	PVT Obote
PVT Padante	PVT Telford	PVT St. Andrew, J.
PVT Watkins	PVT Val d'Or	PVT St. Andrew, S.
PVT Xiaoping	PVT Yaobang	PVT Yat-sen

Appendix E
South Point Academy Code

To honor my god or gods, be loyal to South Point, and be faithful, honest, and sincere in every act. I will come to understand that honorable failure builds character. Unfairness or cheating does not.

To perform every duty with allegiance and to the best of my ability.

To obey all orders and regulations of South Point and of proper authority.

To be at all times polite and courteous in my deportment, bearing, and speech.

To be determined in my academic studies and in my military training.

To take pride in the noble traditions of South Point and never commit an act that would compromise them.

To cultivate poise and a quiet, firm demeanor.

To improve my mind by reading and participation in intellectual and cultural activities.

To keep my body healthy and strong and to refrain from intoxicants and narcotics of any kind.

To be helpful to others and restrain them from wrongdoing.

To face challenges with courage and intestinal fortitude and not to complain or be discouraged.

To be worthy of the sacrifices of my parents and colony, the generosity of the alliances, and the efforts of all those who teach and administer to me.

To carry what I learn into my military career and always place right above personal gain, integrity above power.

To remember that being a South Point cadet imposes upon me the responsibility to live up to these ideals.

(Gen. Sheila A. Sothburg, Ret., Commandant, South Point, 2278–88)

Appendix F
Appointment of Cadet Officers and Noncommissioned Officers at South Point Academy.

Cadet officers and noncommissioned officers are appointed by the commandant of cadets, with recommendations from company, battalion, and regimental commanders.

To be selected to receive cadet rank at South Point is a privilege and high honor. Only the most deserving cadets are recommended to hold rank. Cadets unworthy or incapable of obtaining rank shall be denied the honor. Any cadet who holds rank and abuses or disgraces him or herself shall summarily and irrevocably lose that privilege.

Under the rank system employed at South Point, corporals and sergeants are selected from second- and third-year cadets, commissioned officers from third- and fourth-year cadets. Only once in the academy's history has a cadet from first year been recommended for the rank of corporal. That officer is your current regimental commander: Colonel Michael James Bryant.

Once each year, the cadets in each company are rated by their peers, commanding officers, and company tactical officers and are placed in their respective companies. The Order of Merit list shall reflect such promotions and demotions and yield cadet corps recommendations to be considered by battalion, company, and regimental commanders.

Second-year cadets with clean disciplinary records and overall GPAs of at least 9.0 will be automatically recommended for the rank of corporal during their first semester.

NOTE: Racinian conditioning is reserved for those cadets who hold the rank of second lieutenant.

Appendix G
First•Year Cadet Weekday Schedule at South Point Academy

"Time is a precious commodity—even with Exeter's twenty-eight-hour day. It'll take some getting used to. Pace yourself, or you will *dust out."*

—Commandant Marxi

0600: First call
0605: Cadets on line
0610: Squad physical training
0630: Reveille, march to breakfast
0700: Mess formation
0730: Morning classes begin
1100: Drill
1305: Mess formation
1335: Afternoon classes begin
1605: Free time, intramurals, tours, confinements
1700: Mess formation
1730: Retreat
1830: Combat training begins

2230: Last mess formation
2300: Evening study period
2700: Taps
2800: Lights out

Appendix H
Mission of the Seventeen System Guard Corps

The Seventeen System Guard Corps, within the Western and Eastern Alliance Department of the Navy, shall be so organized as to include not less than thirty combat divisions and thirty air/space wings, and such other land combat, atmospheric, space, and other services as may be required.

The Seventeen System Guard Corps shall be organized, trained, and equipped to provide fleet guard forces of combined arms, together with supporting air/space components, for service with the fleet in the seizure or defense of advanced military bases and for the conduct of such land/sea/space operations as may be essential to the undertaking of a naval campaign. The Corps will also engage in security and defense operations for all primary colonial settlements.

The Seventeen System Guard Corps shall provide detachments and organizations for service on armed vessels of the Alliance Navy, shall provide security detachments for the protection of naval property at naval stations and bases, and shall perform such other duties as the Alliance Assembly may direct. However, these additional duties may not detract from or interfere with the operations for which the Seventeen System Guard Corps is primarily organized.

The Seventeen System Guard Corps shall develop, in coordination with the Alliance Armed Forces, those phases of extrasolar operations that pertain to the tactics, techniques, and equipment used by interplanetary forces, and shall, in accordance with integrated joint Alliance plans, work toward the expansion of peacetime components of the Corps to meet the needs of security, antiterrorist operations, and war.

An EOS Interview with Ben Weaver

EOS: What got you interested in writing?

WEAVER: When I was a freshman, my composition instructor told me that I had talent and that I should pursue a writing-related career. I told him I had thought about writing a war novel. Being a literary type, he told me to read *A Farewell to Arms* by Hemingway. I did. After the course, I began writing short stories. I bought a copy of *The Writer's Market,* did research on the magazines, and sent off stories to the small press.

EOS: Which writers would you consider your major influences?

WEAVER: Of course the literary giants like Hemingway and Fitzgerald, whom I studied in college. Some of my favorite Science Fiction authors include Asimov, Clark, Bradbury, and Le Guin. I also enjoy military Science Fiction authors like David Drake, David Weber, and David Feintuch (especially the latter's *Midshipman's Hope*). I'm also a fan of Joel Rosenberg's work, particularly a novel entitled *Emile and the Dutchman.* John Steakley's

Armor is a very interesting read, as is Bernard Cornwell's *Rebel* (from the Starbuck Chronicles), though it's not SF and set during the American civil war.

EOS: Is there any single novel or author who most inspired you?

WEAVER: Joe Haldeman's *The Forever War*. The sense of desperation that comes through in that first-person narrative is amazing. People talk about novels "speaking to them." That one spoke to me.

EOS: What was the process of writing *Brothers In Arms*?

WEAVER: I started with the basic notion that I wanted to write a military SF novel. Then I asked myself questions like Who's the story about? What does this person want? Why? What stands in the way? Drama equals danger plus desire. So I began with that and created the characters Scott and Jarrett St. Andrew, two brothers who have conflicting ideas about what they want for themselves and each other. I began developing an outline—a basic summary of each chapter. I guess I spent nearly a year or more working on the story, honing it, trying a scene a dozen different ways until I was satisfied with it.

EOS: We notice that the novel contains several appendices. Did you create those before or after writing the book?

WEAVER: The appendices came before the novel. I had to create the infrastructure first so that as I wrote the book, I could consistently rely on my charts and tables of organization. I spent many, many months doing research on birthmarks, military academies, the search for extrasolar planets, and the exploration of our solar system, among other things. Creating seventeen different star systems turned into a monumental task because I insisted on being as a faithful as possible to real science by using the real names for planets or naming them after the actual scientists who discovered them (see: Gatewood-Callista in the novel for an example, and that added much more time to my research. Hemingway said that you need to know the whole iceberg as a writer, but you only show the readers the tip. Well, sitting below *Brothers In Arms* is a sizable iceberg, and it was only with that berg in place via my charts and tables that I began writing the first chapter.

EOS: So, how long did it take to write the actual manuscript?

WEAVER: About six months after finishing the appendices I had a first draft in hand. I wrote five days a week and spent between three and eights hours per day, depending on other commitments. Now I try to set a page count that I must hit each week. This is a great way for me to remain disciplined. I tried Stephen King's method, but it didn't work for me. He says he writes each day until "beer o'clock." All I got was a hangover.

EOS: What is it specifically about military stories that intrigues you?

WEAVER: I mentioned earlier that drama equals danger plus desire, and those elements are inherent in military/war stories. War provides a great backdrop for fiction because all of the emotions are heightened and your sense of time speeds up. Knowing someone for a week during wartime is like knowing that person for a year. Though my poor eyesight prevented me from joining the military, I've interviewed many folks who attest to this fact. Another aspect of military fiction that I appreciate is the idea of characters struggling for a greater good—then questioning whether there really is a greater good. What's worth dying for? What is loyalty? Bravery? Courage? Honor? For many of us, they are just words. In military stories, you can explore these intangibles and make them concrete for characters and readers.

EOS: We understand that you are married and have children. How do you balance writing with the demands of being a husband and father?

WEAVER: (grins) Very carefully. I've heard other writers say that their profession is a mistress with which no woman can compete. I don't subscribe to that. I also don't subscribe to the notion that writing is a mystical or God-given talent. It's a craft you can learn. Some of us get better at it than others. In truth, writing and being a parent are very similar. You nurture your children as best you can, then send them into the world. One distinction I like to make is that when I'm writing, I'm at work, and you can't come in and ask me to take out the garbage. My boss is a gunnery sergeant with the managerial skills of a bulldog, and he will snap at you. When I finish, I punch the clock, close the office door, and I'm a husband and father. I won't neglect my family for my work. Then again, I don't have to worry about that—my family is very understanding of the demands of being a writer. It's a comfortable fit.

EOS: What projects are you working on now?

WEAVER: I might write another novel set in the *Brothers In Arms* universe. I've been toying around with a number of different story ideas. I would love to do a novel about military folks conquering a forbidden or inhospitable territory or planet, a story not unlike the great race to the north pole. My subconscious is still working on that one. I'd also like to write other military SF books and perhaps write an original screenplay or two.

EOS: Do you have any other advice for aspiring writers?

WEAVER: When you begin a career in writing, you must remain focused. If you stray from your target, you will not get published. You should also continue your education, as I did. Remember three words: read, read, read. My old composition instructor told me that a writer is a reader. Read anything you can get your hands on. And don't limit yourself to a single genre or type of book. The best training is a diverse training. When I was writing Brothers In Arms, I read other military novels, I read military magazines, I read poetry, I read a lot.

EOS: Well, Mr. Weaver, we thank you for taking the time to speak to us. We look forward to more work from you in the future.

WEAVER: It's been my pleasure. Thank you. You're dismissed.